Those Five Kids

Those Five Kids

By

Marlon Cozier

Strategic Book Publishing and Rights Co.

Strategic Book Publishing and Rights Co., LLC
USA | Singapore
www.sbpra.com

ISBN: 978-1-62857-230-8

For information about special discounts for bulk purchases, please contact Strategic Book Publishing and Rights Co. Special Sales at bookorder@sbpra.net.

Contents

Chapter 1

Randomly Kidnapped

In the year 2009, there are five members of the Fallon family. The oldest Fallon is named Joe. He can act very childish at times, but he is a mature 2008 college graduate. He was born on August 30, 1979. He is married to a woman he met in New York nicknamed Kay-Lo, a crazy girl who acts like a spoiled kid. She was born on March 24, 1981. Joe and Kay-Lo currently reside in Florida. Their youngest son, Joey, was born on November 2, 2000. He likes to bring peace to people. Another kid, Jake, was born on January 7, 2000. He loves sports and solving mysteries, and he dreams of becoming a detective and a basketball player when he gets older. Jake also loves figurines. There is one last Fallon, named Joseph, born on February 6, 1978. Joseph is Joe's older brother and is a fitness coach at a local gym.

Inside a nice-looking two-story house, Kay-Lo is feeling very hot. She tries to turn on the air conditioner, but it hasn't been working since Joey accidently bumped into the unit and knocked the fan blade loose while playing inside with his neighborhood friends earlier in the summer.

Joe is outside in the hot weather, listening to music while detaching the hose, which seems to have burst, from the faucet connected to the house. Kay-Lo goes outside and takes the white earphones out of Joe's ears, letting him know that she is about to go shopping. After Joe finishes dealing with the hose,

Kay-Lo wants him to go inside to fix the air conditioner. Joe thinks about how he always has to do everything himself. Kay-Lo thinks that when people do things for themselves, they build up more experience.

Kay-Lo grabs her purse and leaves the house, leaving Joe alone. Joey isn't home at the moment; he is sleeping over at his cousin Frankie's house, which is just four blocks away. They both live on Quinver Avenue. Joseph and Jake have been living in New York, but they are moving to Florida tomorrow.

While Kay-Lo is out of the house doing some errands, Joe is all alone inside on this hot, cloudy Friday. It is August, and summer break is almost over for them. Because Kay-Lo refuses to fix the air conditioner herself, Joe goes up to the attic for the red toolbox. He accidently drops a ladder, and a box holding six crystal necklaces opens and falls out onto the floor.

Joe had forgotten that he had these necklaces. They had been a gift for him and Joseph when they were little kids. The crystals are magical objects that were made at the High Production factory in Georgia. Each crystal has one ability: underwater breathing, morphing, invisibility, future sighting, teleportation, and creating a force field of protection. The teleportation crystal is the only crystal necklace that can work its magic for two people at once.

Each crystal has its own number at the bottom of the necklace, from one to six. This way, Joe, or whoever else, will know which crystal is which. The person has to wear the crystal necklace around his or her neck to receive its powers, except the future sighting crystal. Sometimes the owner doesn't have to wear the future sighting crystal around his or her neck for it to work. The six crystal necklaces are called the Crystals of Power.

Joe doesn't remember who gave them the gift. He won't allow Joey and Jake to use the magical crystals because they are too young. He has to try his best to keep the magical crystals out of their sight. At the moment, Joey and Jake don't know about the crystals. Joe and Joseph weren't supposed to know about the crystals when they were little kids, either.

Although he forgot about them many years ago, Joe now remembers what each crystal necklace does. He takes out the future sighting necklace, removes the white earphones from around his neck, and wraps the future sighting Crystal of Power around his neck to get the feel of it again. Then he takes the red toolbox so that he can fix the air conditioner.

Joe goes back downstairs, throws the white earphones on the computer desk, and picks up a small flashlight from the computer desk to see inside the air conditioner while he is fixing it. When he is done, he turns on the air conditioner, and it looks like it's working once again. The fan from the inside is spinning and a nice, cool breeze settles in the house. Before Joe goes back in the attic, a bright white light blinds him for a few second and then fades away. He wants to know what just happened.

Joe puts the flashlight back on the computer desk and goes back up to the attic to put one of the Crystals of Power back inside its rectangular box. The box is black and gold on the outside and red on the inside. Joe notices that it's a jewelry box, possibly meant to keep the Crystals of Power safe. When Joe is finished, he closes the attic. Then he goes on the computer and does a little searching to see if he can find anything about the Crystals of Power. He has no luck with that.

All the other crystals shown on the screen are just regular ones. Joe goes back to search, but then freezes for a second when he sees something related to his parents. It says, "The kidnapping of José and Joanne Fallon." Joe knows that this is about his parents. He clicks on the link and starts reading about it.

As he is reading, he finds out that his parents were kidnapped from Finger Lakes National Forest in New York, but there was another place before that. The first kidnapping location is unknown. He can't believe that they were actually kidnapped. He hopes that they are still alive.

A couple of minutes later, Joe starts to wonder what, if anything, this has to do with the Crystals of Power that he holds. He does some more research about the Crystals of Power, but he still can't find anything. He feels like the Crystals of Power don't exist, but they must because he has them in his attic. Joe does a search for his parents but can't find any more information about how and why they were kidnapped, or who kidnapped them. He gets up, goes to the phone, and calls Joseph, but it isn't Joseph who answers the phone. It seems to be Jake, whom Joe hasn't seen since he was born nine years ago.

"Hello!" Jake answers.

"Joseph?" Joe says.

"Joseph? No, no, this is Jake. By the way you sound, I expect that you're Joe Fallon. You're my dad that I haven't seen in years. Remember me? Last time you saw me was at Atlantic Hospital in New York. The place where I was born."

"Of course I remember you, Jake Roland Fallon."

"Okay, it wasn't necessary to mention my middle name."

Joe asks, "May I speak to Joseph?"

"Sure." Jake gives the phone to Joseph.

Joe talks to Joseph about what he has just found on the computer. After he finishes explaining, he hopes that Joseph will understand and won't take it too seriously. Joseph promises that he will handle it. The person who kidnapped their parents is probably still around.

Joe and Joseph have no clue how that person kidnapped their parents. Joe needs to find a way to gather some information about this. He sees now that his parents were never dead. He feels relief, but he doesn't understand why they were taken. He wonders where they are right now.

Before they hang up, Joseph says that he hopes Joe will have some good news when he and Jake arrive at the house tomorrow night. But nothing is on Joe's mind, which is a huge bummer for Joseph.

After the phone conversation is over, Joe lies on the couch watching some television. That afternoon, Kay-Lo comes back to the house with a few blue shopping bags. She places her purse on the living room couch and reaches inside one of the blue shopping bags to show Joe the clothes she has bought for Joseph and Jake. She was going to buy some clothes for Joe and Joey, but she decided that they already have too many clothes. She is going to stop buying them clothes for now.

Kay-Lo says, "These are very nice clothes. Jake told me that he likes cool clothes that don't look raggedy and outdated. He loves to dress cool, and he's a funny kid." She puts the clothes back inside the blue shopping bag. "Now, then, did you fix the air conditioner while I was gone like I asked you to?"

Joe gives her a true answer, which she doesn't really believe. She goes over to the air conditioner and starts to inspect it. She is happy that there aren't any scratches on it. It seems like Joe has the skills to fix water pumps and other appliances. Joe had originally planned to be a mechanical engineer, but the job he wanted rejected him. Now he works at a day care center.

Joe tells Kay-Lo that Joseph and Jake are coming tomorrow night, and that Joseph has some expectations of them and Joe told him no.

"Why say no?" she asks.

"If I said yes, he would know what to expect when he gets here. But since I said no, he has no clue what he is up for. I am going throw him a fantastic party tomorrow. This means we need to start planning this party today. I'll get the decorations from the party store, and you can call a few friends, family, whoever, to see if they would like to come."

Kay-Lo agrees to do as Joe says. Later that afternoon, Joe backs the black car out of the garage, closes the five-window garage door, and goes to the party store to get some decorations for tomorrow night's party. A short time later, after he has found a few things, he goes up to the cash register to pay. A man standing in line behind him keeps looking at him and can't stop staring. On the way out of the store, this man stops Joe and stands right next to him.

"Joe Fallon?" the guy says with surprise. "Wow, it took me a while to recognize you. It's incredible how fast you've grown up since I last saw you at your parents' community speech."

Joe asks, "Who are you?"

"Let's not get into any details. Last time I saw you in person, you were just a tyke. Look at you now, all grown up. So, uh, do you have kids?"

"Yeah, what's it to you?"

"What school do they go to?" the guy asks.

"One of my kids goes to Sea Sight Elementary School. Why do you need to know? Who are you?"

The man doesn't respond to those two questions. "Listen, I apologize for staring at you. There are people who do that for no reason, and they need to mind their business. But I know something about you, Joe, and I am on my way to my partner's headquarters to spread the news. I'm so glad that I saw you as soon as I arrived in this state—such good timing. I'm going to be here for a while, and you will never have a chance to find me." He pushes Joe, then runs away.

Joe wonders if this was the guy who kidnapped his parents. It is such perfect timing that he has just done research about his kidnapped parents; otherwise, he wouldn't have the idea that some random guy kidnapped them. He starts to go after the man who seems to know him so well. He chases him back inside the store. Joe is quick, but not quick enough. He is a bit behind the guy. They run up and down a few aisles in the party store.

The random guy has dropped food cans and moved a shopping cart into the aisle to slow Joe down, but it doesn't work because Joe is an athletic person. He does a flip over the shopping cart without touching it and continues to chase the random guy. Joe's eyes are focused on the guy, who looks back at him to see where he is. He notices that Joe is catching up with him. He continues to throw down more shopping carts and to pelt him with hard items, but Joe dodges them all, not slowing down one bit. He continues to chase the random guy.

The random guy can't believe what he is seeing, and he quickly runs out of the party store. So does Joe. The random guy gets into his Jeep and drives away. Joe stops to look at his own black car. He doesn't want to crash it because he has had it for a very long time, and he isn't ready to get rid of it just yet. But if he wants to find out who the guy is, he might as well use the car. He gets inside the black car, puts the three shopping bags with the party decorations in the back seat, starts up the car, and drives off in a hurry. They are so lucky that the police have gone on strike. Nobody knows why they are on strike.

Joe is inside his car, gaining more speed to catch the random guy. The Jeep's powerful engine allows him to drive fast, but the car is very filthy and not attractive. The guy looks at his side mirror and sees that Joe is gaining on him. The random guy doesn't know why Joe won't quit chasing after him. He makes a left turn that will lead him to a highway. Joe turns, too, and puts more pressure on the gas pedal to help him catch up to the guy.

During the chase, they approach a road that requires people to take a few sharp turns. When they get close to it, the random guy doesn't slow down; he maintains the same speed while taking the turns. Joe thinks that the random guy will crash his Jeep after the rough turns, but he doesn't. Joe thinks that if the random guy can turn his automobile like that, he can do the same. He does exactly what the random guy did when he was going through the turns, but when Joe reaches the second turn, his car goes skidoo and hits the right barrier, making a huge scratch on the right side of his car. He notices that he has just damaged his car, but he doesn't stop to look at the damage. He can still see the guy's Jeep, so he continues chasing him down.

The only problem is that there are too many cars in the way. Joe takes a nearby exit and goes the other way. He takes a shortcut he knows and makes his way back to the highway. The shortcut gives Joe a better view of the random guy's Jeep.

The guy starts to go insane inside his car, banging on his steering wheel. He cannot believe this; he doesn't understand why Joe won't give up chasing after him. He started to get frustrated, until he comes up with a plan that he doesn't really want to do: make a U-turn on the same area of the highway. The random guy is now going in the wrong direction while the other cars are going in the right direction. Joe sees him again, his eyes wide open, and he can't believe what he has just seen.

Joe knows that what he is about to do is risky. He makes the same kind of U-turn the random guy did, but he does it more slowly. Besides making a proper U-turn, Joe turns his scratched-up car like he is parking it in a parking lot. He keeps shifting gears over and over again, and hitting his back bumper against the street barrier. Cars keep honking at him, and one guy starts yelling at him in a croaky voice. Joe hears him but doesn't say anything. When he has turned around completely, he drives off, trying not to hit anyone's bumpers to avoid getting in trouble.

More vehicle horns are blowing. Later on during the chase, Joe finally reaches the random guy again. He sees him exiting the highway. Maybe Joe can finally catch up to him. When Joe gets off the highway, he sees the Jeep, and it isn't moving. He has him now.

Joe crashes his car into the Jeep, destroying the guy's back bumper and destroying his front bumper. He wants the guy to be trapped inside his car.

Joe goes inside his car trunk to take out a length of chain, then goes over to the guy's car. He wants to tie up the guy with the steel chain, just in case he has the chance to escape his vehicle.

Joe quickly runs toward the guy's Jeep.

Something seems to be wrong; the random guy isn't inside the car. Joe starts to scream. He can't believe that he has done more damage to his own car than was necessary. Passersby start to look at him, wondering what is going on with him. A little girl thinks he is a zombie. Joe looks around the area quickly to see if he can spot the guy, and he does. The man is running away into a crowded area. There are so many people. Joe sees where he is headed and starts to chase after him again, this time on foot. He and the random guy push and shove people out of the way.

Across the street they go. Although there are cars driving through, Joe and the random guy safely make it across the street. Joe wonders if the guy is really making his way to his partner's headquarters. Where is his headquarters located? Joe can't let him arrive there.

Joe sees a bicycle on the ground, picks it up, and starts to ride it. Some little kid is looking at him. Joe now gains more speed than he had walking. He continues to chase after his target, focusing on his breathing. His target runs over to a pier, then stops at a rail that prevents people from falling into the water. Joe finally has him. He gets off the bicycle and runs toward the random guy, throwing them both into the water together.

Joe and the random guy start fighting in the water while people on the pier look at them. The random guy tries to swim away from Joe to reach a motorboat, but Joe doesn't allow him to do so. He keeps pulling him back and continues attacking him. He isn't going to stop attacking the guy until he tells him who he is.

The random guy splashes some salt water on Joe's face, which allows him to escape to the motorboat. The man quickly starts up the motorboat and begins to drive away. Joe doesn't have a chance of catching him now.

"So long, Joe-Loser!" the guy says as he takes off. "Thanks for dumping me into the water!"

The random guy leaves the area. Now Joe won't be able to figure out who he is. Joe quickly gets out of the water and goes back on the pier to see if he can still spot the random guy. The boat is quite blurry in the distance, so Joe decides he might as well forget about it for now and heads back to his car.

Suddenly, a little boy yells at Joe, "Hey, nitwit, that's my bike you just took! Get your own!" He kicks Joe in the left leg then rides away.

"Kids!" Joe says.

Joe goes back to his destroyed black car, dries off a little, and then makes his way to the auto repair shop to see if he can get his car fixed. When he arrives there, he learns that the cost to fix the car is $600. He looks in his wallet and sees that he only has $340 on him. Not too bad, but he still needs more to get his car repaired. He leaves the auto repair shop with his party decorations inside three shopping bags and makes his way back home on foot. Later that afternoon, Joe finally arrives back home.

Inside the house, Kay-Lo wonders why Joe is wet. Joe lies to her, telling her that kids sprayed him with a hose. He goes to the kitchen to put down the decorations for the party tomorrow. After putting on dry clothes, he sits down at the computer desk in the living room and thinks about the event that just took place. He wants to find out who the guy he chased down is and how he knows Joe. He also wants to know where his partner's headquarters is and what that place is. Joe regrets telling him which school Joey goes to. He wasn't thinking clearly, but the random guy doesn't know Joey or what he looks like, so Joe knows that Joey will be safe.

Kay-Lo says, "Joe, there is no time to rest. I want you to come and help me set up the decorations. I'll pay you fifty dollars."

"Since when do you loan me money? There's a reason I don't loan it to you."

Because Kay-Lo has said that she will pay him, Joe takes the party decorations out of the three shopping bags and starts to help her put up the party decorations all around the house—except in the bedrooms and the bathroom, of course. During the evening, they finally finished setting up. The living room, kitchen, and the front of the house are finished, and a few balloons hang from the garage door. But Joseph and Jake won't notice them.

For whatever reason, there isn't a dining room inside the house, probably due to lack of space. They usually eat at the kitchen counter and sometimes on the living room couch, which is close to the front door and the front windows. Outside the house, Kay-Lo finishes setting up the decorations in the backyard, since the party is taking place back there, as well. The back door is locked, so Kay-Lo goes around the house to go back inside. She notices something odd.

"Where is the car?" she asks Joe.

"The car?" he says nervously. "Oh, it needed an inspection. Yeah, it needed to get checked out, and thank goodness I remembered that."

"How come you never told me it needed to get inspected?"

"I keep forgetting! I had it written down on a piece of paper and left it inside the car, and that's how I remembered. We're not getting it back for a week or two."

Kay-Lo, who doesn't know how long a car inspection takes, figures that she will have to start taking the local bus again. She hasn't been on a local bus in years. She hopes that the police will hurry up and come back from their strike before something happens.

After telling Kay-Lo another lie, Joe goes to stow the rest of the party decorations in the messy garage that he needs to clean, and then he goes to the bedroom, thinking about what he can do before Kay-Lo finds out where the car actually is, because he knows that she isn't that stupid. He has to try to make things as easy as possible.

That evening, in the kitchen, Kay-Lo uses a stepladder to reach a foil pan atop the cabinets so she can finish making dinner. Joe finally comes out of the bedroom, his eyes red.

"I haven't seen you in a few hours," she says to Joe. "Why are your eyes so red?"

Joe answers, "I think I just woke up. I didn't know that I ended up going to sleep. I must have been tired. I had to do a lot of thinking when I went to the bedroom, so maybe that's why I went to sleep. I also had this strange dream about Joey, I can't get over it."

When Joe and Kay-Lo have just finished eating dinner, Joe takes a hot shower. Later, he sits back down on the couch next to Kay-Lo to watch a movie. After the movie is over, it looks like

Kay-Lo is already asleep. Joe sees her knocked out, so he puts a pillow underneath her head, covers her up with a blanket, and then gives her a little kiss on her left cheek. Then he goes to bed.

Early the next morning, up in the attic, one of the Crystals of Power inside the black and gold jewelry box has a white beam coming out of it. The light is bright, and this time it starts flying around the dark house. It passes by Kay-Lo, through the kitchen, and goes inside the bedroom, where Joe is asleep. The white beam flies inside Joe's right ear and then fades away.

When the mysterious light vanishes, it is still early in the morning. Joe wakes up and nervously looks around the bedroom as if someone is in there with him. He gets out of bed and goes to the kitchen to fetch himself a glass of water. After he finishes drinking the water, he looks at the couch and starts making his way back to bed when he notices something. He looks at the couch again and notices that Kay-Lo isn't there. He wonders where she has gone.

It is slightly dark inside the house, so he hits the light switch, but none of the house lights come on. Joe is starting to get freaked out. He continues to search the slightly dark house for Kay-Lo. He looks in the attic, basement, and backyard, but Kay-Lo is nowhere to be found.

From the kitchen window, Joe sees ambulances and fire trucks passing through the neighborhood. He goes to the front window, wondering what's going on at this hour. He goes outside and follows them in his black car. How did the car reappear at his house? Joe follows the ambulances and fire trucks until he reaches the spot where a local bus has flipped over. Joe watches the scene, and he sees firemen and paramedics pulling people out from the local bus. It looks like they all are survivors. The strange part about this is that most of them are asleep for reasons unknown.

A surviving little boy, who is wearing a pair of sunglasses, writes on a piece of paper that he was sitting next to a woman, but then she turned into a monster just before the bus flipped over. He was the only kid on the bus.

Joe looks more closely at the accident and sees a fireman trying to control a woman who looks familiar to him. Once he's focused on the woman, he realizes that it is Kay-Lo. Apparently Kay-Lo was inside the local bus before it flipped over. Detectives start investigating what flipped the bus over.

Joe quickly gets out of the car and rushes over to the accident. He looks at Kay-Lo, who is acting like a devil. Joe doesn't know what is wrong with her, so he tries to calm her down, but Kay-Lo can't. She bites Joe on the right shoulder really hard, and he starts to feel a bit woozy. A fireman pulls her away from him.

Joe falls on the ground with blurry vision and sees something on top of the flipped-over bus. It seems to be a person covered with hair, but he can't see the person properly. He blinks, and the person with the long hair from head to toe has disappeared. Joe goes back inside the car and puts his head down on the steering wheel, still feeling woozy. He looks at the flipped-over bus. He thinks about Kay-Lo becoming a devil and wonders if she is possessed. He can't think correctly and has no clue what is going on. He wants to know what happened on that bus.

Once Joe lifts his head from the steering wheel, he looks at his rearview mirror and sees Kay-Lo sitting in the backseat right behind him. She grabs him, her forearms dragging him to the back, but then a white flash appears, making Joe wake up in his bed!

What is this? Joe has woken up. He looks around the bedroom, wondering if it was all just a dream. He doesn't know what kind of dream it was. He quickly gets out of bed and runs to the couch to see if Kay-Lo is there. Yes, she is, and she is still sleeping. Joe breathes nervously, not understanding what happened moments ago. He looks at Kay-Lo and hopes that everything will be okay.

Chapter 2

Revealing

On a hot Saturday morning, Joe wakes up, exits the bedroom, and goes to the living room to make sure Kay-Lo is all right. She is still on the couch sleeping. Joe goes to turn on the air conditioner because it is fairly hot in the house. He starts to make breakfast for himself, Kay-Lo, and Joey because he knows that Joey is coming back home this morning. He wonders how he is doing.

At Frankie's house, Frankie gets up from his bed and sees Joey packing up. He is surprised that Joey is leaving so soon.

"I have to go back home early," he says to Frankie, packing his clothes inside his book bag. "My mother called me last night before I went to sleep, saying to come home in the morning because she has a few things for me to do before the party they are having tonight."

Frankie didn't know that they were having a party; he hasn't received any message about it. Joey apologizes to Frankie for not telling him about it. He forgot to mention it to him. Joey tells Frankie that the party is for his brother and his uncle. Frankie wonders if Jake is visiting until Joey tells him that they aren't visiting; they are moving to his house, meaning that they are staying. He can't wait to see them. Joey has spoken to Jake so many times on the phone and on the Skybot video chat network. Jake rarely uses the Skybot video chat because he doesn't have any friends. Tonight Joey will finally be able to see his brother, Jake, and his Uncle Joseph in person.

One day while talking on the Skybot video chat, Jake tells Joey that he loves to do detective work and solve mysteries. Joey learns that Jake is amazing at solving puzzles. Joey doesn't really know what his Uncle Joseph does, but he would love to learn more about him while he's in Florida. Frankie will have the chance to join the party tonight. He is excited about meeting his cousin Jake for the first time in person.

Joey has to get going; he's got some work to do when he gets home.

"Before you leave," Frankie says to Joey, halting him, "you should go down to the school today. I'm going there right now so I can get my schedule, textbooks, and other equipment I need for school."

"Oh, yeah, I forgot they called yesterday. I'll head down there later on. I hope Principal Russ remembers me."

"Of course he will. You know how adult brains are. That's why I can't wait to become an adult."

Joey says, "What's so special about being an adult? They act worse than kids, I think. Well, Frankie, I will see you again tonight. Don't forget to bring those playing cards to school on Monday so that you, Matt, Baron, and I can play during lunch. Thanks for letting me sleep in your bed. I hope your parents' blanket was comfy for you."

"How come you didn't eat the grilled cheese I made for us last night?"

"I thought you already knew that I don't eat cheese," Joey replies. "You can have it for yourself—that way you won't go hungry."

Frankie thanks his cousin Joey for staying over. Joey exits Frankie's house and makes his way back home with Frankie's dad, Harold.

Frankie Bennett is Joey and Jake's cousin. He is ten years old. He was born on March 27, 1999. Frankie considers himself a technology expert because of his love of science and his scientific knowledge. He impresses the people he knows with that knowledge. Frankie has one fear, and that fear is boats because of how they rock, how seasick he can get, and how afraid he is of falling into the ocean. Margaret is Frankie's annoying mother, and Harold is his dad, who is sometimes polite.

Later this Saturday morning, Frankie takes five dollars out of his wallet, leaves the house, and gets on his bike, making his way to school to get his schedule and his textbooks. When he arrives at the school, he accidently bumps into a kid and apologizes to him. On the way to the main office, he sees his principal, Mr. Russ, who has been the principal for six years. Mr. Russ realizes that Frankie has received his voice message from yesterday. They start to chat for a bit.

After Frankie finishes talking to Mr. Russ, he makes his way to the main office once again, to get his things for school before he leaves. After one of the school secretaries gives Frankie his schedule, textbooks, and other equipment, he starts to make his way out of the school building to head back home. He sees the kid he accidently bumped into earlier talking to his mother about something to do with the name Fallon. Frankie isn't too sure if this is the Fallon he knows. To make sure, he pretends to read one of his new textbooks so that the kid and his mom won't know that he is actually listening to their conversation.

The boy says with sorrow, "But, Mom, I don't want to do this. It might take me the whole school year to find out more about

Dad's old friend, and besides, I still can't get over the fact I lost that art competition yesterday."

The woman wants the kid to be quiet and put something inside his right ear that will change his attitude. She tells the kid to make sure that no one can see what's in his ear. The woman wants the kid to listen up about what he has to do while he is here at this school.

The woman explains to the kid that there is this boy whose last name is Fallon, and what she wants her son to do on the first day of school, which is this Monday, is find him. Once the kid finds him, he should ask him a couple of questions, but he'd better not tell his name to the Fallon kid. Before the woman drops the kid off at this school building on Monday, she will give him a smartphone so that he can give her or his dad a brief update on the kid that he must find.

The kid says, "So what you want me to do is find the boy whose last name is Fallon, ask him some questions, and give you or Dad an update on the kid? How am I going to remember that? Who's my dad again?"

"You don't need to know who your dad is. You will not forget what to do because I will write it down in a note. I often write notes for myself because I don't like forgetting things. Look here; I am going to give you two smartphones so that we can reach each other. The reason I'm giving you two is because I know you are not a responsible kid and will probably lose one," the woman says.

"You should've let my sister, Bianca, do this instead if you think I am not responsible. Bianca is more arrogant and annoying than I am."

"I was thinking of her, but I think you will do a better job. Now, since I am a genius with a high IQ, let's get back to the house to plan things out."

Before they leave, the kid's mother goes to pay the registration fee for her son to attend the school—or did she?

Frankie really hopes that they aren't talking about Joey. If so, what can he do? Because he doesn't know, he decides not to mention anything to Joey.

Luckily, Frankie knows a lot about safety and privacy for a ten-year-old. This will be useful in keeping Joey safe from whatever the kid and his mom are planning to do. Frankie knows they are talking about Joey because he is the only kid at Sea Sight Elementary School whose last name is Fallon. Frankie will see what he can do about this.

Frankie starts making his way back to the house on his bike, but first he needs to buy some breakfast. A few blocks down from the school, Frankie sees an ambulance passing by that looks like it is stopping in front of the school building. He just left the school; what could've happened? Frankie wants to see what is going on, but he doesn't want to kill any time and it is none of his business. He stops at a local store to buy some breakfast with the five dollars he took from his wallet earlier on, and then he makes his way back home.

When he gets home, Frankie goes to his parents' bedroom to put back the blanket he slept on last night. While he is there, he sees the bedroom window half open. He goes to the window and pulls away the black curtain so that he can push the window down, but it seems to be stuck.

"What are you doing in my bedroom?" Margaret yells at Frankie, startling him. "How many times must I tell you, don't come inside this bedroom unless you ask for permission."

Frankie says, "There's no need to yell. I was only giving you back the blanket I slept on last night since Joey was sleeping in my bed. Do you mind telling me what's wrong with that window?"

"It won't close, so I'm using black curtains to make it look like it's closed. Now leave the bedroom before I ground you for two weeks."

"You know," Frankie says, "I really wish that someday you and Dad would leave the house and never come back."

"Don't ever say that again, or you will live with your grandfather in the retirement home until you reach college! Now step out of the way and let me get my pocketbook. I'm about to go over to Kay-Lo's house to help set up for this party tonight."

"Is Dad going to be there tonight? Where is he right now?"

"Yes," Margaret answers. "He's coming tonight and he's in the living room watching little league. I'm leaving now, so make sure the door is locked. Bye!"

Frankie knows that Margaret is the most immature mother he has ever seen. She leaves dirty tissues and other things on the floor and on the kitchen table. Frankie wants to stay at Joey's house until his parents get a bit cleaner.

Later that morning, after eating breakfast, Frankie starts to wash up the dishes. Then he starts cleaning his bedroom. When he is finished cleaning, he will stop by Joey's house to have a little talk with him before the reunion party tonight for Joseph and Jake.

At the auto repair shop, Joe paid a total of $340; he gives the mechanic $50 more, the money that Kay-Lo gave him yesterday. It still isn't enough; he still needs a lot more if he wants his car back before Kay-Lo figures out that the car was actually damaged, not being inspected. Kay-Lo bought the black car for Joe for $6,299. Joe is afraid of how she will react if she finds out that it was badly damaged.

Half an hour later, Joe leaves the auto repair shop and makes his way back to his house. Joe opens the front door and sees Joey at the computer desk drawing something. Joey loves to draw; it is one of his favorite hobbies.

Before Joe goes to watch some television, he notices that the attic staircase is open. After closing it, he asks Joey if he opened the attic, and also where Kay-Lo went.

Joey answers, "No, I didn't open the attic. Mom went out with Frankie's mother to buy some more supplies for the party tonight. But I can tell you this—when Mom and Frankie's mother left this house—half an hour later, I believe—I heard this eerie sound coming from the attic."

"Why are there always such strange noises coming from the attic?" Joe asks.

"I don't know, but something creepy happened when I was alone here in the house. While I was lying on the couch, I heard the attic staircase opening. I turned around and saw this thing floating right in front of me. Then, *boom*, there was this huge flash of light. After that, I suddenly woke up in a dark forest wearing black and red pajamas. I felt lost and was thinking that I didn't have much time left. What do you think would have happened if I had died in that forest?"

"I don't want to think about that. Please don't think about dying in that dark forest," Joe says. "Are you sure the floating object behind you caused you to have this dream? What did the object look like?"

Joey exclaims, "A crystal necklace! It had the number four on it. I don't know if I was seeing things, but it's getting to me. That crystal necklace is what I was drawing at the computer desk."

Joe knows that the object Joey saw was the future sighting crystal, one of the six Crystals of Power. Luckily, Joey doesn't know what kind of necklace it is. Joe is still trying his best to keep the six crystals away from both Joey and Jake.

Something doesn't make sense. Joe doesn't know why the future sighting Crystal of Power came to Joey. There might be a way to find out, and that is to call the High Production factory, creators of the Crystals of Power and other high-quality objects.

Joe picks up the phone and starts to call the High Production factory to find out more secrets about the Crystals of Power that lie inside the black and gold jewelry box. This is the second time Joe has called the factory by himself. Last time he called was in 2003.

One of the factory workers remembers him. The worker asks what Joe needs help with. Last time Joe called them about his parents, but they had no clue how they were kidnapped. This factory worker also didn't know, but he did tell Joe that his parents were great soldiers and factory workers before they retired. Joe now has a different question to ask. This time it is about the Crystals of Power.

The factory worker knows what Joe is talking about. He explains that the six crystals known as the Crystals of Power were made for Joe and Joseph's parents. It was a gift for them when they retired from the High Production factory after trying to give Joe and Joseph the most powerful protection of all time. After many years of failed attempts, other factory workers finally finished their longtime experiment and kept it a secret from José and Joanne until the day of their retirement, when the workers gifted José and Joanne with their greatest invention yet, the six Crystals of Power. They told them what the crystals did and how they would provide the best protection for their family.

José and Joanne are the only two who held them. Nobody but them and their families is supposed to know about the crystals. The reason is their family's safety and privacy. When Joe was a little kid, he wasn't allowed to know about them until he got older. Now that Joe has kids of his own, he knows they should not take hold of the Crystals of Power because something bad might happen if they find out about it. They might tell other kids about them.

The most important Crystal of Power is the future sighting crystal. It knows when something evil or deadly is coming, and if that happens, a bright flash of white light will come out from the crystal. The white flash only happens when the owners are really close to the crystal necklace, so it can surprise them. When they are far away, the future sighting crystal will fly toward them, and when the owners notice it, it will flash. When the owners are sleeping, a white beam will fly out of it and enter one of their ears, and it will go into their mind. Once the bright light fades away, the owners wake up in a random spot about to witness something bad that might happen to them or their families in the future. What the factory worker means by "the future" is that the owners have a real vision, not a dream.

"So that's what happened to me when I was sleeping last night, and that must be the reason my son woke up in a dark forest and didn't know what was going on. I wonder what his vision means," Joe says.

"If your kid is young, he isn't going to understand. Don't tell him that he had a vision, because then he will know that it will happen, and it will cause him anxiety," the factory worker tells Joe. "There's something I want to tell you, and it may sound confusing, but I will try my best to make it easy to understand. The visions you and your son had will happen—or they won't happen. If it doesn't happen, it means that you guys prevented it from happening. If it does happen, it means that you failed to stop the evil against your family. You should know what I am talking about eventually."

"I assume that these visions can be very creepy. I don't know what made Kay-Lo get on the bus after midnight in my vision.

Also, in my vision, a kid with sunglasses wrote that before the bus flipped over, Kay-Lo became an out-of-control psycho maniac. Well, actually, that's how she acts in real life, anyway. There was also something on top of the bus. I don't know what it was. The whole body was covered in hair. Right now I want to forgive my parents because I want that future sighting crystal destroyed. Is there any way to destroy the crystal?"

"Unfortunately, no," the factory worker tells him. "For some strange reason, the crystals can't be destroyed. The future sighting crystal isn't the only Crystal of Power that can't be destroyed, but don't worry—we'll find a way."

Joe asks the factory worker to keep him up to date, just in case they find a way to destroy the crystal. The factory worker promises to do so. Before ending the conversation, the factory worker explains to Joe how the Crystals of Power got their magical powers: a lightning bolt operator set them on a platform in the lab, raised the platform, and hit the crystals with electricity that would imbue each of them with a different powerful ability. It became a successful experiment that was only for Joe's parents.

The factory worker understands that it sounds crazy, but they did it for José and Joanne because they spent most of their time inside the factory working on only one thing for their kids. The worker tells Joe that there is a secret inside one of the Crystals of Power that he cannot mention. The factory worker thanks Joe for calling the High Production factory and reminds him that they try their best to provide the best information they can.

After talking to the factory worker, Joe wants to know what he meant about a secret hidden inside one of the Crystals of Power. The good news is that he has found out some secrets, and now he is going to make sure that his and Joey's vision doesn't occur.

Joe now understands why he saw his parents in the search results when he typed in the Crystals of Power. They knew how these objects work. They were the ones who held them.

Suddenly, Joe remembers something about his parents from a Christmas holiday two decades ago. On that particular Christmas, Joe found out from Joseph that their parents were kidnapped. Their parents' friend, Ms. Parkinson, told him; that's how he knew. Their parents were taken to the Finger Lakes National Forest in New York, Joe now remembers. But he doesn't remember who entrusted him and Joseph with the six Crystals of Power. It couldn't have been his parents since they had already been kidnapped. Joe sits down at the kitchen counter, trying to think, until Joey comes in.

"Hey, Dad!" Joey greets him. "Slow day, isn't it? When Jake and Uncle Joseph come, this house should be livelier. How was Jake back in the day?"

Joe replies, "To tell you the truth, I don't really know Jake that well, which is sad for a dad. I talk to him on the phone often, but only for a short period. The last time I saw him in person was at Atlantic Hospital back in New York. Joseph, Kay-Lo, Jake, and I were born at Atlantic. You were the only kid who was born here in the southeast."

"What?"

"Your mom, uncle, brother, and I were all born in New York. You were born down here because your mom and I were living here when you were born. We moved to this house sometime after Jake was born. I had to quit my old job."

"Weird!" Joey says. "Anyway, I'll be in the living room watching little league. You can do whatever adults like to do." He walks away.

For a quick moment, Joe sits at the computer desk and goes online. He wants to find a few original creations that the High

Production factory workers produced. He clicks on a link and gathers some information about the factory. Construction of the High Production factory started in 1951 and finished in 1959. Since then, factory workers have invented several high-quality objects. They once created a device called the HC Mind Chip, which was supposed to give users better control over their brains. But it was a failed experiment: the device gave users *no* control over their brains, and it made them very heartless, even if they originally were not.

One day, all eleven HC Mind Chips went missing from the High Production factory; a blue and white cyborg went missing that same day, too. To this day, none of them has been found. Factory workers are still searching for the eleven missing HC Mind Chips, and the blue and white cyborg. They still can't figure out how they went missing.

Joe continues to read more about what's been made in the factory throughout the decades. When he is done, he sits back in the secretary chair, trying to get the Crystals of Power out of his head. He hopes that his vision about Kay-Lo won't come true. He doesn't want Joey's vision to come true, either. He knows for sure that the future is upon them.

Chapter 3

Family Reunion

Minutes later on this Saturday afternoon, somebody is knocking on the front door. Joey opens it and sees that it is Frankie, who needs to talk to him right away. He wants to get the conversation over with. In the living room, Frankie is about to explain something to Joey.

"I want to ask you something," he says to Joey, turning down the television volume. "If you were the only Fallon at Sea Sight Elementary School and someone was looking for you, would you tell that person about yourself or your family?"

"No, unless it slipped out by accident. Also, if I know that person very well, I guess I would tell him a tiny secret."

"Good. Now, if you had a fake last name, what would it be?"

Joey says, "Hmm, I guess I'll say Jarrett."

"Cool. So what I want you to do when we go back to school on Monday is to use your fake last name, only if it's necessary. I'll tell you if I see that person."

"I don't know what you're talking about, but okay, I will do it. Are you trying to keep my identity from someone?"

Frankie replies, "Maybe, maybe not. I'm trying to protect your privacy. I'm trying to help."

That afternoon, Joseph and Jake's plane has just taken off from New York. They are now making their way south. Meanwhile, Joe is knocked out on the couch. Joey leaves the house and makes his way to his elementary school while Frankie stays at the house.

When Joey arrives at the school, it looks like there is almost nobody there. He goes to Mr. Russ's office, and the principal is there. They talk a bit about whom to believe just in case someone gives Mr. Russ or Joey a different story about something. Joey goes to the main office to get his schedule and his textbooks. After that, he starts making his way home.

Later that evening, Kay-Lo has returned back home, spreading the news that Joseph and Jake's plane has just arrived in Florida at the Orlando Stanford International Airport. A few moments later, a lot of people from the neighborhood start to arrive at the house. Neighborhood kids bring gifts for Jake. Joe is a bit nervous that Jake won't make any friends while he's here in Florida. He doesn't want him to feel alone while he's in Florida. Jake might not have a great childhood if he doesn't have any friends. Joe goes over to Joey to do him a favor—to help Jake make as many friends as he can during the party.

After that, even more people arrive at the Fallons' house for the party. Some of Joey and Frankie's friends are there, including Dakota, Matt, Baron, Uriah, Dale, and Ian. Some of their families are there as well: Margaret, Harold, Gerald, Brunson, Sasha, Trish, and others. Gerald and Brunson are the only two in the house who are from a different country, the United Kingdom.

Matt and Baron's parents make it to the party as well. Matt's older brother couldn't make it because he is busy with college, and Baron's two sisters are not in Florida. They are in Newcastle, England, for their vacation, which ends today. They will be back in Florida tomorrow. Baron didn't go to England with them because he has to do summer school. Joe is a great friend of Baron's parents and Dakota.

Later on during the party, Joseph and Jake make it to the block where their new house is. Kay-Lo sees them coming when she looks out the front window and tells everybody to hide so that they all can surprise them both. Kay-Lo shuts off all the lights inside the house before Joseph and Jake actually make it to the front. When they arrive at the front of the house, Joseph and Jake admire how it looks.

Joseph and Jake start taking their first steps toward the house. Joseph checks the front door to see if it is unlocked, and it surely is. He slowly opens the front door, having no clue what is about to happen. Joseph finds the light switch, and when he turns on the light everyone pops out, yelling, "Surprise!" Jake looks at everyone, hoping that all these people don't live inside this small house. He would feel very uncomfortable about that.

Kay-Lo is glad to see that Joseph is surprised. Joseph gives her a hug. He wasn't expecting Kay-Lo to look this big, but she still looks well proportioned.

It has been nine years since Joe last saw Joseph in person. Joseph has no clue what is going on. He thought that Joe didn't have any expectations of him before he arrived at the house. Apparently Joe had lied—he wasn't going to have a reunion party without inviting their old friends and families. They have new friends now, but Joseph doesn't know them yet. While Joseph is staying at the house, he should introduce himself to new people. Jake appears next to Joe and shakes his hand.

"Jake?" Joe says, pleasantly surprised. "Wow, look at you with your long blond hair. Last time I saw you . . ."

"Yeah, yeah, I know. I was just a one-day-old baby. My hair is blond because of Mom. Eventually it will turn into my natural brown color. And I know I need a haircut, so don't mention it. Umm, where's Joey?"

"Right over at the snack table, talking to his friends. He's the one with the dark, spiky hair. You can't miss him."

"Thanks!" Jake says and walks over to talk to Joey.

Over at the snack table, Jake is about to talk to his younger brother, Joey, whom he has never seen in person. He has only talked to him on the phone and on the computer through the Skybot video chat. He looks really nervous as he goes over to talk to Joey. He relaxes himself and takes a deep breath. "Hi, Joey, I'm Jake," he greets his brother shyly. "Jake Fallon!"

Joey says, "I know who you are, big brother. This is the first time in my life I've ever seen you in person. Would you like some meatballs on a toothpick?"

"Sorry, I don't eat meat."

"Oh, okay! Hey, let me introduce to you these three kids right here. This is your older cousin Frankie, and this is Matthew, but we call him Matt. And this sarcastic kid right here is Baron."

Baron says, "Pleasure to meet you, kid. You know, you look kind of familiar. Have we met before?"

"Not that I know of," Jake replies.

"Oh, it's probably just me, then. Here, I got you a present. It's a clown doll that represents me, because I'm funny. Be aware that Joey's a chicken—he's afraid of clowns."

Now Joey wants to introduce Jake to the other half of the family, including some of his friends. Joey knows almost all of his families and what they look like, so he won't think that he doesn't know any of them.

Joey promises Jake that his family and friends will love him. He is going to make sure that Jake makes a lot of friends while he's in Florida. He has been employed to do so. Joey tells Jake that next Saturday night he is having a video game night to help Jake make a lot more friends.

"There's another event before that," Baron says to Jake. "One of my little sisters, Madelyn, is having a birthday party on Monday, so I am inviting you to come if you'd like."

Jake says, "Sounds cool. That'll be fun."

Jake is starting to feel like he is home again. He starts wandering around and talking to a few new friends that he's made thanks to Joey. He knows for sure that he is going to have a wonderful time in his new house and in his new state. He hopes that it will be better than New York.

About two hours have passed, and the party is still going on. Now Jake has met the other half of his family, a few of Joey and Frankie's friends from the neighborhood, and a few of their school friends. He has already made a lot of friends in one night. The party is still rocking after midnight. A lot of people are still inside the house jamming. Joseph talks to Joe while Kay-Lo dances to salsa music.

This is by far one of the best parties Joseph has been to this year. Earlier this year, in March, he went to an old friend's party, and it wasn't that good. The house was a bit empty; there wasn't that much food, and it was boring. Ms. Parkinson was also there with a friend named Ophelia. Joseph still doesn't know her last name, but he knows that she used to be married. He has heard that she got a divorce.

During that bad party, when Ms. Parkinson went to take her vitamins, Ophelia mysteriously appeared next to Joseph, saying, "I know who you and your brother are." Then she walked away. Joseph wondered how she knew who he and his brother were if she had never met them. After Ophelia disappeared, Joseph didn't know where she had gone. A couple of weeks after the boring party, Ms. Parkinson came up to Joseph and Jake's old house. She was wondering if Joseph knew where Ophelia was. Joseph didn't know her, so he said no. Ms. Parkinson told Joseph that Ophelia had randomly disappeared two days after the party. That is all Joseph can remember.

"Hold on," Joe said to Joseph. "If you went to that party by yourself, where was Jake?"

Joseph replies, "I left him with his maternal grandmother, who still lives at our uncle's house, but now he's in a better place. Remember, he passed away in 1972 after a fight he had with someone. He died from his injuries."

"Too bad our parents didn't have a chance to tell us a story about him!"

"I know," Joseph says. "But don't worry about Jake—he is a good kid, and he is doing great in school, including with his basketball training. Jake used to go to Volotont Elementary before moving to Florida. Usually I drop him off at basketball practice before school starts, but he quit for some reason."

Joe knows that quitting sports isn't always good because people will lose their basic training and exercise. The same thing happened to Joe when he used to run track and field, when he was Jake's age. People start getting lazy after quitting. Joe is going to make sure that doesn't happen to Jake. He will make sure Jake becomes a tough kid.

Joe says to Joseph, "Well, enough talking about the past. I want to show you something quickly so we can enjoy the rest of the party."

Joe wants to show Joseph something up in the attic. First, he makes sure that nobody is near there. The coast is clear. He pulls down the attic staircase and climbs it, bringing Joseph along with him. He starts telling Joseph about when he chased down the random guy on Friday. Later during the conversation, he takes the future sighting Crystal of Power out from the black and gold jewelry box where he is storing it and shows it to him.

Joseph figures out what Joe is trying to do. He wants to find the person who kidnapped their parents. Joseph decides to join Joe on this mission; he knows Joe cannot do all this work by himself. He is going to need some assistance.

After a few hours have passed, Kay-Lo waves good-bye to the partygoers, thanking them for coming and bringing the party to life. Now she has to clean up the mess that has been made in the house.

It is the middle of the night, and almost everyone has gone to bed. Joseph, Joey, and Jake are already asleep. Joe and Kay-Lo are still up cleaning the house. When they are done, Kay-Lo goes to bed and Joe lies down on the living room couch, thinking about how he and Joseph are going to find out how their parents were kidnapped and who kidnapped them. Joe still believes that the person he chased down on Friday is the kidnapper, but he isn't completely sure because he doesn't have enough proof.

Joe finally goes to sleep at nearly four in the morning. Hours have passed, and so far Joe is having a normal dream rather than a dream or vision that will come true.

Here's to a new day!

Chapter 4

Early Mission

The sun is shining on this beautiful Sunday morning. This is the last day of freedom for the Fallons before they start heading back to work. Joseph and Jake are the only ones who are staying home tomorrow because they have just arrived in Florida. Jake gets out of bed, tripping over the clown doll he got from Baron at last night's party. He forgot that he left it on the floor; now he picks it up and puts it in his closet. He turns on the television to see if any fantasy cartoons are on. There is nothing for him to watch, but there is barely anything to watch on television on Sundays. Jake leaves the bedroom and goes to the kitchen, where Kay-Lo is talking to Joe and Jake while she makes breakfast for everyone.

Kay-Lo had gotten up before seven o'clock and didn't feel like going back to sleep, so she went for a nice early-morning jog. When she came home, she was pumped. Joe knows why she is so sweaty: she went jogging because of what Joseph said last night at the party about how she's gotten big over the years. Now Kay-Lo feels that she is fat and needs to lose weight. She plans to go jogging three times a day—in the morning, afternoon, and evening.

Kay-Lo has given herself a mission, and that mission is to slim down. It is best for her to go out and exercise. She sets a goal of five to six months to see how thin and fit she can get. She knows that she will be looking better than ever by then. Right now, this is the best she can look. Jake thinks that she can't look like that forever.

While jogging around the area, Kay-Lo comes up with an idea of something they all can do today. She wants everyone to go to Sandy Beach to end their summer vacation in a well-deserved way.

Breakfast is ready. Kay-Lo sees that Joseph and Joey are still sleeping. Jake has just came from Joey's bedroom, and he is the only one who's awake. He isn't too sure whether or not his Uncle Joseph is still sleeping. Jake goes back to the bedroom he's now sharing with Joey to tell him that breakfast is ready.

Minutes later, after Jake has told Joey that breakfast is ready, Joseph wakes up and starts to make his way out of the house. He will see his housemates later. Since Joseph left his job back in New York, he is going to try looking for a new one in Florida. He's looking for a job that pays lots of money.

By the time they are finished eating their breakfast, Joe, Kay-Lo, Joey, and Jake are about to start making their way to Sandy Beach. Joseph is already in the city looking for a job. Frankie can't go because he has to go out with Margaret, his annoying, selfish mother, to do a bit of school shopping.

Sandy Beach is way too crowded for a Sunday. They try for seven minutes to find a good spot in the sand, but they don't find one and end up close to the water.

The waves are calm, so Jake doesn't have to worry about that. The water is sky blue with sailboats floating by. People riding speedboats pass by, making a few waves. On land, there are several kids playing beach volleyball. Joey and Jake start making their way toward the water. Kay-Lo warns them not to go in too deep.

Joe and Kay-Lo are lying on the towel over the hot sand. They are talking about Jake. They want to plan things out soon so that they don't take too long deciding what to do with him. Kay-Lo wants Joe to remind her to go down to Joey's school tomorrow so that she can talk to Mr. Russ about Jake. She is planning to register him at Joey's school.

Joey is a really nice kid. There is only one thing that Joe doesn't like about him: Joey cannot stand up for himself. He doesn't know how to take revenge on people who pick on him. One time, Joey told Joe that he doesn't like fighting and that he usually bites. Joe doesn't think that biting is strong enough. He will have to do something about Joey. Even if Joey is a kindhearted kid, he will have to defend himself at some point. With any luck, in the future Joey will do more to take revenge on people.

Kay-Lo doesn't know Joey's circumstances that well because she has been in the United Kingdom visiting her elderly grandmother for months. She wants Joe to visit her just in case he goes there.

When a few more minutes have passed, Joe and Kay-Lo go in the water to have fun family time along with Joey and Jake. Later that morning, they come out of the water to rest on the sand.

After resting for a couple of minutes, Joey and Jake go over to watch several kids play beach volleyball. After a foul play, Joey picks up the volleyball and asks one of the kids if he can play. One of the kids just laughs and starts making fun of him. Jake tells the kid to leave him alone. The boy laughs, says some mean things to Jake, kicks sand in his face, pushes Joey into the hot beach sand, and then walks away. Jake picks Joey up and tells him to forget about it, that the kid is just rotten.

At noon, they leave the beach and make their way back to the house on foot. Later that afternoon, Joe is sitting on the living room couch. Jake comes out of the garage after parking his bike there and joins Joe in the living room. He asks Joe if there is a basketball hoop because he saw a basketball in the garage. He wants to get out of the house and play. He wants to stay active and healthy.

"Sorry!" Joe apologizes. "Don't worry; either your Uncle Joseph or I will buy you one later this week. A little advice for you, Jake—never eat junk food before playing sports. It can make you sick and it will make your breath smell bad. Eat healthy snacks to stay healthy, and always wash your mouth."

"I already know that, silly! This may sound dumb, but when I was four or five, I used to think that detergent was something you gargled in your mouth because it's considered a cleaning substance. Then I was introduced to something called mouthwash."

"Uncle Joseph really messed up your mind back then!" Joe exclaims.

Jake says, "That I believe, but at least he didn't mess up my face when I was afraid to go on the plane yesterday and embarrassed him. There is a reason I didn't want to go on the plane, but the strange part is that I don't remember why. But it's lucky I went on, or else I wouldn't be here in Florida. I wouldn't have had a chance to explore this place."

Joe comes up with an idea. When he comes home from work tomorrow, since Jake will be home, he is going to take him to explore the area so that he will get to know his environment well before Joe gets Joey from school. After getting Joey from school, they will head over to Everyday Gym to get some exercise.

Joe goes into the bedroom, leaving Jake alone in the living room. Jake is about to take a step when someone rings the doorbell. Jake opens the front door and sees Frankie. Frankie comes in, apologizing that he couldn't make it to the beach. Jake says that he didn't mind and that it was okay. Frankie was with his mom getting ready for school. Jake thinks he's lucky; he still needs to get his supplies for school just in case he starts this upcoming week.

Frankie wishes Jake luck in finding a new school and tells him to make sure nobody bothers him. He wants him to act tough and to be brave.

Frankie walks away, making Jake remember the kid that bothered Joey at the beach. For some reason, the kid he saw looked very familiar. He wonders how people from the past can meet their old friends and know where they are. He remembers something Joe told him on the phone a year ago, that over the summer he saw one of his coworkers at Ezra's Creek. He was exploring with his coworker because he kept hearing rumors that there was an underground cave with something hidden inside of it. He told Jake that people he knows from years ago, old enemies and friends alike, can appear out of nowhere and surprise him. Jake finds that weird.

Inside, the house is very bright and clean with a delightful atmosphere. Later on, Joe goes on the computer to write a blog on some website until he notices that there is a video message for Joey. Joe calls out to him, but he is in the basement washing his clothes from the past week. Kay-Lo was going to tell him, but she had to get Joey and Jake ready for school. Jake will tell Joey that he has a video message. He is mad that Joey received a message and he didn't, and he is older than the kid. Joe warns him that getting messages isn't always good; they can bring bad news. He will find out when he gets older. Jake is relieved, at least he was told. He goes downstairs into the basement.

"Hey, you spoiled fool," he says to Joey. "Dad said that you got a video message on the computer."

"Really? I'm surprised."

"Me, too!"

"I wonder who it's from," Joey says.

"Why don't you go upstairs on the computer and see for yourself, slowpoke?"

"Gee, thanks for the sarcasm. You and Baron should use that on one another. Baron is such a sarcastic kid, so I think you and he should hang out with each other a lot, get to know each other better. That's if you like to hang out with a kid who is very dumb, of course. And don't call me a spoiled fool again."

Joey goes upstairs to the computer and finds out that the video message is from one of his classmates, Dakota. This is the first time Joey has ever received an e-mail. When he clicks on the envelope icon, a video message of Dakota appears.

"Hello, Joey Fallon and Frankie Bennett. Yes, you should already know who I am. I'm your classmate, Dakota Ora. There is something that I would like to tell you. I won't be coming to school this week because one of my cousins seems to have had a panic attack. I will explain what happened. While I was at the hospital with him, he told me that he saw this kid that he knew. He is the kid who bullied and beat him up in school almost every week back in 2007. If you would like to know where he saw this kid, it was at our school. Yes, I'm talking about Sea Sight Elementary School. While he was there at eleven o'clock Saturday morning, he was alone, getting his belongings that he's going to need for the school year. After he got his stuff, he saw the kid, and the kid made eye contact with him and started to smile. He walked up to my cousin, but some woman happened to call him before he did anything. The kid walked away, and my cousin couldn't control his breathing. His heart was racing and he dropped to the floor. Principal Russ tried to calm him down, but he was still panicking. Principal Russ brought him to the infirmary for medical treatment. Later, the ambulance arrived at the scene and they had to take him to the hospital, where he could receive proper treatment. My cousin knows the boy very well and doesn't know why he was bullying and beating him up, but it looks like he needs to get revenge. I'm asking you guys if you can do to the boy exactly what he did to my cousin. I want you guys to bully and beat him up. Teach him a lesson that it is not cool to bully other people. Before I end this video message, there is one last thing I would like to tell you guys. My cousin told me that he can appear out of nowhere. He is also sneaky, and from the sound of all this, it sounds like he's about to enter our school as a new student. I don't know, but if he is, then kids in that school should be careful when they're around him. He can be a bully. My cousin also heard that the kid is up to something. I don't know what that means, so another thing I want you guys to do is try to gather some information from him to see what he is up to. I just want to make sure that he isn't up to something that has anything to do with my cousin or me. That's the reason I want you guys to do that. Well, have a pleasant first week of school. I should be back soon. Bye, kids!"

That is the end of the video message. This is going to be a long school year for Joey. He gets up and goes into the bedroom, unable to believe that he and Frankie have been given a mission. Joey isn't looking forward to it, but Dakota is his best friend, so he might as well help him. Joey and Frankie are going to team up to make it easier to see what the new kid is up to.

A few minutes have passed, and Joseph has returned home from his job hunting. There are no decent jobs for him. He did see one place that was nice, a restaurant near a creepy manor, but they aren't looking for any employees at the moment. To take things easy, Joseph decides to take a nap so he won't feel worn out. He makes his way to his own bedroom to take an hour-long nap.

After an hour has passed, Kay-Lo enters the house with school supplies for Joey and Jake. Joseph has woken up from his nap and gone to the kitchen to get some ice cream. Once he has his ice cream, he sits down next to Joe on the couch. Joe wants to know how Joseph's job back in New York was.

Joseph says, "It was the best job I've ever had. I loved being a gym coach!"

It is nice to hear that Joseph's job was the best he's ever had. Joe currently works at a day care center. They put on puppet shows for the kids, give them food, make sure they take their naps, and make sure that they are safe and in good health. They need to have fun during their young lives. He gets paid seventeen dollars an hour.

Joe wants Joseph to help him with something money-related. He told him that while he was chasing down his suspect, he destroyed the black car. The car is at the auto repair shop at the moment. He's already given them more than half of the money, but he still needs to give them over two hundred dollars.

Joe says to Joseph, "I would give them the money from my bank account. But that money is for the five of us Fallons. Right now, I'm broke. The day care center pays good money, but it is stressful to receive it sometimes. Good thing I don't work there on Thursdays, so I can rest. What do you say? Would you help me?"

"Okay, I will help you pay the rest of the money for the car repairs. I still have a lot of money from my old job. How much money do they still need to get?" Joseph asks.

"So far I gave them $340 on Friday and $50 yesterday. That means they still need $210. Simple addition and subtraction. Oh, and do you mind buying Jake a new outdoor basketball hoop?"

"I sure will. I'll buy one some time this week so he can practice his basketball skills."

First, Joseph needs directions to the auto repair shop, which is near a building called the S.S. Security building. He can't miss it. He will see what he can do. Before he goes to the auto repair shop, Joe warns him that the mechanics will think that he is a fraud, so Joe will leave his ID card on the table tomorrow. When Joseph takes it to the shop, the mechanics will look at the last name and know that Joseph is related to Joe. Joseph will see what happens when he gets there. Joe can count on him.

Later on, inside Joey and Jake's bedroom, Joey and Frankie are eating ice cream. Joey explains to him about the video message Dakota sent earlier about the new kid at their school. They share their thoughts about the mission, which is going to start tomorrow at school. They wonder how long this mission is going to take.

"Something just hit me," Frankie says to Joey, putting the bowl of ice cream on the dressing table. "You said that Dakota's cousin was inside the school building yesterday morning before noon?"

"Yes," Joey replies. "Then, after he saw the kid who bullied and beat him up two years ago, he started having a panic attack. Later the ambulance came to take him away."

"Ambulance? Joey, I think I know the kid that made Dakota's cousin panic. It's the same kid who is looking for a person whose last name is . . . I'm not going to say it. You might get ideas. After I left the school, I did see an ambulance approaching the building. That means it was Dakota's cousin who made them appear. How come I didn't notice his cousin?"

"That's because you don't know him."

"Oh, right," Frankie says. "So Dakota gave us a mission to see what the new kid is up to?"

"Yes, once we find out what he's up to, we have to tell Dakota. If we don't see him on the Skybot video chat or at school, we will simply send Dakota a quick message. So what's the plan, since you're so smart?"

So far, Joey knows that Frankie is the smartest kid he has ever known, which is why he always asks him for help at school or asks him what to do. Today is one of those days, so the first plan Frankie has in mind is to introduce themselves to the new kid. That way, the kid will become great friends with them and talk to them. Then he might give them some helpful information to help them see what he is up to.

The whole purpose of that first plan is so that Frankie knows the kid can trust him and Joey. Then maybe they can help him find the person he is looking for. If that doesn't happen, they might as well move on to something else. Another thing that Joey and Frankie need to find out is what the new kid is planning to do once he finds the person he's looking for.

"What else did Dakota say?" Frankie asks Joey, with ice cream all over his bottom lip.

"He wants us to find out who the kid is. You already know who he is, but I don't. Once we find him, he wants us to avenge his cousin by bullying the kid and beating him up to teach him that it's not cool to bully or beat up other kids. I have a problem with that. I don't like fighting or hurting people, and I don't like bullies."

Frankie says, "I think you're right. If we fight or bully the kid, we will have to take responsibility for our own actions. It's best for us to find out what he is up to. That's all we have to do. This mission shouldn't be too hard. We will just have to wait and see what happens when school starts tomorrow."

"Okay, I get it. Do you mind wiping the ice cream off your bottom lip before it turns into an icicle?" Joey says.

Frankie's next plan is to find out the kid's name and to make sure Joey uses his fake last name. That's all he has to do. Finally, during lunch they will sit next to the new kid and have a little chat with him. This way, they should be able to learn things about him. After school is over . . . well, Frankie doesn't know about that part yet. There is nothing else planned for tomorrow—those are all the plans Frankie has for now. What will happen during the school week?

Joey goes back on the computer to send Dakota a video message on Skybot. Dakota isn't online, so he won't see Joey's video message until he logs back in. Joey has sent Dakota the plans for the new kid that he and Frankie are going to carry out at school tomorrow. That's just about it. Joey logs off of the Skybot video chat.

There isn't much to do for the rest of the day. Joey packs his things for school tomorrow inside his book bag, and Frankie goes home to do the same. Everyone else in the house doesn't do anything but try to make this Sunday last.

That night, everyone is in the living room watching their favorite Sunday night sitcom, *4 Rich Girls*. The show is about four rich girls who are forever fighting because each girl thinks that her stuff is better than the other girls' stuff. The show's rating is 2.1 out of ten. Later, when the show is over, Joe, Joseph, and Kay-Lo go to bed while Joey and Jake stay up with the bedroom door closed and the light on.

Joey asks Jake, "How did you like your first weekend in this lovely house?"

"The weekend was excellent," Jake replies. "Sandy Beach happens to be the cleanest beach I've ever been to. There's a beach in New York that is full of junk. And the seagulls, for example—how rude can they be?"

"I've never been to New York, so I wouldn't know. Okay, enough blabbering. Time for bed. I've got school in the morning."

Jake says, "I can't wait to see my new school, whenever that is. I'm not looking forward to middle school in the next two years. Middle school is wack—there are more bullies, the teachers are meaner, and the kids smell like they shower with rotten tomatoes."

"Was that supposed to be funny?" Joey asks.

"Kind of."

"Listen, middle school isn't going to be all that bad. The thing that I don't like about it is that the work gets harder and the kids act very stupid. That's not going to happen to us. We'd better make sure that we make ourselves look adorable. Uh, I mean cool . . . yeah, cool. So, uh, which school do you think you're going to get accepted to?"

"I hope it's yours. I wonder how southern kids act. I bet they have a different accent. I'll get used to it—I'm pretty good at understanding other people's accents, anyway. Umm, do you mind if I put my swimwear inside one of your drawers?" Jake asks.

"The bottom right drawer is empty. Just take the mega flashlight out of there and put it in the top left drawer on the top left. And don't ask me why I keep a mega flashlight in the drawer."

When Jake finishes unpacking, he turns off the light and cracks open the bedroom door so they can let some fresh air into the bedroom. He goes to the window and looks at the grassy backyard, with a trampoline that is hardly used and a white fence in the back. After viewing the backyard, he closes the curtain, dives into the bed where Joey also sleeps, and goes to sleep. Everybody inside the house is now asleep.

How is Joey and Frankie's mission at Sea Sight Elementary School going to turn out this week? They will soon find out.

Chapter 5

Tricky Questions

On this breezy Monday morning, Joe and Kay-Lo walk out of the bedroom they share and make their way to the kitchen. Kay-Lo is going to make breakfast. Joe is making his way to Joey and Jake's bedroom to wake Joey up when he realizes that Joey is already at the kitchen counter with his head down, snoring. Joe taps him on the head to wake him up.

Joey takes his head off the counter, drool stuck to his left cheek. Joey explains that he had a tough time sleeping last night, so he went out of the bedroom, went into the kitchen to pour himself some milk, and warmed it up in the microwave. He drank the warm milk at the counter, and when he was done, he put his head down and ended up going to sleep.

While Joe is ironing his clothes for work and Kay-Lo is making breakfast, Joey making his way back to the bedroom to change into his school clothes. His legs are still wobbly; he just didn't get enough sleep last night. When he's back inside the bedroom, he sees that Jake is still asleep. Joey is jealous of Jake because he gets to stay home until he finds a school, which he hasn't done yet because he just moved in. Joey figures that his Uncle Joseph is still asleep, as well. Once he finishes getting his clothes on for school, Joey makes his way back into the kitchen again and lays his head down on the counter. He doesn't like getting up early in the morning.

"Start getting used to it again," Kay-Lo says to Joey. "You will be doing that for the next nine months."

"It had to be you to say that," Joey replies.

"Here's your breakfast—eggs with sausages."

"Jake told me that he doesn't eat meat. I don't think you should give him sausages. Hey, at least your food looks appetizing. Those lunch ladies in school cook like garbage. I wonder what their husbands say about their food."

"Please, I know what I would like to say about Kay-Lo's food," Joe says.

Kay-Lo responds, "Say it and I won't make you any more."

"I'm just kidding."

"Eat my dust!"

After Joe has finished eating breakfast, he looks at his watch and sees that it is time for him to leave. Before he goes, he places his ID card on the living room table so that Joseph will see it before he goes to the auto repair shop to pay more money for the repairs. Joey finishes eating his breakfast just as the school bus arrives in front of the house.

Joey exits the house and makes his way onto the school bus. Kay-Lo then exits the house to go for her morning jog to work. She works at a local hotel. Before Joe leaves, he washes the dishes so he won't see anything in the sink when he gets home later, unless Jake puts something in the sink and doesn't wash it. Joe leaves the house, closing the front door and locking it, and makes his way to the day care center.

Meanwhile, on the school bus, Joey sits down next to Frankie, who is putting two bottles of water inside his string bag. Frankie always carries around one or two water bottles so that he doesn't get dehydrated in hot weather.

Frankie feels very excited this morning. Before he left the house for school, he drank a cup of coffee in a kid's mug. Joey wonders why Frankie didn't have eggs and orange juice. That would've been the best breakfast for him.

Frankie drank a cup of coffee because he went to bed late last night; he couldn't sleep at all. He wasn't too sure, but he probably went to bed at around four in the morning and woke up around six. He was too hot and had too many things on his mind. He was nervous about school today. Joey had the exact same problem: he had trouble sleeping last night. Frankie figures that this new mission they are about to start caused both of them lack of sleep.

Halfway to school, Matt and Baron sit down on the other side of the bus aisle, talking to Joey and Frankie. Matt Wilkins is nine years old; his birthday isn't until April. He was born in Florida. Matt's preference is to be an optimistic kid because he knows that when people don't think optimistically, they won't have a chance at a successful life.

Baron Jeremiah is ten years old, only one month older than Matt. Baron's nickname is "Freaky Baron" because of the way he acts sometimes. This is his second year at Sea Sight Elementary School. Baron was born in Newcastle, England, and moved to New York at the age of six. Then he moved to Florida at the age of eight. Baron has a rude, sarcastic sense of humor, but what's amazing about that is that some people don't know whether he is being sarcastic or not.

On the school bus, Matt looks inside his leather knapsack to make sure he has everything he needs for school. He is all set; the only thing he doesn't need is this set of binoculars he rarely uses. He must remember to take them out when he gets home today. Seeing that he is all set, he asks Joey and Frankie if they are ready for their first day back to school.

Joey says, "The beginning of the school year might be a bit challenging, but it should get better as the year goes on. Our friend Dakota gave us a mission to find out what the new kid in our school is up to. That's all we have to do."

When Matt finds out that they are about to do some detective work, he wants to join. Joey is most grateful, but he doesn't want Matt to buzz off on the mission too soon, just in case something bad happens.

Joey starts explaining to Matt why Dakota has asked them to see what the new kid is up to. Matt saw someone else experiencing a panic attack, and it wasn't a good feeling for him. It was one of the most disturbing things he has ever seen in his life. He hopes he will never see anything like that again. Joey thinks that everything is going to turn out as they've planned. He promises Matt that he won't see any more panic attacks.

Baron is curious to know what the kid looks like; he wants to get a description of him. Because Frankie is the only one who saw the kid in person, he explains what he looks like. The kid is about his size, with brown eyes, black hair, and both ears pierced. The kid's earrings are shaped like stars. After hearing the description, Matt and Baron agree to watch out for the kid for Joey and Frankie. Frankie appreciates their kindness.

The school bus is almost in front of the school building. Frankie reaches inside his string bag to take out two devices that will help him and Joey with their mission. Since Matt and Baron agreed to help them today, he will kindly lend them their own devices tomorrow. The device is a voice-to-voice radio.

Joey has always wanted a voice-to-voice radio. It is something that he has nagged his parents about since it came out in 2007, but his mother, Kay-Lo, won't get one for him because she is too cheap.

Frankie gives the device to Joey so that they can keep in touch with one another if they come up with something. No one else in the world who owns a voice-to-voice radio will hear Joey and Frankie's conversation because there is a different connection installed in every device.

The voice-to-voice radio works by sticking the voice chip inside their ears and talking through mini handheld radios. The voice chip allows the person to hear the other person's voice. It's impossible for the voice chip to go too deep inside their ears. The voice chips are waterproof, so they don't have to worry about taking them out unless they need to clean their ears. The weird thing about the voice chip is that it can also pick up smartphone conversations, so they can only hear the person talking through a smartphone. Frankie has no idea why.

This is a perfect device to help them with their mission, but Frankie isn't too sure if using the voice-to-voice radio is worth it. He will have to wait and find out. Matt and Baron can't wait to start this mission and see how it will turn out. There is one more thing that Frankie wants them both to know: they cannot foil their plans and end up doing their dirty work with the kid.

"I doubt that will happen," Baron says to Frankie. "Listen, Matt and I are your best friends. We will never foil your plans."

Frankie says, "You'd better not. We have to do this for Dakota and his cousin. Dakota is our best friend, so we should never let him down. Best friends should always trust one another. If they break that trust, it means they are not your true friends."

"Why is this boy so smart?" Baron asks Matt.

The bus stops in front of the school. Kids get off the bus and make their way inside the building, which has an almost all-white scheme with a white and blue flag that represents the school. Sea Sight Elementary School has been around for over seventy-five years. For about twenty years, the school had an assistant principal named Mr. Clang, who retired last year.

This current school year, they have a new assistant principal named Mr. Griffin. Joey, Frankie, Matt, and Baron will be able to meet him very soon. The school building was renovated in the nineties to create more space and fewer safety hazards for the kids. Another known fact is that the school doesn't require uniforms, but only decent clothing is permitted within.

Joey, Frankie, Matt, and Baron stand next to each other, about to enter their second year at Sea Sight Elementary School. They'll get to meet new kids, teachers, and the new assistant principal, and they have new books with lessons to learn. But three of them are not looking forward for it.

"Welcome back to jail, guys," Joey says to Frankie, Matt, and Baron. "A long year is ahead of us. This is going to be a fun year. Hooray."

Baron says, "I like your sarcasm. Don't worry—the school year will go by fast. Our education is very important. What would we do without it?"

"Nerd!" Frankie exclaims. "By the way, since when do you care about our education? You didn't care at all last year."

"Are you trying to say I'm heartless? For shame!"

Inside the school building, the hallway is filled with a lot of new kids. It is time for Joey, Frankie, Matt, and Baron to begin the school year with a mission concerning the new kid.

While they make their way to their lockers, someone pushes Joey to the floor, causing someone else to trip over him. Joey quickly gets up, wondering who just pushed him. There are too many kids in the hallway, so he isn't sure. When Joey reaches the lockers, Baron sees that his hair is messed up. Joey doesn't want to hear any questions from him; he just wants to know who pushed him just now. He hasn't even been inside the school for a minute.

While the kids are waiting for the school bell to ring, Joey, Frankie, Matt, and Baron go to the school cafeteria since Baron missed out on his breakfast before leaving his house. He has a quick bowl of cereal while he plays cards with Joey, Frankie, and Matt.

Frankie says, "It's nice to come to the cafeteria for breakfast. Hey, Joey, I thought Jake was going to be here today."

"Not yet. He hasn't found a school yet since he just moved to Florida. Eventually he will find one, and I hope it's this one."

"Your brother sure does have a lot of hair on his head. You can barely see his eyes. Well, actually you can, but he needs one of these to straighten out his hair," Baron says, taking out a comb from his knapsack.

"You carry a comb with you?" Frankie asks.

"Yep. You see, I don't like my hair to be messed up while I'm out in public, so I carry this comb just in case. Another reason is that if I see a girl having a bad hair day, I will loan her a comb. If the girls want to make their hair look better, I will give them one of my mother's hair products, but those girls had better pay me for it first. I also have makeup just in case the girls look ugly. One more thing—I brought along some gum, so when I give it to the girls, they can chew it and look cool at the same time."

"At least you can see the humor in girls," Frankie comments.

When the school bell rings, Joey, Frankie, Matt, and Baron leave the cafeteria and make their way down the hall to their first-period class. All the other school kids are making their way to their first-period classes as well. Two kids run by, and one of them knocks Joey to the floor. The kid starts laughing at him, which means he purposely knocked him down. Again, Joey doesn't see who the kid was.

Frankie and Matt do not have first period with Joey and Baron; they have no classes together. Joey and Baron's first-period class is art with Ms. Winchell. She has been doing art since she was seven, and she is now a teacher to help kids develop a more creative mind. That is what this class is mostly about; it is very simple for the kids.

By the time first period is over, it is time to move on to second period. Mr. Griffin has made his first appearance in the hallway. He is looking around for a kid named Baron. Baron nervously walks up to Mr. Griffin and introduces himself to him. Mr. Griffin greets Baron and says he wants to speak to him in his office. Baron knows that today is the first day of school, and he feels that he is already in trouble. What does Mr. Griffin want from him?

Joey, Frankie, and Matt will catch Baron later. They start to make their way to their second-period class. While Baron is walking with Mr. Griffin, he keeps his head down, hoping that he isn't in trouble. Baron doesn't even know what he did. When he's near Mr. Griffin's office, he comes across something. He walks back to the room he passed to catch a glimpse of the room from the outside. Mr. Griffin calls Baron and wants him to continue walking with him to his office.

Baron walks into the office to see why Mr. Griffin needs him. Later, during second-period English class, Baron enters the classroom and finds a seat next to Joey.

Baron says, "Hey, Joey I didn't know we had this class together."

"Isn't that something?" Joey replies. "Why did that new assistant principal need to see you in his office?"

"His name is Mr. Griffin. He wanted to see me because my mother sent my glasses to school. My eyesight is terrible when I'm reading, so she is afraid that people will think I can't read."

Joey says, "That's a dumb reason for Mr. Griffin to call you into his office."

"It really is. He has a lot of keys on a split key ring hanging on his office wall. Listen here; while I was making my way to his office, I came across a high-tech room. I don't think it was there last school year. When class is over I will show you, Frankie, and Matt. By the way, Mr. Griffin has an enormous forehead."

After their second-period class is over, Joey stands as close as possible to his locker; he knows for sure that the same random kid is going to pass by again and purposely knock him down to the dirty floor. Baron and Joey are talking, and they are waiting for Frankie and Matt to arrive so that Baron can show them the newly installed room.

Baron is still talking to Joey. While he is talking to him, he spots a security camera hanging from the ceiling. He looks around the hallway and notices that there are more. Later, Frankie and Matt join Joey and Baron. Baron shows them the incredible high-tech room on the other side of the hallway.

They explore inside the room, which they discover controls the security cameras throughout the building. The monitors show live footage of what is taking place inside and outside the building. This means that they are being watched and won't be able to sneak out of the building or escape from doing illegal things inside the school—sooner or later someone will find out about it from the security footage.

This is an amazing room, but their time there is over. Mr. Griffin walks toward the monitor room, and he spots the four kids. He wants to know what they are doing in the monitor room. He wants them to come out of there this instant. Once Joey, Frankie, Matt, and Baron are out of the monitor room, Mr. Griffin closes the door.

Baron says, "Apparently, we are not allowed in there."

Mr. Griffin replies, "Yes, Baron, you are correct."

"Hey, he remembered my name. That's awesome!" Baron exclaims. "Who works in that monitor room?"

"We have a security guard who will work in there to monitor the whole school building. She will be here in a matter of minutes."

Joey says, "We apologize for trespassing, Mr. Griffin. We won't go in there again. What are the consequences for going inside that monitor room?"

"Students will serve detention for a week during lunch and after school," Mr. Griffin answers.

Baron says, "Whoa, two detentions each day for one week? You've seriously got demons in your head."

"Quit it, Baron, before we get two weeks of detention," Joey warns him.

It is 9:39 a.m., and that is when third period begins. Frankie has math, his least favorite subject, and he is now with Baron. Joey has gym, and he is with Matt this time. Frankie and Baron's class has already started. Inside Ms. Nancy's classroom, Frankie has claimed the desk in front of Baron's so he doesn't have to feel uncomfortable with the kids he doesn't know.

Ms. Nancy, their math teacher, greets everyone in her class. Because today is the first day of school, Ms. Nancy would like to know her students better. She gives them each a piece of paper and asks them to write down some details about themselves. When that is done, she starts to explain to the class about the activities they are going to be doing throughout the school year. Any time Baron hears the word "activities," he thinks he is going to be doing something fun like arts and crafts, but that fun ends up being hard schoolwork with questions he has trouble answering. Sometimes he just leaves the question blank or guesses an answer that doesn't relate to the question.

Inside the gym later, during third period, Joey and Matt are playing a game of basketball. When they finish, they take a rest on the bleachers. Matt feels devastated that he didn't win the game. Last school year, when they were playing the same sport, they kept losing. But Matt isn't going to take it too personally. Joey admits that they stink at basketball. He tells the truth, that he doesn't like basketball and prefers playing baseball, one of his favorite sports. Matt likes football, where he can make a touchdown. Football has all the action.

While looking around the gym, Matt sees the gym coach putting some dumbbells underneath a bleacher. Then he happens to see a random boy sitting on the same bleacher all alone. Joey can't see him, so Matt points the kid out to him. Joey, a kindhearted boy, feels that the kid is all alone and needs some friends. Matt has always admired Joey's heart and will do anything for anyone, unless that person is a kidnapper or does other illegal things.

Joey jumps off the bleachers. He will return to Matt after he finishes talking to the kid. He goes across the gym and sits down on the bleacher. He sees that the kid is nervous, so he calmly introduces himself and asks the kid how he likes his first day of school.

"I . . . I guess it's going okay," he nervously answers Joey. "I'm only here to look for another kid."

"Another kid?" Joey asks. "Who are you looking for?"

"I don't know. My mom told me to look for a person whose last name is Fallon. Do you know any Fallon kid in this school?"

"Fallon kid? Tell me more about this Fallon kid you speak of, since you mentioned your mom."

"I don't know anything about him," the kid says.

"Why are you looking for this Fallon kid? I can help you find him . . . maybe!"

The boy sighs. "I'm looking for him because my dad happens to know his dad. I'm not allowed to mention my dad's name, if you were going to ask. To be honest with you, I don't even know my dad's name."

"How do you not know your own dad's name? What's your name?" Joey asks.

The kid takes a deep breath. "My name is . . . Scram Bumbleberry."

Joey almost starts to laugh. "Sorry, I'm not laughing. That's a nice name." He almost laughs again. "How does your dad know this Fallon kid's dad?"

Scram doesn't know how they met, so he only tells Joey that they met once back in New York. Joey thanks Scram for that piece of information. He steps off the bleachers and starts to laugh. He rejoins Matt on the other bleacher and tells him what he found out: the kid's name is Scram Bumbleberry, and he said something strange about his dad knowing Joey's dad from New York. Matt laughs at Scram's last name. Although Scram said that strange thing about his dad knowing the Fallon kid's dad, he believes that it can't be Joey. It's probably another Fallon.

Joey believes that it isn't another Fallon, because he remembers that on Saturday afternoon, before the reunion party, Frankie asked that, if Joey was the only Fallon at Sea Sight Elementary School and someone was looking for him, would he tell that person about himself or his family. Joey is going to speak to Frankie in the hallway before fourth period.

When third period is over, Joey and Matt make their way back to the hallway to meet up with Frankie and Baron, and to tell both of them what he found out from this kid. Baron nearly dies of laughter when he learns Scram's name, and Frankie laughs a bit. Baron doesn't know why Scram's last name is Bumbleberry. Joey then explains the news that Scram's dad knows this Fallon kid's dad. Joey remembers what Frankie said about his last name this past Saturday, and now he wants to know who Scram is. Why is Scram looking for this Fallon kid? Joey knows that it's him.

"It's a short explanation," he says to Joey. "I was at school on Saturday to get my schedule, textbooks, and other boring things I need. Before I left, Scram and I guess it was his mother were talking to each other. His mom told him to look for the person whose last name is Fallon—which is you, Joey—and ask you some questions. I don't know the full story about why they need to find you, but you have to try your best to protect your identity. Keeping your privacy to yourself is the most important thing anyone can do."

"I think it's coming together. Is this why you asked me what my fake last name would be?"

"Now you know, and you said Jarrett. If you had said Fallon, I'm pretty sure Scram would do something to you that nobody would notice, but don't worry about that."

Joey says, "I still want to know what they want with me."

Frankie guesses that since Joey is a little kid, he knew that little kids can sometimes spread the word. Perhaps Scram is looking for Joey to do just that—ask Joey some tricky questions to expose private information about him or someone else. If Scram wants to do that, Joey and Frankie should do to the same to him—ask Scram some tricky questions to see what they can find out.

"To keep you safe from accidently exposing private details to someone, I'm going to let you in on a little secret," Frankie says to Joey. "You've got to be careful when someone asks you a tricky question. Sometimes you don't know whether you're being asked a tricky question. That's why you must keep your answers short, smart, and simple."

The school bell is about to ring. Frankie and Baron go to their next class. Joey is with Matt again for the next class. While

Joey and Matt make their way to their fourth-period class, Joey thinks about what Frankie just explained to him. He feels nervous because he isn't sure if he will be asked a tricky question and end up spilling the beans. He is going to try his best not to expose any secrets to anyone.

Fourth period has started. Joey and Matt have history with Mr. H. Frankie and Baron have class together again. Their fourth-period class is science with Ms. Olive. When fourth period is over, it is time for lunch. The cafeteria is a bit crowded. After fighting through the crowd of kids, Joey, Frankie, Matt, and Baron reach their lunch table. The kids are still acting like wild animals. Frankie notices that they have opened up the other side of the cafeteria, creating more space for them. Joey still wants to know why he's the only one who keeps getting pushed to the floor.

Baron says, "Maybe because you're too short and nobody can see you."

"I'm going to flip your chair over," Joey replies.

"Sorry I offended you."

Frankie says, "Okay, so Scram said that his dad knows Joey's dad from New York? I don't know what he means by that. If Scram is looking for this Fallon kid, who is Joey, and Scram's dad knows Joey's dad from New York, that means we will have to ask Scram a few more questions about this."

"I'm not too sure about this, but I'm thinking of two things that Scram might be trying to find other than me. He's either looking for my dad or he is looking for something else that is related to me or my dad."

While the kids are eating lunch and trying to figure things out, Kay-Lo enters the school to talk to Mr. Russ in his office. He is delighted to see Joey Fallon's mother again. She takes a seat in the chair across from Mr. Russ's desk. Mr. Russ asks what has brought her here. Kay-Lo tells him that her son from New York, Jake, just came to Florida, and she is wondering if he can come to the school. Mr. Russ is surprised that Kay-Lo has another boy; he thought she had a girl.

Mr. Russ will see what he can do, but first he has to have Kay-Lo fill out a few forms. It isn't that much for her to do. Once she hands it back to Mr. Russ, he says he will call and tell her if Jake is accepted at the school. If he is, she will have to pay the tuition of $750. Kay-Lo thinks that her bank account will be empty, but she thanks Mr. Russ. She hopes that Joey would like for his older brother to come to the school. If he doesn't, he will be upset. She will just have to wait and see.

Before Kay-Lo leaves the office, Mr. Russ starts to explain a few things to her about Joey's behavior. Joey is one of the best kids he has ever seen. He always keeps himself out of trouble.

"He's never like that," she says to Mr. Russ. "Jake, well he's a different story. His Uncle Joseph told me a lot about him. He can be very bad at times, but he's not really a bad kid. He told me that he likes to solve a lot of puzzles, and he also likes to help other people. That's what I like about him."

Mr. Russ smiles. He likes that Jake likes to help other people. After that little conversation, Kay-Lo thanks Mr. Russ for his time. She is all set to head back to work by jogging.

Back in the cafeteria, Matt notices that Scram isn't there. Frankie thinks that he might have gone to the bathroom. Joey looks at Frankie, wondering why he just said that. Frankie thinks this because, since they are elementary school kids, they aren't allowed to leave the cafeteria unless they need to use the bathroom, which is right near the cafeteria. Baron is relieved that he hasn't said that stupid opinion Frankie just shared.

Frankie decides to make more plans by himself since no one else is coming up with one while Scram isn't in the cafeteria.

Frankie's next plans are for tomorrow. They need to ask Scram a few questions while they are on the school bus—if they see him, that is. It's like what Joey did earlier today when he was at the gym talking to Scram.

Frankie's second plan is that while they are in the hallway before any class starts, they have to make sure that Scram goes into the classroom, nowhere else. If he doesn't go into the classroom and goes elsewhere instead, they have to make sure he isn't up to something that nobody knows about.

The next and final plan is for Joey and Matt only, and it may be a bit challenging for them. Since both of them have gym with Scram, Frankie wants Joey and Matt to break into Scram's locker and search his bag to see if they can find anything that might help them with this mission while they are in the locker room. After they finish searching, they'll have to remember to put his stuff back, or else Scram will know that it was them and they could get in serious trouble. Joey doesn't like that plan—it sounds too risky—but he is going to take the chance and break into Scram's locker.

There is only one thing that can help Joey and Matt break into Scram's locker, and that is to use a lock picking kit. Frankie used to have one, but since it broke, he will have to buy a new one at a shop.

Those are all the plans Frankie has for now. Matt notices that Scram has just entered the cafeteria. It is time to go talk to him to see if they can get more information about his dad and Joey's dad. All four of them sit down at the lunch table across from Scram. Scram already knows Joey, but he doesn't know Frankie, Matt, and Baron.

"Oh, how rude of me!" Frankie says to Scram. "I'm Frankie."

"I'm Matt, but it's short for Matthew."

"And I'm Baron, Scram," Baron shouts at Scram as if he is slow and stupid.

Joey says, "Just in case you can't remember our names, feel free to call us the four kids. It'll be five kids if my older brother gets accepted to this school."

It is a pleasure for Scram to meet three more kids. The way Scram is talking to them makes it seem like he is nervous, but he isn't; he just made a couple of new friends in the hallway just now. Matt figures out why they didn't see him in the cafeteria earlier during lunchtime. Joey wants to know what Scram is doing after school.

"Well, I'm not sure," Scram answers. "Besides, I've got a lot of work to do when I get back home. I got to clean my room, stack up papers, and help my mother do some shopping for the house. That's all I got to do. My dad is also going to meet up with his home dude today."

Baron laughs. "He said 'home dude.'"

"Yeah, and I remember that he said to me on Saturday that he goes to a place in southern Florida. I don't know what the place is called. Actually, I'm sure that the place doesn't have a name."

Baron asks, "What kind of place doesn't have a name? The place I live in is called 'home.' That has a name."

"Anyway, what do you do during your free time? I apologize for asking you so many questions. We just want to know you better," Joey says.

Scram replies, "It's okay, as long as I don't spill out too much personal information."

"I wish he would," Baron whispers to himself.

During Scram's free time, he likes to be with his friends and take walks. Another thing that he does during his free time is take a few photos of the places he sees. He's taken pictures of a few amazing buildings, including the apartment building where his dad lives. Scram has also taken pictures of Village Park on Planet Avenue and of the seashore.

Sometimes, at Village Park, Scram likes to plan things out with his friends so that things can go his way. He needs new friends now to work with him. Scram's biggest fear is not having any friends.

Joey finds the things Scram has just said about not having any friends very touching. He tells him about his fear of clowns; they can be very scary at times. He wishes that they never existed. Scram started to do all his walkabouts when summer started. Frankie thinks the things Scram does are very normal. It almost sounds to him like he isn't up to anything. They go back to their own lunch table wondering if they've found out anything about Scram. Frankie thinks that they haven't found anything at all.

"What about the things he said about his dad?" Matt asks Frankie.

"Yeah, you're right. He said that his dad goes to a place in southern Florida to meet up with his friend. Why does that sound so mysterious to me?"

Matt still wants to know the name of the place where Scram's dad goes, but Scram said that it didn't have a name. Baron doesn't think that's true. He thinks that Scram does know the name of the place; he just doesn't want to tell them the truth. But if he's not going to tell, how are they going to find out the name of the place? Matt didn't realize that this mission was going to be so hard, but he is a very optimistic kid and knows that they will pull off this mission somehow.

After lunch is over, the next class is about to begin. They have three more classes left. They are up to their fifth period now. Joey goes to his fifth-period class with Baron. They have Ms. Karol, who teaches writing, the same class Frankie and Matt had first period. Frankie and Matt are still in the hallway. Matt tells Frankie that Scram has just entered the classroom, so he won't be doing anything suspicious.

During fifth period, Mr. Griffin makes an announcement for all students and staff members. He wants them to meet him and Mr. Russ in the auditorium during last period. After sixth period is over, the whole school makes its way toward the auditorium. Joey, Frankie, Matt, and Baron sit in the back row of the auditorium. Frankie makes sure that Scram is there; if he isn't, he will start to think that Scram is already up to something.

Mr. Griffin says, "Welcome, kids! In case you didn't know, I am Mr. Griffin, the new assistant principal of Sea Sight Elementary School. Are you guys enjoying the first day back to school?" The kids moan and grumble. "Well, it's only the first day of school. I bet by the second day, you all will get your school spirit back."

"Listen to this joker," Baron says to Joey. "He said school spirit. I'm sure none of us has a school spirit. I've never even heard of that. He's such a dummy with that enormous forehead of his."

Joey laughs.

The kids wonder why Mr. Griffin has summoned them to the auditorium. Nothing bad has happened, so they don't have to worry about anything. Now that the first day of school is almost over, he would like to give them something special. When the kids receive their envelopes and open them, they find certificates to the history museum. It is an educational field trip for them. They are going this Friday, which Frankie thinks is pretty sweet—he loves educational activities. Mr. Griffin hopes to see all of them there. The next thing he would like to talk about is the rules when they go to the history museum.

Baron says, "Of course there have to be rules for this trip. I mean, come on, it's a museum. A museum has its own rules. Mr. Griffin is such a nerd. Only nerds make up rules."

"Are you talking to Frankie, Matt, and me, or are you just talking to yourself?" Joey asks.

"I don't know why, but I'm actually afraid to answer that question."

Mr. Griffin explains a few rules to the kids about what to do and what not to do during the museum trip. After he finishes explaining the rules, he is about to show the kids a video presentation about the museum. This is Baron's chance to go to sleep until school is over. When the boring video presentation is over, school has ended for the day. Joey wakes up Baron, and together they leave the school building.

Outside of the school, on the front steps, Matt is glad to see his old friends again. Tomorrow they can start fresh with their mission. He gets on the school bus to go home while Baron takes a local bus to get to his house. Joey and Frankie are still near the building, talking about how proud of themselves they are. They did pretty well today, having found out two things about Scram. Two is better than one. They will continue with their mission tomorrow and find out more secrets from Scram. Right now, they are done for the day.

Chapter 6

Weak Kid

Joe arrives in front of the school to get Joey and Frankie. They ended up walking with each other and having a talk. Joe drops Frankie off at home to change into his gym clothes, because he has decided to go with them to the gym. Joe and Joey go back to their house to do the same. Joey first lies down on the couch, so glad to be back home. He is never going to leave this house, even if it catches fire, like last year when Kay-Lo burnt food on the stove. They still use the stove, but Jake doesn't like the food that is made on it.

There is no time for resting; they have to hurry and change into their gym clothes. When they are in their gym clothes, about to head over to Everyday Gym, Jake says he doesn't feel like going because there is no point of exercising if he can't lift the heavy gym equipment. He doesn't understand the point of going to the gym is to exercise and gain strength. He used to do that a long time ago until he stopped because of an accident he had. He ended up losing his stamina and strength a couple of years later. Joe promises Jake that when they go to the gym, he will train him hard and advise him not to stop with his training. Jake hopes that going to the gym is worth training for.

Before going to the gym, they pick up Frankie. When they arrive at the gym, Jake isn't feeling it. Joseph is, though, and he is about to start doing some exercise, hoping that he will become buff some day and stay fit. He fears becoming an unhealthy person and wants to help people who feel that they are not healthy enough, which is one reason he is a gym coach.

For the next couple of hours at the gym, Joe helps Jake build up his muscles, because he's going to need the strength someday. Later on during the training, he is going to show Jake how to block attacks. It's very important for him to stand up for himself. While they are doing that, Kay-Lo goes on the field to do more running. Joey and Frankie go on the treadmill to get their blood pumping. They will feel great after that.

Joe teaches Jake how to stand up for himself by blocking attacks and taking down his opponents. He also helps him build up his strength by doing push-ups and sit-ups. Joe is trying to turn Jake into a tough kid.

There is a move that Joe would like Jake to learn: how to perform a spin kick. Joe is teaching Jake how to perform this move because he believes that it causes people to feel dazed, making it more likely that the fight will end without anyone stopping it. One condition: Joe doesn't want Jake to perform it unless he is getting attacked by someone he doesn't know. Jake knows that he will never get attacked by a random person, so it is probably unnecessary for him to learn this move. Still, Joe insists on teaching him.

Jake has a hard time with his training, but he just has to keep practicing. He will pull it off eventually. Later at the gym, Joe has just finished teaching Jake how to defend himself and how to take down his opponents. They start making their way to the treadmill.

When Joe and Jake get to the treadmill, Jake refuses to get on it. Joe tells him that it's a treadmill and he will have a lot of fun on it. Jake wonders if Joe thinks that he is stupid and doesn't know what a treadmill is and what it's for. He still refuses to get on it because of his fears of being on a moving platform.

Jake is afraid of treadmills because he fears falling off them. He also doesn't like escalators because he thinks they will eat up his foot. Those aren't Jake's only fears: he is afraid of robots, and there was also his fear of boarding the plane when he was making his way to Florida, a fear that stemmed from an incident at his old school. Jake doesn't remember the details of the incident, though. After what happened to Jake at Volotont Elementary, he never got inside any vehicles until this past Saturday. Jake is still terrified of them.

Joe says, "To be honest with you, I don't think a plane is a vehicle. I think it's only considered an aircraft."

"You graduated from college and you're saying that you think that a plane isn't a vehicle? I think you need to go back to school!" Jake replies.

Joe thinks Jake has a rude mouth, but at least he has learned that Jake's fears are robots and another random fear that Jake cannot remember. Joe understands now, so he goes back with Jake to make him do more exercise. Jake thanks Joe for what he is trying to do for him.

Later on at the gym, everyone is ready to head back home. After hours of training for strength, Jake's arms have started to hurt. It is good for him; as long as he's doing his exercises, he will build the strength he needs for the future. Joe is doing all this training for Jake because he wants him to defend himself against other people. He wants Jake to prove to him that he is a tough kid and not a weak one.

They leave the gym and make their way back home. Frankie reaches his house first. Then the Fallons arrive back at their house. Joey is glad that he's made it back home in one piece.

First he is going to shower and then take a nap; he is feeling exhausted. Jake tells everyone that he's going to play one of those racing games on the Xbox game console.

When Jake says something about racing, it reminds Joe of something. He asks Joseph if he went to the auto repair shop. Joseph was there earlier that morning when he was home. He used the ID card and everything went okay. The mechanic told him that he needed to give them a hundred dollars. He paid more money for Joe today. There was more news: they won't be getting the car back until next Sunday. The repairs will be done on Friday, and then they will take it for a test drive to see if it is running smoothly.

Joe can't believe that he has to wait until Sunday to get the car back. They just need to keep on stalling Kay-Lo to make sure she doesn't find out the truth about the car.

It is getting a bit dark outside. On the computer, Joe is writing a blog on a blogging website. He usually writes about his past, present, and future life. A lot of other bloggers like his work, so he continues to share more with them. While Joe is writing his blog, someone is calling from the Skybot video chat. It's for Joey, but he is napping. Joe decides to pick up.

"Hello?" he answers. "Oh, it's you, Baron."

"Joey? Wow, you grew up fast. I wish I could hit puberty like that."

Joe laughs. "I'm not Joey. It's me, Joe. Baron, don't you recognize me anymore?"

Baron says, "Oh, Mr. Fallon, it's you. Please accept my apology. For a minute there I thought I was talking to Joey."

"No, he's asleep. Would you like to leave a message? I can give it to Joey when he wakes up."

"No, thank you. It's a bit private. It's about … girls. Yeah, let's go with that. They can be so weird sometimes, the way they wear their makeup. You should see how hideous they look when they wear that. Ooh, it feels like Halloween all over again."

"Uh, okay," Joe says. "Jake is awake. Would you like to speak to him?"

"The kid that looks familiar? Umm, no, I don't want to speak to him. Anyway, you keep cool and make sure you tell Joey that I called on Skybot. Bye!" Baron logs off the Skybot video chat.

An hour later, Joey wakes up. When he steps out of the bedroom, Joe tells him that Baron called and wanted to speak to him on the Skybot video chat. Joey thinks that the news was *so* one hour ago, and he hopes that Baron is still online. When Joey logs into Skybot, Baron isn't online. Frankie, Matt, and some other random friends are online. He only calls Frankie and Matt. They talk more about their mission. Joey moves the mini flashlight, takes the white earphones from the computer desk, and plugs them into the computer speakers so that Joe, Joseph, and Kay-Lo won't hear their private conversation.

Matt finds out that Baron learned something about Scram. Now they can hear exactly what Baron heard. But there is just one little problem: Baron isn't online at the moment. They decide they might as well wait for him to get back online.

While the three of them are waiting for Baron to return to the Skybot video chat, they have a quick conversation about what to name their team while they are on a mission. Joey still can't think of a decent name.

Baron still has not returned online. What could be holding him back? Joey, Frankie, and Matt all want to know what he heard from Scram. Could it be that Baron is lying and feels guilty, and that's why he hasn't come back online yet? Joey, Frankie, and Matt decide to wait a little bit longer, so they talk about something else that isn't mission-related.

An hour goes by and Baron still isn't online, making Joey, Frankie, and Matt more impatient. Joe, Joseph, and Kay-Lo are in the living room watching a movie. Jake is still playing a racing game on the Xbox console in the bedroom.

Back at the computer desk, it looks like Baron has forgotten all about Joey, Frankie, and Matt. It looks like the three of them won't be able to find out what Baron heard from Scram earlier today when they left school. They might as well wait until the second day of school tomorrow.

They log out of the Skybot video chat to do their own business. Joey goes to the bedroom and joins Jake in playing a multiplayer racing game.

When Joey and Jake finish playing video games, the movie Joe, Joseph, and Kay-Lo's were watching is over. They get ready for bed.

While everyone else is sleeping, Jake is the only one up. He's in the living room when Joe comes out to get some water and notices that the television is on. He is about to turn it off when he notices that Jake is lying down on the couch watching television.

"Little Moth, what are you doing up this late?" Joe asks Jake, putting down the glass of water on the small living room table.

"I couldn't sleep," he replies. "I've been having these bad thoughts in my head. If you want me to tell you, I will be most grateful. This has something to do with you. I don't think I will ever be able to stand up for myself. I appreciate everything you did for me at the gym today a lot. I just don't think that it's going to work for me. I don't think I will never become a strong person like you."

Joe says, "Of course you will. As long as you keep training hard, you will end up feeling like a new kid. You will be better than ever before."

"Thanks for that. By the way, did you just call me a little moth?"

"Yeah, it's your nickname," Joe says. "I've used it since that January day when you were born. I quit my last job because of you. You were one of the tiniest babies I've ever seen."

"It made absolutely no sense for you to quit your job because of me. You must've been a very stupid person back then."

Joe thinks that Jake needs to work on his rude mouth, but he isn't going to do anything about it because he wants Jake to take responsibility for himself. Joe knows for sure that this is a great parenting technique.

They are still in the living room at three a.m. watching late-night shows. Jake is feeling a bit thirsty, but he doesn't want to drink water; he wants to drink coffee. Joe wonders how he knows about coffee. Joseph told Jake about it. Back in New York, in some weird neighborhood, Jake was watching fantasy cartoons while Joseph was up making something with a delicious smell. Jake loved the smell, so he asked him what he was making. Joseph told him that it was coffee.

Jake wanted to try the coffee; he swore he would be able to handle it. Joseph gave him a sip, and he loved it. Joseph gave him some more, and he finished the whole thing in less than five minutes. That was enough for him. It was so good that he wanted some more, but Joseph wouldn't allow him to have any more for some reason.

"Since you're so fascinated with coffee, I'm going to bring you to the Star-Bright coffeehouse next Monday night. You'll find out what true coffee tastes like," Joe says.

"I would love to go, but why on a Monday?" Jake asks.

"I'm busy with work on Saturday afternoon. The coffeehouse isn't open on Sundays. Next Monday night should be the best time, especially with that bright full moon."

"Oh, well, that's fine with me."

Joe and Jake will finally have some father and son time. Jake really likes the idea of going to the coffeehouse with his dad next Monday. It is a bit far off, but Jake has the patience to wait. He already knows that it's going to be a fun night with Joe. Jake gets so excited that he yells, waking up Kay-Lo and making her run out of the bedroom with a blue baseball bat in her hand. Her hair is all messed up.

"Oh, it was you who made that noise," she says to Joe and Jake, resting the blue baseball bat on her left shoulder. "What are you guys doing up this late at night drinking coffee?"

"What are you doing up this late at night holding a baseball bat?" Jake asks.

"Don't be mouthy. You are too young to be drinking coffee. It's not good for kids."

"Look, Mom—Dad and I were just here having a little talk, and you are never too young to drink coffee. I have seen a lot of kids younger than I am drinking coffee. Kind of strange, though!"

Joe says, "Jake and I are going to the Star-Bright coffeehouse next Monday. I would bring Joey, too, but he doesn't like coffee. I have no clue why not. I keep forgetting to ask him."

"People are different in their own way," Kay-Lo replies. "Well, I'm going back to bed. See you guys later, when the sun is out. Good night, my two loves." She walks back to the bedroom.

Joey doesn't drink coffee because if he drinks a cup, he will start seeing things during the day and he will have bad dreams at night. Joey makes sure to keep himself unharmed. He hopes that he will remain that way during his mission with Frankie, Matt, and Baron in the morning.

Chapter 7

Not a Care

The sun has made another appearance in Florida on this Tuesday morning, and so far, it is the hottest day of the week. Joe has woken up on the living room couch, where Jake is also sleeping. Joe goes to the kitchen to make some breakfast before he gets a move on. Before he finishes making breakfast, Kay-Lo enters the kitchen, surprised to see Joe up before her. Joe still feels a bit tired, but sleeping on the couch felt good. Jake still seems to be enjoying it.

Joe offers Kay-Lo some breakfast food. This is the third breakfast of the week. He made bacon and some cheesy eggs with a little bit of milk. His food is for enjoyment, and it will give them a lot of energy. He knows that today is going to be a big day for everyone.

Joey runs out of the bedroom, nervous that he has missed the bus because Jake isn't in bed. Then he remembers that Jake hasn't found a school yet. The school bus hasn't arrived in front of the house yet, so there is nothing for Joey to be worried about, other than his mission, which will continue at school. He is relieved because he thought he overslept. If he had missed the bus, he wouldn't have been able to get more information on what Scram is up to.

At the kitchen counter, Joey is about to eat Joe's wonderful work of art. He actually doesn't like the eggs because Joe put cheese in them. Joey doesn't like cheese, so he decides to have a yogurt instead. Joseph leaves to go to Everyday Gym. He wants to see if they will accept him as a gym coach.

While Joe and Kay-Lo are eating breakfast and Joey is eating yogurt, Joe asks Joey what he did in school yesterday. Joey doesn't want to tell him that he spent the whole school day trying to find out what Scram is up to. He is afraid that he will get in trouble, so he gives Joe a different answer. He explains that he has a new assistant principal, did some arts and crafts, and almost flipped Baron's chair over while he was sitting on it.

Jake wakes up on the living room couch and comes to the kitchen for breakfast. While he's eating the eggs, the school bus arrives in front of the house. Joey exits the house and makes his way onto the school bus. He sits next to Frankie while Matt sits in the seat behind them this time. They talk about what they are going to do today while they are in school.

If they were paying attention to their surroundings, they would notice that Baron isn't on the bus with them. Joey starts thinking that Baron has chickened out of the mission. He could've been afraid of what might happen to him during the mission, but nobody is going to do anything to him. Scram doesn't know what they are up to, which means that there is nothing for Baron to worry about.

Once Scram has gotten on the bus, Matt thinks that they should talk to him since this is one of their plans for day two. Scram is sitting in the back of the bus wearing an orange shirt, blue jeans, and white and blue sneakers. Joey, Frankie, and Matt move to the back to talk to Scram.

Scram greeted Joey, Frankie, and Matt. He started explaining to them how he dislikes some of the school kids because of how they made fun of his name yesterday when he was trying to make friends, and he didn't appreciate it one bit. Joey, Frankie, Matt, and Baron weren't around when this happened.

When Scram went back home yesterday, he cleaned his room before he went out with his mother. He thought about what the kids had done, and that got him so mad. He started screaming at the top of his lungs and knocking things over, and he broke one of his bedroom windows with a rock by accident. He couldn't stop thinking about what the kids had done to him. When he went to bed last night, an idea popped into his mind. He thought that he should start picking on the bullies to give them what they deserve.

They shouldn't have made fun of Scram's name. Now that they have disrespected him, he will get his revenge by picking on them. This will teach the kids not to disrespect one another. By the end of the day, a lot of the school kids will be afraid of Scram. If they tell Mr. Russ, Mr. Griffin, the teachers, or any of their parents, they will be in for a treat.

Scram doesn't tell the boys what he is going to do to the kids. Joey starts to feel afraid of making a wrong move with Scram after all the things he just said. It would be best for them to heed his words before Scram does something gnarly to them. Matt realizes that he is a bully who will pick on anyone, not just Dakota's cousin. It looks like there is no way of stopping Scram from doing that. To move things along, Joey asks him how his dad is doing.

Scram smiles because he just loves to answer questions. He explains to Joey that his dad is doing great. Yesterday his dad told him that he is going to a big house on Habitation Avenue to test some kind of metallic device. His dad can be a random person sometimes.

Frankie starts to figure out something. Just as Joey is about to ask Scram some more questions about his dad, Frankie pulls him back to their seats. Joey wants to know what that was all about, as he wasn't done asking Scram questions. Frankie tells him that Joey asked the most needed question to Scram. Joey asked Scram how his dad is doing. Having just found out that Scram's dad is going to Habitation Avenue and has a metallic device with him, he starts to get more clues. Matt hopes that the device isn't explosives.

Frankie thinks they should go to Habitation Avenue to see if they can find Scram's dad and see what kind of device he has. Joey completely disagrees with him. It is too dangerous for little kids like them to go to the city on their own. He's keeping himself safe in their area. If they go down there, they are just asking for it.

The bus arrives at school. They get off the bus, but Scram is actually the first one out of there. He doesn't waste any time before going inside and starting to push kids out of his way. Joey, Frankie, and Matt are still outside wondering what they are going to do about that boy. Who can stop Scram from acting like a complete fool?

Inside the school, while waiting for the bell to ring, Frankie reaches inside his string bag and takes out some tweezers. He also takes out the lock picking kit that he bought after he went home from the gym yesterday. Joey and Matt are going to use this to pick Scram's lock since they are in the same gym class. It's a very simple task for them to do. They have to take care of the lock picking kit; it may not be the last time they will ever need to use it. Joey puts the lock picking kit inside his pencil case for safekeeping. Frankie then gives Matt his very own voice-to-voice radio, which he thinks is wicked cool.

When the bell rings, Joey, Frankie, and Matt enter their first-period classes. Frankie has class with Matt. Joey is by himself in Ms. Winchell's art class, a class that is all about writing, drawing, crafting, and coloring nice pictures.

Joey has always wanted to be good at drawing, so this is his chance. Later on, in Ms. Winchell's class, Baron comes into the art room and sits behind Joey. Joey asks him where he was. Before Baron is able to speak, Ms. Winchell tells them to stop talking. Baron will tell Joey after Ms. Winchell finishes talking about something that Baron doesn't care about.

Once Ms. Winchell finishes telling the kids what they will be doing during the year, she gives them coloring papers to color. Today's picture is of a statue of a young kid skipping with a balloon in her hand. All they have to do is color it.

While they have free time to color, Joey wants to know why Baron wanted to speak to him but didn't get back on Skybot yesterday. Frankie and Matt were waiting as well. Baron stops coloring and looks Joey in the eye. He says he is completely sorry for what he has done; he completely forgot about them because it was his little sister Madelyn's birthday. They were partying until eleven o'clock at night. Baron wants Joey to forgive him, and Joey does.

Now that Baron has told Joey the truth, he can tell him what he heard from Scram yesterday, but he isn't going to tell him now because Frankie and Matt aren't with them. They will have to wait until all four of them meet in the hall. Baron tells Joey that he has something else to do today. Baron needs to sneak inside Mr. Russ's office, and he wants Joey to be on the lookout to make sure he isn't caught. Baron explains to Joey what he needs from Mr. Russ's office.

Joey, Frankie, Matt, and Baron meet with each other in the hall. Baron is about to tell them what he heard from Scram. Before he can even tell them, Scram himself walks up to them, making Baron nervous to say hi to him.

So far, school has been going great for Scram; he is starting to love it. He shows them a wristwatch that he took from some kid. It is the most valuable watch there is, and he just loves getting free stuff. Before Scram leaves to go to his class, he wants to introduce the four kids to the other friends he made yesterday during lunch. Scram will have to wait until next period is over to do that, though. He has to go to his next class.

Once Scram is gone, Baron tells them what he heard from Scram yesterday as he was leaving school. As he was making his way home, he noticed this kid in front of him; it was Scram. He heard Scram talking on his smartphone, and Baron assumed that he was talking to his dad. He heard Scram say that his dad has a duplication system that can clone almost anything. He also heard that Scram's dad goes inside a mansion on Habitation Avenue to test out the system with his wife, and it seems to be working. One thing that was surprising: all they need is to find Joey's dad and then that will be it, but to do that they must find this Fallon kid first.

When Joey hears that, he is in complete shock, with his mouth half open. He wonders why it is always his dad. Baron knows the name of the place. It's called Haunted Mansion World. It's the only mansion on Habitation Avenue, and it's been abandoned for many decades. Baron doesn't remember exactly how long it has been abandoned. He only knows this from his parents.

Baron knows that Scram knows the place; he just didn't want to tell the four of them, probably because he wanted to keep it private. Frankie is surprised that Baron figured that out all by himself; it is a good one for him. Baron feels like he has finally become a smart kid.

Frankie gives Baron his own voice-to-voice radio, which he kindly accepts. Joey starts shaking his head side to side with his eyes closed, wondering what Scram's dad wants with his dad. Could it be something dangerous? He tries to take his mind off it, but he is having a hard time doing so.

Joey wonders what Scram's dad could be doing with a duplication system. Matt guesses that he wants twins. The school bell rings then; second period has come. Frankie and Matt are in their class feeling very bored because their teacher won't stop talking about her life, which nobody needs to know about. Later, during second period, Mr. Griffin comes inside the classroom to talk to the teacher, finally bringing peace and quiet for the kids. Frankie overhears Mr. Griffin saying that he is going out right now to meet with his boss, so he won't be staying in school today. He will be back tomorrow. When he leaves the classroom, the teacher continues with her life story, irritating the kids once again.

After second period is over, Matt spots Scram bullying another poor kid in the hallway near the water fountain. Scram is picking on the kid because, apparently, the kid accidently stepped on his foot, messing up his new white and blue sneakers. The next time he does that, Scram will kick the kid so hard in the legs that he won't be able to stand for months. The kid quickly ran away from Scram while Scram was making his way to meet up with his four kids. Before second period starts, Scram mentions to the four kids that he would like to introduce them to his two new friends. One kid is named Leonard, and the other one is named Rodney. They are with Scram, so they can both help him make the school kids' lives miserable. Scram will see the four kids later.

Frankie wonders where Scram is going with his two friends. He is supposed to be going to the gym, but Scram is headed in a different direction. Matt doesn't want to get involved, so he simply walks away; Joey does the same and leaves with him to go to the gym. Frankie wants to see what Scram is up to right now, so he lets Baron tag along with him. It looks like Scram and his friends have gone into the school library.

The school bell rings yet again, meaning that it is time for the next class. Frankie and Baron run into the library. It so quiet that Baron feels like he's gone deaf for no reason. While Frankie and Baron are in the library looking around, they start hearing voices. Someone is having a conversation, and the voice definitely sounds like Scram's.

Frankie and Baron don't know where in the library Scram is. They search around to see if they can spot Scram's face, but they cannot let him see them or he will know that he is being stalked. They can't find Scram or his friends anywhere, but they can still hear his voice. If they follow the voice, they should be able to find Scram, so they do just that until Baron accidently drops a few books from the bookshelf onto the floor, alerting the kids who were talking that someone else is in the library. They start searching the library to find out if anybody is there.

Frankie pushes Baron for his stupidity; now they don't know how to escape the library without getting caught. A couple of minutes later, Frankie and Baron are sitting near the last bookshelf. When Baron peeps around it to see if they are coming, Rodney surprises him, grabbing him by his rock 'n' roll shirt and pushing him onto the wall. Leonard does the same to Frankie. He wants to know what those hooligans are doing, and Baron accidently blurts out that they are looking for Scram. It is tough luck for both of them; Scram isn't in the library.

Frankie truly thought that he saw Scram go into the library and that he heard his voice. He must have been wrong. Rodney says something to Baron that makes him upset. Leonard starts picking on Frankie, calling him a girly-boy. Frankie knows that he doesn't look like a girl. His hair isn't even long. Leonard started playing with his hair, and Frankie doesn't like it. He pokes Leonard in the left eye, making Leonard release him. Frankie then stomps on Rodney's right foot, helping Baron run away. Now Leonard and Rodney are chasing after them.

After Frankie and Baron have escaped the library, they make their way to their class. When Frankie turns his head back, he notices that Leonard and Rodney are chasing after them and warns Baron about it. They run as fast as they can to reach their classroom, but there is one problem: their third-period class is around the corner in the hallway.

Before Leonard and Rodney ran out of the library, they picked up a few hardcover books to chuck at Frankie and Baron and slow them down. The one book Leonard throws hits Baron on the left ankle, and Baron trips over the book. He falls on the floor. Frankie, however, helps him back up quickly before they get caught, and they keep running away, trying to reach their class so they don't get hurt.

When Frankie and Baron reach the area where their classroom is, Frankie notices that Mr. Russ is at the door talking to their teacher. This is a huge problem for Frankie and Baron. They decide not to go that way because they don't want Mr. Russ and the teacher to know what's going on. They go up stairwell A, which leads up to the second floor. Leonard and Rodney see them going up the stairs and follow them. On the second floor, Frankie and Baron run inside a different art room with no lights on, but Leonard and Rodney see them go in there. Frankie is smart to place a few chairs and a table against the door so that Leonard and Rodney can't get in.

Rodney starts banging on the door, trying to enter the art room, but the door won't open because of the furniture Frankie put there. They aren't going anywhere; they are staying right there until Frankie and Baron exit the room. They can be there all day, which is a huge problem for Frankie and Baron. Rodney keeps trying to open the door. He warns them to open it before he busts it down. Baron wants to see him try because he knows that the door weighs more than he does. Frankie corrects him. He thinks that the door doesn't matter; it is the hinges supporting the door that matter. Baron seriously wants Frankie to stop being so smart.

Outside in the hallway, Rodney continues ordering them to open the door until he notices another door to the room. They are so dead now. Frankie peeps through the door window, thinking that Leonard and Rodney must have given up chasing them. He moves the items that he used to block the door and slowly opens it. As soon as he does, Leonard busts open the other door that leads into the art room, rushing to catch Frankie and Baron before they escape again. Frankie and Baron quickly rush out of the art room. Baron trips over a chair and falls to the floor. Leonard grabs Baron by the foot, but Frankie saves him by stomping on Leonard's hand. Baron gets back up quickly while Leonard's hand is still in pain. Rodney continues chasing after them.

There is another stairwell ahead. They go through the door and up stairwell B. Now they are on the third floor, which is the top floor of the building. Frankie realizes that they should have gone back downstairs to the first floor instead. Rodney is still following them.

On the top floor of Sea Sight Elementary School, Frankie and Baron go through double doors. They don't know where they are now because it is pretty dark. Frankie finds the light switch and realizes that they are in the science laboratory. They've never noticed the lab because they've never had class on the third floor of the school. Leonard reaches the lab and joins back up with Rodney. They both go through the double doors to look for Frankie and Baron.

Frankie and Baron are hiding behind a lab table, talking quietly to each other. Frankie can't believe what is happening to them. They are going to be in so much trouble because they are being chased around the school building, and surely some security cameras have caught them. They are not supposed to be running around the school building being chased by other kids.

Frankie has nothing to worry about, though. Baron tells him that the female security guard isn't in the monitor room today. He saw a paper with the list of people absent from school in Mr. Russ's office, when Mr. Russ was taking something away from Baron before he met Joey in Ms. Winchell's class earlier today. Frankie is relieved that the security guard is absent. Frankie asks Baron for the security guard's name. Baron doesn't quite catch the first name, but he does catch the last name: Torres.

Frankie peeps over the lab table and notices that Leonard is getting closer to their table. To make sure they aren't caught, they crawl to another table so that their position won't be exposed. Rodney is smart; he is standing on top of the tables so that they won't see his feet. He notices a few chemical drops on the table, so he avoids them. He gets lucky; he puts his hands underneath one of the tables and finds them. Frankie and Baron both scream and get out from underneath the table. Baron forgets that he is underneath the table and accidently bumps his head. This time they aren't able to escape.

Frankie doesn't know what is going on. He wants to know what they want from him and Baron. Leonard and Rodney want to beat them up. Before Leonard and Rodney are able beat up Frankie and Baron, Baron notices something unusual on Leonard's right hand. Leonard isn't going to fall for it until Rodney tells him that there is actually something on his hand. While looking at his right hand, Leonard notices bumps spreading around. He starts to get agitated and goes to the sink to wash his right hand. Once he finished washing his hand, more bumps continue to spread. He hollers and then leaves the science lab. Rodney wants to help him, but he doesn't want Frankie and Baron getting away, so he decides to take care of business.

Baron asks Rodney, who is holding him and Frankie by the shirts, why he can't go and help his friend before his allergic chemical reaction gets worse. Rodney starts to think about it and then lets them go. This isn't over for him; he will be back. When he meets Frankie or Baron again, there will be pain. He pushes Frankie and Baron to the floor and leaves the science laboratory. They both leave the science lab and make their way to their third-period class.

Baron yells at Frankie, "Can you please tell me what the point was of going to the library?"

"I thought Scram was in there with those kids who just chased after us, and I thought we were going to find out more information from him. I guess I was wrong, so I apologize for making those kids, who I believe are in the fifth grade, chase us. If you hadn't been stupid enough to drop the books from the bookshelf and tell them that we were looking for Scram, none of this would've happened."

"I apologize. If you noticed, those two kids who chased us are big. Look at us—we look like skeletons. They need to pick on someone their own size, those two big toffee-nosed goons."

During third-period gym class, Joey and Matt almost win their game. They have a lot of fun. Matt thinks the game has gone better than yesterday. While Joey and Matt are sitting on the bleachers, Joey notices something really random. He didn't see Scram in the locker room before class, and he doesn't see him in the gym now. He hopes that the situation isn't serious. He contacts Frankie through the voice-to-voice radio. Frankie asks if Scram has found out what Joey is up to.

Things still seem to be okay, but that isn't the end of it. Joey tells Frankie that he hasn't seen Scram in the locker room or in the gym. Frankie and Baron haven't see him either; they thought Scram was in the library, but then things started getting out of hand and they ended up being chased by Leonard and Rodney. Frankie wants Joey and Matt to stay on their guard because Scram may still be in the building.

After they finish talking through the voice-to-voice radio, Frankie immediately remembers that he and Baron were spotted by the security cameras while they were being chased. If they want to keep themselves from being spotted by the security guard before she comes back, they will have to sneak inside the new monitor room during lunch and delete the recording. Frankie hopes this plan will work out.

If that plan fails and the security guard finds out about it, Mr. Russ or Mr. Griffin will end up being told about it, and this may result in Frankie and Baron receiving detention— or, worse, suspension. Then they will not be able to help Joey and Matt find what Scram is looking for. Frankie wants to prevent this from happening, so he and Baron must find a way to delete the recordings of them being chased down the school hallway.

Before third period is over, Joey and Matt play some basketball just for fun, and without them noticing, Scram comes into the gym. After gym is over they go back to the locker room. This time, Scram is there. Joey and Matt notice him.

Scram has seen them playing basketball and tells them that they've got some skills. Joey asks him why he was so late for class. Scram explains that Mr. Griffin called him into his office before he went to meet Leonard and Rodney in the library. He called Scram into his office because his dad called to tell him that he's going to be with his wife for the rest of the week, meaning that Scram will have to stay at a friend's house or stay home and let his grandfather take care of him.

Matt thinks it's lame that he didn't find out more about Scram's dad. Joey remembers what Scram said to him about his dad and this Fallon kid's dad. He wants to know where in New York Scram's dad was when he met this Fallon kid's dad. Scram remembers that his dad met this Fallon kid's dad somewhere in the east of New York City. They used to work together at a place called Empire Hall.

Joey keeps on saying "Fallon kid's dad" because if he says "my dad," Scram will realize that he didn't say anything about Joey's dad and figure out Joey's last name. Scram actually isn't that dumb.

"I just noticed something," he says, walking up to Joey. "Why do you keep asking me questions about my dad?"

"I simply want to know your family better," he lies.

"I have a mother, too."

"I don't care. She doesn't sound important."

Scram leaves the locker room. Joey and Matt can't get into his locker to see what he has inside his bag besides school equipment. At least they've found out something: Scram's dad used to work with Joey's dad at Empire Hall in the east of New York City. After Joey and Matt finish changing, they hurry to the second floor to meet back up with Frankie and Baron. When they find them, Joey explains what he heard from Scram and where he was when Frankie and Baron were in the library. After hearing what Joey says, Frankie thinks he is kidding. Joey isn't kidding, though; this happens to be a true story.

A thought forms in Joey's head, and he realizes that Scram isn't trying to do anything to Dakota or his cousin. Scram and his dad are after Joey's dad, but Joey doesn't know what they want from his dad. He wants to warn Joe, but Matt advises him not to do that but doesn't explain why. It isn't over yet; they need to get more information from Scram. Matt is very optimistic that they can do this. When the school bell rings, they make their way to their fourth-period class.

Later on, during fourth period, Mr. H. assigns his students a book to read and announces that next Tuesday they will be writing a two-page essay about what they have read. While writing the essay, the kids won't be allowed to look at the book; they will have to memorize it and write the essay in their own words, full of details. This exercise will improve memorization and prove to Mr. H. that they read the book. The name of the book he is assigning is *The Mysteries of Captain Broach*.

After fourth period is over, it is lunchtime. In the cafeteria, Joey, Frankie, Matt, and Baron sat down at Scram's lunch table. Scram greets them again. Scram is wondering where his friends Leonard and Rodney have gone. Baron is pretty sure that they are somewhere using extreme caution. Before eating lunch, the four kids decide to talk to him.

Joey is nice enough to tell Scram that he needs more friends; he can't have the four of them and Leonard and Rodney as his only friends. He needs to introduce himself to other kids. Scram likes Joey's idea. He needs to find more kids tomorrow, and he will have to see how it turns out.

So far, the school kids are showing Scram a lot of respect. None of them disrespected him today because he has been picking on them, and he will not stop until every kid in school respects him. He doesn't do anything to his four kids—Joey, Frankie, Matt, and Baron—because he knows that they are generous to him. Baron covers his mouth with his left hand and starts to laugh quietly, making sure Scram doesn't hear him. Baron knows that he, Joey, Frankie, and Matt are only pretending to be generous to Scram so that they can get more secret information about his dad and why they need Joey.

Scram loves being a bully; it makes him feel so alive. He doesn't care what anyone says. Before he came into the cafeteria, he took some kid's lunch, which he is about to eat right now: a burger and strawberry milk. It is the best food of the day. The kid that he took the lunch from is named Uriah. He thinks that's a stupid name.

"Look who's talking," Baron whispers to Frankie.

"I promise I will pay you twenty dollars for the lunch after school today."

Scram has a deal with Frankie. Frankie isn't going to eat the food; he is going to return it to Uriah when he finishes talking to Scram. Joey tries to think of more questions to ask Scram about his dad, but he can't think of anything, and neither can Frankie, Matt, or Baron. They are done talking to Scram for today.

The four kids don't know what they are going to do next now that they are out of questions for Scram but, surprisingly, Baron knows what to do. He knows that Joey doesn't like stalking people, so he is going to do it. After school is over today, he is going to follow Scram since he goes in Baron's direction, just to see if he can get more secrets out of him without asking any more questions. It sounds risky, but Baron is going to do what is right for Joey. Baron knows that he may be a slow, stupid, sarcastic kid at times, but he actually has the guts to do detective work by himself. He's played those video games. Joey, Frankie, and Matt wonder if Baron can truly get more secrets out of Scram by himself. Baron is also going to try not to get caught.

Chapter 8

Sneaky Youths

When lunch is over on this Tuesday afternoon, the four kids make their way to their next class. Then Frankie remembers something: he and Baron forgot to sneak into the monitor room to see if they could find a way to delete the recording of them being chased by Leonard and Rodney. They plan to go there right now. They cannot get caught while they there. Baron isn't worried because he thinks that no one would be there besides the female security guard, who isn't in the building at the moment.

They both wait for the hallway to empty so that they can make their way to the monitor room. When there aren't any kids left, Frankie and Baron make their way to the room. Frankie notices a security camera atop the monitor room door. Luckily, Baron has gum, which he can stick on the camera lens so that it won't catch any footage of them while they are inside the monitor room—just in case they can't find a way to delete the recording. Baron starts chewing a piece of gum and blowing bubbles.

Frankie yells at Baron, "Can you hurry up and stick the gum on the camera?!"

"Sorry, this gum is so good."

Baron takes his piece of chewed-up blue gum out of his mouth, grabs a step stool so that he can reach the security camera, and sticks the gum on the camera lens. Then he gets off the step stool, closes the monitor room door, and locks it. Right now all they need to do is find a way to delete the recording of Leonard and Rodney chasing them so they won't get in trouble.

Frankie doesn't know what to do; there are tons of buttons inside that room. He and Baron must find the one that can delete the recording. There are several buttons: one disables the cameras and keeps them from rotating, while the other makes the cameras rotate. There is another button that turns on the cameras' lights at night since the camera cannot pick up anything in the dark. The lights are installed at the bottom of the security camera just in case an intruder breaks into the school at night.

There are no buttons inside the monitor room that will delete the recording from the camera. This could be a really sticky situation for Frankie and Baron. Frankie starts looking underneath the machine control panel to see if there is anything there. It looks like he was wrong—there's nothing but a picture of a female security guard stuffing her face with a chicken wing. The picture is taped underneath the controls. Frankie starts to get nervous as he realizes that there is nothing inside the monitor room that will delete the security recording. He and Frankie start making a mess. They don't want to do this, but they feel they don't have any other choice.

In the hallway, Mr. Russ is passing by the monitor room. He hears the noise Frankie and Baron are making inside the room. He knows where it is coming from. He grips the monitor room doorknob and shakes it, but it won't open. Mr. Russ knows that the monitor room door isn't supposed to be locked while the security guard isn't there. He wonders if there is an intruder in there. He starts talking to see if anyone inside will answer him. Frankie and Baron hear his voice and, when they realize who it is, they start to get more nervous.

Because nobody answers Mr. Russ from inside the monitor room, he goes to Mr. Griffin's office to get the monitor room key, which is hanging on his office wall. After retrieving Mr. Griffin's keys, he makes his way back to the monitor room door. Inside the monitor room, Frankie and Baron quickly clean up the mess they've made and are trying to find a place to hide before Mr. Russ catches them there. They hide underneath the machine control panel that has a picture of the security guard attached to it. This isn't a great hiding spot; their whole bodies are visible.

Mr. Russ comes back with the keys to open the door. Frankie knows that this is the end of his streak of no detentions or suspensions, and he is ready for it. He looks up, praying, until he notices something on the side wall that is touching the ceiling. He grabs Baron to make sure he isn't exposed. Mr. Russ finally finds the right key and opens the door. He goes inside the monitor room and looks around to see if anyone is there. He can't find anyone, so he looks around just to make sure that everything is still in place. He opens up the cabinet drawers, making sure that nothing is missing. When he opens one of the cabinet drawers, Frankie spots something.

Mr. Russ is still inside the monitor room, looking around and making sure that everything is in order. There is only one little problem: Baron has to sneeze because the dirt is getting into his nose. He can't hold it, and Frankie can't grab his nose to prevent him from sneezing because he is in front of Baron and their hiding spot is very narrow. Baron holds both of his nostrils and lets out a quiet sneeze, bumping his head on the ceiling. Luckily for them, Mr. Russ doesn't hear the sound. Once Mr. Russ has finished searching the area, he leaves the monitor room without closing the door. Mr. Russ wishes that Mr. Griffin didn't have so many keys on one split key ring; it would be easier to find the monitor room key. Mr. Russ will get his own key for the monitor room soon.

Inside the monitor room, Frankie and Baron come out of hiding and close the door. They've been hiding inside the air-conditioning vent that is on the sidewall near the ceiling. They had to use the step stool to reach it.

Baron is never going back inside that vent again; he wonders how he'd been able to fit inside there in the first place. He doesn't think that hiding up there was worth it. But while they were inside the vent, Frankie spotted something as Mr. Russ opened one of the cabinet drawers. He doesn't remember which drawer it was in, so they start searching through all of them. There are a total of eight cabinets, with thirty-two drawers packed with papers; each cabinet has four drawers.

Frankie opens the third drawer of the sixth cabinet and finds what he saw. He picks up the item and sees that it's an instruction booklet. He opens up the booklet and starts to read it. He figures out that there isn't any button that will delete the camera recording. He thinks that the technicians who installed the monitor room and the security cameras are sneaky. The security camera deletes the recording once a month to free up memory. Frankie can't wait that long; the security guard will spot them before a month has passed. This isn't helpful at all. Frankie wishes that there was a button to delete the recording manually.

A plan forms in Baron's mind. If the security guard can watch security recordings from previous days, this obviously means that there are memory cards installed in every security camera in the building. If they prevent themselves from getting into a lot of trouble, they can continue helping Joey and Matt find out why Scram is looking for Joey. They can take a chance and replace the old memory cards inside the security cameras with new ones.

Frankie placed the booklet back inside the cabinet drawer and actually agrees to Baron's plan. Frankie finds that Baron is on a roll today. Baron starts to smirk. Luckily for them, they aren't dome cameras; they wouldn't have any idea what to do if they were. Frankie starts tidying up the room some more while Baron looks at the recordings taken earlier that day. After a couple of minutes, they see the recording of him and Frankie running around the school. It doesn't look good. Almost every camera in the school has spotted them. Some of the cameras didn't catch them running, but Frankie thinks they should still change the memory cards, just in case. He doesn't know why he had that idea.

Frankie is about to leave the monitor room when Baron starts playing around with the buttons. They could get in trouble for that. Before Frankie tells him to leave the controls alone, he spots someone on the screen who looks familiar. Baron notices the person, too. The person they've spotted on the screen is Scram.

The video of Scram was captured at around 9:39 a.m. today. They wonder what he was doing inside the school laboratory at that time. Baron presses "play" to watch the tape. A few seconds into the recording, two double doors open, revealing Scram inside the lab. He is looking around the room. About two minutes into the recording, at 9:41 a.m., Scram releases some wires from the walls, accidently knocking over a beaker and spilling some chemical onto the table. After Scram takes the wires, he leaves the laboratory.

Frankie, having just found out that Scram's dad has a random duplication system, thinks that Scram has taken the wires for his dad to use, to make his system work. During that video when Scram knocked over the beaker with the chemical, Baron figured that's how Leonard had that allergic reaction; he accidently touched the spilt chemical.

Earlier today, inside the slightly dark lab, Leonard probably didn't see the spilt chemical, so he ended up touching it. Frankie also figures out something. The time, 9:39 a.m., is when third period starts, and that was when he and Baron went to the school library to see if Scram was there, but he hadn't been. Frankie also remembered that Joey found out he wasn't in the gym, but later on he was. Right inside the locker room, Scram told them that Mr. Griffin had called him to his office because of his dad, but Frankie remembered that Mr. Griffin left the school earlier today to see his boss, meaning that Scram was actually inside the lab while Frankie and Baron were being chased by Leonard and Rodney. Before they made it into the lab, Scram had probably already left the area. Frankie finds Scram to be a very sneaky kid.

Frankie and Baron leave the monitor room and make their way back to the classroom. First they make sure that the hallway is clear. After fifth period is over, the four kids meet up with each other in the hallway near the lockers. Frankie tells Joey and Matt that they weren't able to delete the recording, but they did figure out a way—by replacing the old memory cards with new ones. Frankie's dad knows a place where they sell memory cards for security cameras, and Frankie knows where it is. He tells them that it was lucky that he and Baron went inside the monitor room, or else they wouldn't have found out more about Scram. He tells Joey and Matt everything that happened while they were inside the monitor room.

Joey gets the point. With this information, they should be able to find out what Scram and his dad are up to and why they need to find Joey's dad after they find this Fallon kid (Joey).

Two class periods later, school is over. Joey, Frankie, Matt, and Baron are in front of the school building. Before Joey, Frankie, and Matt leave, they tell Baron to please be careful while he is sneaking up on Scram and trying to get more secret information from him. They are shocked that Baron is doing this. Sneaking up on someone is the worst thing Baron has ever done in his life, and he hopes this is the only time he ever has to do it. Joe comes to get Joey and Frankie, and they leave the school area. Matt gets on a local bus. The three of them hope that Baron will be all right while he is out trying to find out more secrets from Scram.

While waiting for Scram to leave the building, Baron remembers that he forgot to take off the chewed-up piece of gum that he placed on the camera lens inside the monitor room. He goes back inside the room, grabs the stepping stool, and pulls the gum off of the camera lens. After he throws it away, he spots Scram on one of the monitors, putting on his bag and making his way out of the school building. Baron quickly leaves the monitor room to follow him. He is focusing on his mission rather than doing something stupid or goofing off.

Baron and Scram get on the same local bus. Scram sits in the center, while Baron sits in the back, listening to what Scram is saying. Scram has no clue that Baron is on the bus listening to his conversation.

Baron's voice-to-voice radio can pick up smartphone conversations, so he is able to hear Scram's dad. Luckily for Baron, no other smartphone conversations are going on, but Scram needs to hurry up and talk to his dad before another conversation begins. Scram is on the phone again with his dad, telling him that he found some wires that will help him with his system.

Scram's dad says, "Great work, Scram." He applauds through the phone. "I want you to take your time finding that Fallon kid. Once you find him, I will get what I want. Then I will be set for one of my master plans. Good luck finding him."

Scram ends the smartphone conversation. Baron wonders what Scram's dad's master plans could be. How many master plans does he have in store?

Scram gets off the local bus, and so does Baron. Scram goes inside his house, closing the door but not locking it. Baron waits a few seconds before opening the door. Then he slowly opens the door and tries to enter the house quietly, but the door keeps on creaking. Baron hushes it, hoping that Scram hasn't heard it. Instead of opening the door all the way, Baron goes through the half-open door and then closes it. The inside of Scram's house is dirty. Baron covers his nose because the house has a very bad odor. He hopes that it isn't him who smells like that, but it can't be because he takes a shower three times a day.

Baron already wants to leave Scram's junky house, but if he does he won't be able to find out more secrets about Scram. The house is small and smells like a garbage dump. Baron thinks that this is bad for the environment. He tries to find a place to hide before he gets caught. If he gets caught, he will be in a lot of trouble. Luckily, he finds a perfect place to hide underneath the kitchen sink, where there are no cleaning substances. Baron hopes that there isn't a roach underneath the sink.

Scram comes to the kitchen and goes into the refrigerator to take out his favorite snacks. He accidently drops a snack bag near the spot where Baron is hiding. Scram picks it up, noticing that the sink cabinet door is cracked open. When he left the house for school that morning, he closed the cabinet door all the way in. His grandfather wasn't home just yet, so how did the door crack open?

Scram is about to open the door, making Baron extremely nervous, but the phone rings. Scram pushes in the sink cabinet door and then answers the phone. It's his mother. Baron is already sweating, trying to calm his nerves after almost having a real panic attack. This isn't the right place to hide, so he sneaks out from underneath the kitchen sink to find another hiding place while Scram is in the living room talking to his mother.

Baron goes to a different area in the house. He wonders why Scram was so concerned over a cracked cabinet door. After looking around the house, Baron notices that he is in Scram's bedroom. Surprisingly, his room looks very clean; everything looks nice besides the busted-up window that ha⌐ been boarded up halfway since Scram threw a rock at it Monday night.

Baron starts looking around to see if he can find anything related to Joey's dad and Scram's dad. The dressing table is packed with stacked papers. Maybe Baron can search through the papers to see if he can find any clues. Three piles of papers are stacked from the left of the dressing table to the right. Baron searches through the middle stack first. Before he reaches the last paper in the stack, he sees the picture of a mansion, which he supposes is the mansion where Scram's dad goes. He notices something strange standing on the staircase in front of the mansion: a portrait frame with a completed portrait. The portrait in front of the mansion has to mean something, or else it wouldn't have been necessary to include it in the picture. Baron knows he shouldn't take the picture, but he takes it anyway and puts inside his knapsack, just in case. Now that he has finished looking through the stack of papers in the center, he is about to start on the right-hand stack.

The stack of papers on the right is smaller than the one in the center. Baron looks through all the papers and doesn't find any information. Then he looks through the final stack of papers on the left. Baron finds something in the middle of the stack that doesn't look too good. He starts reading the paper, which is about the Fallons' house. As he is reading, he starts to get the idea that Scram isn't looking just for Joey, but for his house as well. After reading that, Baron starts to understand why Scram has been looking for Joey all this time. Scram wants to find out where he lives so that he can sneak inside the house and take something that doesn't belong to him. This has nothing to do with finding Joe once they find Joey. This must be why Scram's mom sent him to Sea Sight Elementary School.

Baron contacts Joey, Frankie, and Matt through the voice-to-voice radio. After he's done explaining, Joey asks what they need from inside his house. What do they want? He realizes that it's best for them not to ask Scram any more mission-related questions. They will simply have to leave him alone for now. After talking through the voice-to-voice radio, Baron is about to leave the house when Scram comes to the bedroom. Baron slides underneath the bed so that Scram won't notice he's there. Scram sits down on the bed and takes off one his dirty socks, dropping it on the floor near Baron's face is. Baron holds his breath, trying not to inhale the stinky sock smell.

Scram turns on the television, which was left on the CC7 news channel. He leaves the bedroom to get his food. This is Baron's chance to escape the house. He comes out from underneath the bed to exit the house. He opens the creaky front door. Scram hears it and runs to the door to see who is there. Luckily, Baron closes the door fast and hides behind one of the garbage cans before Scram looks outside to see who was trying to come through the door. When he doesn't see anyone, he closes the door, locks it, and turns on the dome security camera that is mounted outside the house. Baron has just noticed that the camera's red light has come on, meaning that he can't move away from the garbage can. For now he will have to wait until something happens.

About six minutes later, Baron is doing his homework behind the garbage can. A few kids walk by. This could be his chance to escape Scram's house. He quickly puts his work inside his knapsack and shelters his face using the side of one kid's shoulder. This kid, who is wearing a sky blue shirt, has no clue what Baron is doing. When Baron is away from the dome security camera, the kid pushes him off, making him trip over a garbage can. He falls on top of it. The kids start laughing at him.

Baron wonders why there are so many garbage cans on the block. Today must be garbage day. Baron knows that he is not garbage, so he quickly gets up and runs away before the sanitation workers mistake him for garbage. About twenty minutes later, Baron has made it back to his block in one piece. He goes inside his house to meet up with his cool British family. His parents are two of Joe's best friends.

At the Everyday Gym, Joe continues training Jake to help him better defend himself, gain more strength and momentum, and perform a spin kick. Joey is talking to Frankie about what Scram and his dad want from inside his house. He understands that Scram is looking for this Fallon kid, which is Joey, because they think that he will expose where he lives. There has to be a way to find out what they are looking for inside Joey's house without asking Scram any more questions.

Nighttime comes, and everyone makes their way home. That night the house phone starts to ring, and Kay-Lo answers it. The person on the phone is Mr. Russ, who gives Kay-Lo the good news that Jake has been accepted to Joey's school. He would like to meet with Jake in his office when he arrives at school tomorrow morning. Kay-Lo thanks Mr. Russ very much and hangs up the house phone. Then she gives Joey and Jake the good news. Joey is excited to have his older brother with him in school.

Kay-Lo starts playing some music, singing and dancing while she cleans the kitchen. Jake is in there eating some noodles and celery. Joey goes on Skybot to have a quick video chat with Dakota about what he has found out today. Dakota seems glad to talk to Joey again. He asks him how his first and second days of school went.

Joey tells him, "The first day was nothing. The second day was just a nightmare."

"Wow, I feel your pain."

Joey explains to him that Scram is not doing anything that will harm Dakota's folks, meaning that he is not after Dakota's family. Dakota's cousin is safe from harm. This is not about Dakota; this is about Joey and Jake's dad and Scram's dad.

"There is a problem!" Joey said to Dakota. "I don't know how this is also about my dad if Baron said earlier today that this has nothing to do with him. Hmm, maybe Baron means this has something to do with my house. He said that Scram might want to take something, but I don't know what it is. We've got to continue with this mission to find out."

Dakota replies, "That sounds really confusing! Well, I wish you guys a lot of luck with that. When you guys solve this case, let me know."

"Copy that!" Joey says.

What are Scram and his dad really looking for inside Joey's house? The kids are going to try their best to find out. If they can't figure it out, it might turn out to be an unhappy ending for all of them.

Chapter 9

A Day of Freedom

There is a heat wave going on in Florida on this Wednesday morning. Kay-Lo gets out of bed to make breakfast for everyone and also to make lunch for Joey, who doesn't eat the school lunch. She isn't too sure whether or not Jake is going to eat the school food, so she decides to make lunch for him as well. After she is done making the food, she is about to leave the house to continue with her jogging.

Later on, Joe wakes up and wonders who has left the front door open. When he closes the front door, he goes to make sure that the back door in the kitchen is locked. It is.

Joe is about to make some breakfast when he notices that food has already been made. He figures that it was Kay-Lo who left the front door open. Joe never hears Kay-Lo getting out of bed or leaving the house because he is a heavy sleeper. Joe isn't the only one; Joseph, Kay-Lo, and Jake are also heavy sleepers.

Joe looked at his watch, seeing that he has enough time to go into the garage and clean it up a bit before he leaves for work. He is tired of seeing how untidy it looks, and it also wastes his time when he tries to find his tools that he doesn't keep up in the attic. He has a ladder in there that he only uses when he goes on the roof of the house.

When breakfast is over, the school bus arrives in front of the house for Joey and Jake. Joey heads out of the house for day three of school and his mission. Jake grabs his backpack, about to leave the house. Joe stops him for a quick second. Joe wants Jake to have a wonderful day at school. He warns him that if anybody bothers him, he must not be afraid to tell anyone, including Joe. Jake will try to remember that. He thanks Joe for helping him to become braver. Before Jake walks away, Joe tells him not to forget to meet up with the principal in his office.

"For what?" Jake asks, worried. "What did I do wrong?"

Joe says, "You didn't do anything. Your mother told me yesterday that you need to meet him as soon as you set foot in the school building."

"That woman must be afraid to talk to me. She didn't tell me anything."

"Maybe she was afraid that you were going to forget. It happens. Just go to school, be optimistic like some of Joey's friends, and have fun."

Jake sighs. "Having fun in school? We'll see about that!"

On the school bus, Jake is sitting next to his younger brother, Joey, and talking to Matt and Baron. Matt greets Jake for the second time, telling him that he's going to like it at his new school. It's going to be a lot of fun. Matt explains to Jake what he, Joey, Frankie, and Baron are currently doing in school. He also warns him to be aware of a kid named Scram. Matt explains everything to Jake, from the video message Joey received from Dakota on Sunday to what Baron found out yesterday when he sneaked into Scram's house.

Jake wonders what kind of last name Bumbleberry is. He starts to figure out what Joey, Frankie, Matt, and Baron are trying to do. He asks if he can help because he likes to solve puzzles. What he doesn't know is that this is no ordinary puzzle; it's like a mystery, and they're trying to find some clues. It doesn't matter to Jake; he only wants to help them. Joey decides to let him join the team.

On the school bus, Joey notices something odd as he is looking around. He wonders where Frankie and Scram are. Matt and Baron look around the school bus as well, also noticing that neither of them is there. Joey contacts Frankie through the voice-to-voice radio, but he doesn't pick up. Joey wonders if something has happened to him; he knows that Frankie never misses a single day of school. Even when he has allergies, he still comes to school. Those things aren't going to stop him. Joey finds it weird that both Frankie and Scram aren't on the bus.

"What if Scram kidnapped Frankie?" Baron asks Joey, scratching his head. "He probably brought him over to see his dad inside Haunted Mansion World."

Joey says, "Please don't say that. You're going to make me have bad thoughts."

Frankie has never missed a single day of school. Today is the first time Joey has not seen him on the school bus. Later on, they arrive in front of the school, thinking about what they are going to do today since Scram isn't at school. All they can do for the day is continue with their education and hang around with Jake. Matt and Baron will get to know him better.

"Pleasure to meet you again, kid," Baron says to Jake. "Don't hate me for asking you this, but do I look familiar to you?"

"Familiar? No, I don't think I've ever seen you before, besides that night at the party at my house," Jake answers.

"Sorry for asking you that. It's just that there's something about you."

Joey says, "Hey, since we've got Jake on our team and there are five of us, I think I found a name for our team. We can call ourselves 'The Five Superhero Kids.'"

"Sounds cool, but no!" Baron says. "I don't feel like a superhero, and you shouldn't feel like one either."

"Why, because I look weak to you? I drink milk, you know," Joey replies.

When the school bell rings, it is time for them to head for their first-period class. Jake doesn't have a class schedule yet, so he makes his way to Mr. Russ's office, as Kay-Lo had Joe tell him to go there when he entered the building. Perhaps Kay-Lo knew that Jake wasn't going to remember on his own. This is Jake's first time meeting Mr. Russ. He closes the door behind him and takes a seat across from Mr. Russ's desk.

Mr. Russ welcomes Jake to Sea Sight Elementary School. He gives him his class schedule, and then he wants to know more about Jake. Jake starts to explain a few things, such as how he likes to play basketball, love collecting figurines and to explore places. He also wants to be a detective. He tells Mr. Russ that he isn't afraid of going on dangerous missions; he has the courage for it.

Mr. Russ loves Jake's attitude and thinks his parents must be proud of him. Mr. Russ advises Jake not to go on any dangerous missions at his age; he doesn't want anything bad to happen to him. For now, Mr. Russ wants Jake to have fun in class with his brother, Joey. He has placed Jake in all of Joey's classes. Mr. Russ feels that Joey is one of those kids who will never get into trouble or hurt anybody. He has a bright future.

Jake says, "That's probably why my dad calls him a kindhearted kid, and my mom calls him booby. My mother says the dumbest things. It makes me want to rip my hair out, and I still need a haircut."

"Yes, you do!" Mr. Russ agrees. "Well, if you need any tips about our school, come see me or Mr. Griffin. Mr. Griffin's office is in room 178, which is near the back door of the school."

"Thanks a lot. I will see if I can stop by there during lunch."

Mr. Russ says, "During lunch, we don't allow kids to walk about the hallway by themselves. Ask any teacher to escort you to his office."

"Okay, sounds cool to me. Those teachers had better not ask me any questions about myself, because they don't need to know my business."

Following Jake and Mr. Russ's conversation, Jake heads to his first-period class. In Ms. Winchell's art class, he sits down next to Joey and Baron, who are coloring a picture of an apartment building. Joey welcomes Jake to the class and explains to him what the class is about.

"Beware," Baron warns Jake. "Ms. Winchell is kind of hairy on the back of her neck. Something tells me she's a female werewolf, or maybe she's just like that. There are a lot of creepy things I don't know about humans."

After first period is over, they meet each other in the hallway next to their lockers before next period. This is the day Matt has been waiting for. They don't have to worry about Scram today or figure out what he and his dad need from inside Joey and Jake's house. He knows that their mission will resume very soon.

The five kids make their way to their second-period classes. In Mr. Woods's reading class, Joey, Jake, and Baron are learning a few things that happen when kids don't use the correct grammar and spelling when writing an essay. When second period is over, the five kids meet again in the hallway. Before they are about to leave for their next class, Jake sees Frankie coming through the front doors of the school all sweaty. Joey wondered why he is late for school.

Frankie says to Joey, "Don't get any ideas as to why I'm late for school. I overslept because my dumb parents didn't bother waking me up. I got dressed quickly and ran to school in this dreadful heat."

"If you hadn't been wearing long jeans, you wouldn't have felt hot while running to school. Now, I suppose you have something smart to say back to me, right?" Baron asks.

"No, I am actually taking advice from you!"

"Wow, you really respect me. I didn't see that coming!"

"Hey, there goes the principal. Principal Russ, do you—" Frankie begins.

Mr. Russ interrupts, "Sorry, Frankie, I am too busy right now. I have to go over student files in my office. Talk to me after school." He walks away.

When he's gone, Baron says, "You know, for an old guy with gray hair, Mr. Russ sure does know how to take business seriously."

Frankie was not going to miss a day of school; he never misses a day. He gives Jake his own voice-to-voice radio. He explains to him what it does, and then he decides to go to the bathroom and wash the sweat off his face with the disgusting water; then he will dry his hair with a paper towel. He isn't going to worry about his wrinkled clothes, which don't bother him that much. Baron offers his comb to Frankie to make his hair look better after he washes it. Frankie decides to pass on that. He walks away, going inside the bathroom.

Joey, Jake, Matt, and Baron make their way to their third-period classes while Frankie is in the bathroom, washing his sweaty hair and face. He grabs a dozen paper towels so that he can wipe the water off his hair and face. He then shuts off the water source, dumping the wet paper towels in the garbage bin. With his head down over the sink, he wonders what will happen if they don't find out what Scram and his dad want from inside Joey and Jake's house.

Before Frankie leaves the bathroom, he looks up at the mirror and sees someone standing behind him. This makes him jump, and he turns around quickly. The kid grabs Frankie by his shirt and pushes him against the wall. Then he throws him on the floor, making him land on his front. When Frankie turns around on the floor, he notices that it is Rodney who just attacked him. Frankie is surprised to see him again. He asks Rodney what he is doing, but Rodney picks him up off the bathroom floor with one hand and pushes him near the toilet without an answer. He dunks Frankie's head into the toilet and flushes it twice, giving him two swirlies. Frankie just washed his face and hair, and now he's all wet again. Rodney looks inside Frankie's string bag and finds two water bottles. He takes them out and dumps the water from both bottles on Frankie's legs so that people will think that he's wet his pants.

"W-What did I do?" he asks Rodney.

"That's what you get for stomping on my foot before Leonard and I were going to beat you and that other kid up." He throws the two water bottles at Frankie's head. "That should give you a fresh start."

"That joke was so wack," Frankie says.

"I wasn't trying to be funny, doofus. You thought it was funny when you and that brown-haired kid with dorky glasses attacked Leonard and me yesterday in the library."

"You guys started it," Frankie replies. "Listen, we were only looking for Scram. Since you and Leonard are friends with him, do you know where he is today?"

"Leonard is in the hospital. Scram told me last night that he's going to look for two kids that might help him find this Fallon kid's house and to see if he can find what he is looking for in that house. Umm, I think I shouldn't have said that. If you dare tell anyone, I will break all your teeth. Now that I have you trapped in my clutches, where do you live? If you don't answer, I will bring even more pain to you and that brown-haired kid."

Frankie answers nervously, "I live . . . I live on Quinver Avenue next to a brown and yellow fire hydrant."

"You'd better be telling the truth!" Rodney threatens him. Rodney rudely throws some toilet paper at Frankie, laughs at him, and then exits the bathroom.

Frankie doesn't like what Rodney did to him. He now expects him to be a bully, and this means he's following Scram's lead. He gets the feeling that Leonard is also a bully. This means that there are three bullies in the school.

Frankie is still in the bathroom, trying to clean his hair again and dry off his wet spot. After his wet spot is halfway dry, Frankie makes his way to his second period class, joining Baron. Ms. Nancy doesn't say anything to Frankie about being late, so he knows he is off the hook.

Baron starts laughing at Frankie because of his wet spot. He wonders how he took a leak on himself. Frankie thought that no one would notice it. He tells Baron what he found out from Rodney about Scram not being in school today. He is somewhere in Florida, looking for two kids who might help him find Joey and Jake's house and see what he needs from inside it. Frankie hopes that Rodney was joking about breaking all his teeth if he tells anyone why Scram isn't in school today.

Frankie sits in front of Baron, who notices that Frankie has a little piece of ripped paper towel stuck in his hair. Baron takes it out as a kid next to him watches. Baron looks at the kid and asks him to pretend he didn't see that. Baron flings the little piece of paper towel away from himself.

Joey, Jake, and Matt arrive in the gym, about to play another game of basketball. Jake feels excited. He can't wait to play until he realizes that it is a team match. Joey and Matt put Jake on their team with Uriah, Dale, and Ian. They are going up against the new kids, whose names are unknown. There is one problem: Jake cannot play because he hasn't received a medical form to hand in to the gym coach. Jake doesn't care because he thinks that he wouldn't handle playing team basketball very well right now; he hasn't trained for a couple of years because of a little accident. He sits down on the bleachers and watches the kids play.

Later on during third period, the basketball game is over. Joey and Matt sit down on the bleachers next to Jake. Jake applauds them because they did a great job with the game.

"Yeah, we did great," Matt says sarcastically to Jake. "We did great by losing. This is the third time in a row we've lost a game."

Joey tells him, "You don't have to worry about losing on Friday. The gym coach said today that we're going outside to the soccer field because it's going to be a perfect day. Hey, Jake, how come you didn't receive a medical form?"

"I guess I didn't go to the main office. Once gym is over, I will go there to see if I can get one so I can play basketball once I hand it in. Do I need to give my Social Security number, too?" Jake replies.

"I don't even know what that is," Joey says.

"Shame on you!"

After third period, Joey, Jake, and Matt go back to the locker room to change back into their original clothes. Later, Joey, Frankie, Matt, and Baron are in the hallway on the second floor of the school. They are near their lockers getting ready for their fourth-period class. During fourth period on the first floor, Jake goes to the main office to see if he can get a medical form. The school secretary prints one out for him, and Jake takes the paper from the printer. Everything looks good to him, so he leaves the main office.

While Jake is making his way out of the main office and looking at his medical form, he isn't paying attention and accidently bumps into a kid, who gets mad and shoves Jake. Then he continues walking down the hallway. Jake looks at the kid and sees that he is talking on a smartphone. Jake's voice-to-voice radio picks up a signal from the smartphone, and he hears a voice. He realizes that the kid is talking to Scram when he hears Scram saying something about this Fallon kid. Jake follows the kid, listening to what Scram is saying through the smartphone. The kid Jake is following is Rodney, but Jake doesn't know him yet.

"Okay, about this little wonder," Rodney says to Scram through the smartphone. "Do you think those Fallon people still own it?"

"Of course they do," Scram replies. "Those losers have no idea what kind of fate is upon them. When we find their house, we will break in and take that little wonder when nobody is home. If that doesn't work, we will have to come up with another plan."

"Good luck with that! Is there anything else to do?"

"No, that's it. Oh, and I just found two kids who look like they can help me find the Fallons' house. I can't wait to see what will happen," Scram says.

Jake starts to feel a little anxious after hearing what Scram has said about his family. He can't believe what he's just heard. When Scram's conversation with Rodney is over, Jake hurries to his fourth-period class to tell Joey and Matt the news. When he enters Mr. H.'s class, he takes a seat next to Joey and Matt and tells them what he heard Scram say on the smartphone. Joey doesn't understand the story too well. What is a "little wonder"?

Their fourth-period class is over. At lunchtime, Jake goes to Mr. Griffin's office with a teacher to get some information about the school. Then he receives a permission slip to the history museum and goes to the cafeteria.

All five kids are going to enjoy the rest of the school day, with the exception of talking about Scram and his unnamed dad. Frankie still wants to know Scram's dad's name. It's still bothering him that he doesn't know his name yet. Is Scram lying that he doesn't know his own dad's name, or is he just refusing to tell?

Joey says, "Frankie, remember what we talked about over the weekend? We talked about safety and privacy. Maybe that's why he doesn't want to mention his dad's name, just in case he knew. It's like how you don't want me to mention my real last name. Thanks for telling me about that, by the way."

"You're lucky that I know what safety and privacy are, or you would have been exposed or ended up being kidnapped by Scram or his dad. I was going to tell Principal Russ about it, but I thought that I could handle it on my own, and I did," Frankie replies.

"Principal Russ is thirty-seven years old. I think it would have been wise for you to tell."

"So?" Frankie asks. "He would make your parents worry if he called about what's going on. No, that shouldn't happen. By the way, how do you know his age?"

"From Baron, of course, after he sneaked into Principal Russ's office yesterday during seventh period to get back something called the 'Madonna of Stone.' Baron found it inside a drawer of Principal Russ's desk where he keeps personal stuff. Principal Russ caught Baron with it when he entered the school yesterday. Baron, you should have kept it inside your knapsack. What do you use that stone for, anyway?"

"I use it inside a secret cavern in the United Kingdom where my older teenage cousin keeps his treasure that he finds. The

Madonna of Stone can open up part of the cavern's walls. You guys had better not tell anyone about that secret cavern, or I will smack all of you until I can see the red slap marks on your faces."

The five kids play cards until lunchtime is over. Then they leave to enjoy the rest of their school day without having to do Scram-related things. When school is over, Joey and Jake exit the school building and wait outside, talking to Matt and Baron before Joe comes. Jake is surprised that he had so much fun on his first day back at school; he can't wait for another day. He didn't realize that elementary schools could have lockers and class periods. His old school hadn't. While the two boys are waiting for Joe, Rodney comes out of the building in a hurry.

"Hey!" Jake yells at Rodney. "Where are you going in such a rush?"

Rodney answers, "No time for me to talk to you losers."

Matt says, "Answer his question so we can let you go."

"Fine, as long as it will make you punks shut up. My mom called the school saying that we are moving back to Washington, DC. My father got a new job there. That means I don't have to be at this lame old school anymore. At least Washington, DC, is better than filthy old Florida. Too bad I have to come back here in two years." He walks away.

When he's gone, Frankie says, "Something tells me he's lying. We've seen him in school all day today, and now he has to move back to Washington, DC? Sounds suspicious!"

"Hey, Jake, why didn't you ask Rodney why he was talking to Scram on the smartphone during school?" Matt asks.

Jake answers, "If I did, he would know that I was listening to their conversation. That would pretty much ruin and expose our mission. Roderick will call Scram and tell him about it."

"It's Rodney!" Joey corrects him.

"Whatever!" Jake replies.

The five kids have a wonderful day at school. Joe comes to get Joey, Jake, and Frankie while Matt and Baron are making their way home. After going home to change into their gym clothes, they head to Everyday Gym to do more exercise. Today Joe wants to do something new with Jake, who refuses to go on the treadmill because he is afraid of it. Joe takes him outside to the track and field.

Joe used to run track when he was Jake's age, so he is going to show him how to work on his momentum and how to breathe at the right time while running. This will help Jake run faster and longer. Jake wonders if all this running is worth training for. Because this is his first time, Joe allows Jake to run for only two minutes, to the other side of the field without stopping. Jake thinks he can do it, but what will happen when he starts running?

When Joe says "go," Jake starts running to the other side of the field for two minutes. Before he can reach the other side of the track, he starts to slow down. To his surprise, he still makes it to the other side of the track without stopping. Joe catches up with him. Jake is already gasping for air and asking for some water. Joe isn't going to give him any water until he makes it back to the other side of the field, where he first started running.

Joe wants to challenge Jake some more. He wants to see if he can make it back to the other side of the track in less than two minutes. He gives Jake time to catch his breath, and once he regains some air, he starts running again, making his way back to the other side of the field where he first started. Joe wanted Jake to make it back there in less than two minutes, but Jake fails to do that. It is okay, though; he knows it is Jake's first time, so he's going to give him a pass on that. After a few hours of training outside on the field, Jake is starting to get the hang of it. Joe seems surprised that Jake is doing so well on his first day out in the field. He had thought it would take weeks of training.

When Jake is done training, he sits down next to Joe on the bench on the field. Joe is very proud of Jake. What gets him is that he didn't give up; he kept running and running until he got the hang of it.

Because Jake didn't give up and pulled off the running in one day, Joe will reward him with a cool item: a rocket board. During the reunion party last Saturday night, Joe had taken the rocket board from a neighborhood kid who brought it earlier and hid it. Joe hid that gift away from Jake because he wanted to see how well Jake would do with his training during the week, making his way toward becoming a tough kid.

"I have no idea why these foot straps are attached to the rocket board, but it seems like you can tighten them," Joe says to Jake, giving him the rocket board. "Oh, before you ask me—no, it cannot fly in the air."

"Darn!" Jake exclaims. "Well, thanks. This looks amazing, but I'm not ready for it yet. Maybe I will start practicing next summer. I just need to get the balance for it. You know how my body is sometimes—it gets shaky when I try to balance on something, and then I end up falling like I'm on roller skates."

"Throughout your life, things about you will change. You will get better at things you couldn't do before."

"Puberty?" Jake asks.

"Let's not go there," Joe says. "What I want you to do is believe in yourself, and any time you want me to help you get over any fear, just let me know. Everybody has fears, so you don't have to feel ashamed for being scared of something. You've got to keep on trying. I'm your dad, and I will be there to help both you and Joey every day."

"Unless Mom gets in the way. Now I have my mind back on this bully who used to torture me back at Volotont Elementary. That kid was a menace. He just loved to bother me every day in school. I'm so glad I moved and don't have to see that fool again. You should see this creepy thing he does with his eyes. It's like his eyes aren't placed inside his eye sockets correctly."

The kid who used to bully Jake back at Volotont Elementary is named Dennis. He is from the United Kingdom. He moved to New York in 2007, two years ago, but he moved again to a different location a year ago. He loved making fun of Jake because he was the shortest kid in his class, and also because of the way he used to dress. The clothes Jake used to wear caused him to be bullied some more by Dennis, which is why Jake wants to wear cool and updated clothes now. Before Dennis came to Volotont Elementary, Jake was tortured by other groups of kids. Perhaps this provides a small clue as to why he is fearful about something he can't remember that happened in school.

Meanwhile, at the track and field, it is close to dusk. Jake is doing one full lap around the track without stopping. Joe watches him do his best. He is amazed by Jake's performance. For only one day of training, Jake made it through okay. After hours of training outside the gym, they make their way back home. When they arrive back at the house, Jake starts to feel tired and decides to skip his dinner. He takes a shower and then goes off to bed.

Three minutes later, Joe and Kay-Lo are in the kitchen eating some lasagna when they hear some noises. They sound like they're coming from outside the house. Kay-Lo thinks they are having a thunderstorm outside. Joe goes outside to see if it is, but he knows that it isn't supposed to rain today. Apparently the noise wasn't thunder; it was Joseph. He is bringing in the new outdoor basketball hoop.

"It looks like you remembered to buy the basketball hoop," Joe says.

"I sure did," Joseph replies. "Go tell Jake that I've got a surprise for him."

"Jake is sleeping. He was hyped after hours of training at the gym. I must tell you, I'm very proud of him. He's starting to get the hang of defending himself, and he's gaining more momentum. He still needs to work on his strength. We were on the track for one day and he pulled the running off quickly."

Joseph explains to Joe that Jake is a very athletic little boy. When Joseph and Jake were living in New York, Jake's gym teacher at Volotont Elementary made them train before and after school every day. Teenage cheerleaders were there practicing their dance routines. One day, when Joseph brought Jake home from school, Jake told Joseph that one cheerleader launched him in the air, and he went very high and landed safely on the floor. Joseph didn't believe him; it felt like Jake was telling him a fake story. Jake would come home sometimes and go to his bedroom. He would run in place for at least seven minutes without stopping. He had so much sweat coming out from his sweat glands. He told Joseph he was doing that because he had joined a basketball team and needed as much training and energy as he could get. Jake was only seven years old at that time. Joseph was proud of Jake before he thought Jake was going to turn out to be a lazy kid.

There was a time when Jake told Joseph that he liked to make people smile, especially when he played basketball, but something shocking happened. In late 2007, he stopped and lost half of his endurance. He hasn't trained for a very long time because he had a little accident back then. During a basketball game, Jake twisted his left ankle and was in so much pain. After coming back home from the hospital, he decided to quit the basketball team, but he didn't stop playing. He would only play by himself because he was afraid to have another accident when he played on a team. When he turned nine this past January, he told Joseph that he was ready to try out for a basketball team again for his birthday gift, but he had to wait because he knew that he was moving in the next seven months. During those seven months, he started doing his training again.

"So that explains why he pulled off the running in one day at the gym today," Joe says to Joseph. "He already had half of his endurance back."

"Yeah, as long as he keeps training, he will get a lot better. You can train him some more if you guys go back to the gym. You should push him even harder," Joseph says.

Joe takes Joseph's advice to make Jake train harder to regain his strength and momentum. For now, Joseph stores the outdoor basketball hoop in the garage. When Jake comes home from school tomorrow, the basketball hoop will be right inside the garage. Joe will tell Joey to show it to Jake, just in case he doesn't notice it.

At the computer desk, Joey continues drawing a few pictures. His artistry has been improving ever since he started learning how to draw. While he is drawing and coloring his pictures, he wonders what Scram meant today about finding the little wonder inside the Fallons' house. Joey has been living in this house for almost nine years, and he knows that there isn't a thing here called the little wonder. Joey believes that the little wonder will turn out to be something.

Chapter 10

Smart Device

Thursday is the last day of the week for Joe to go the gym. Joe is off from work for the day since he doesn't work on Thursdays. The first thing he is going to do today is go to the gym and come back home to take things easy. After a huge performance from Jake yesterday, Joe will allow him to take a break today and rest his body. This is why Joe is going to the gym right now—since he won't have to go later on to train Jake. On this windy Thursday morning, Kay-Lo wakes up and does the same thing she did yesterday: makes the kids' lunches and goes out for her morning jog.

Joe makes sure she has closed the front door and locked it. A couple of minutes later, Jake comes out of his bedroom, rubbing his right eye. He joins Joe in the kitchen to have a little talk. Joe greets Jake by calling him Little Moth again. Jake wants him to stop calling him that, as it sounds like he's being called an insect. Joe thinks it is a nice nickname for Jake. They eat their breakfast. This breakfast should keep Jake more energetic when he goes to school today.

Later on, the school bus arrives in front of the house. Joey leaves the house, and so does Jake. Jake is excited to go back to school; it should be a fun day for him. Joe tells them that he won't be getting them from school today. He has to go back to the auto repair shop to see how the car is doing. Joey and

Jake understand. They get on the school bus for day four of their mission. This is Jake's second day.

After the school bus pulls away from the house, Joe changes into his gym clothes and is about to head over to Everyday Gym. This is not the first time Joe has gone to the gym at this time of morning. He goes there every Thursday morning since it's his day off from work.

Joe leaves the house and jogs to the gym. Once he makes it to the gym, he decides to start lifting some weights. As he is about to start doing that, he notices someone he hasn't seen in a long time: his good old friend Lance Perkins, whom he first met in Hawaii on a holiday vacation before he met Kay-Lo.

Joe wants to know what Lance is doing in the gym this early. Most days, Lance goes to the gym in the morning to exercise and feel healthier as the days pass by. He chooses his days randomly, and today happens to be one of them. His old detective partner, Sid Vale, is with his wife today. It's their fifteenth wedding anniversary, so he's going to spend the whole day with her. They're having a party tonight somewhere in Florida. Lance asks Joe if he wants to come. Joe, unfortunately, can't make it because he has kids to take care of, and he is doing something for himself and Joseph as well. He tells Lance that they are on a lookout.

"Who are you guys looking for?" Lance asks.

"Some random person who escaped from me last Friday when he got on a motorboat. I was trying my best to catch him when I had a chain in my hand."

"Detective work. Sid and I are still detectives, but we don't work in New York anymore. We are currently working here in Florida. You would be surprised—we have been trying to solve this mystery about a cyborg, for how many decades, I don't know. That cyborg is nowhere to be found. Hey, before we go work out, just give me a description of that person so I can be on the lookout for you guys."

Joe says, "He has short black hair, lazy brown eyes, and a diamond nose piercing on the right nostril. I don't know the diamond's shape. He's somewhere in southern Florida."

"Okay, I will help you and Joseph with your detective work. If you need me, you can give me a call. I will be at Village Park on Planet Avenue. It's right around the corner, not that far. Usually I'm there at midnight while I'm on duty," Lance tells him.

"Good! I should come visit you some day."

While they are working out at the gym, Joey, Jake, Frankie, Matt, and Baron, also known as the five kids, have now noticed that Scram is sitting in the back of the school bus. Joey does not want to go back there to talk to him. He said on Tuesday that it is best not to ask Scram any more mission-related questions; they should only talk to each other. They arrive in front of the school for the fourth time this week. Tomorrow is their last day before they can spend the weekend without a care in the world, unless they want to continue with their mission over the weekend. It is up to them.

Outside the school building, the five kids are waiting for the school bell to ring. Frankie has finally gotten the sleep he needs after three restless nights, and he feels great. He can concentrate more on the mission now that Scram has returned to school.

The bell rings, signaling that first period has started. They make their way down the hallway and get their books. Inside Ms. Winchell's art room, Ms. Winchell is watching the kids color today's picture. Ms. Winchell appears next to Joey, Jake, and Baron's table. She admires Joey's coloring and encourages him to become an artist. Joey appreciates her words very much, but he doesn't think that his drawing is all that great. He does play a video game about drawing graffiti on the wall without getting arrested by police, but this isn't his type of thing to do. Joey is best at coloring.

Before second period starts, Joey shows Frankie, Matt, and Baron what Kay-Lo made for him and Jake to eat for lunch. Frankie admits that his Aunt Kay-Lo did a marvelous job with the hamburgers. They look better than the ones from McPatty. Jake will never eat a burger or meat, so he kindly gives his lunch to Baron. Baron is pleased with Jake's offer; this whole week he's been feeling loved. He finds it kind of strange!

Scram comes out of nowhere, greeting the four kids until he notices that there is a new kid. He wants to know who he is. Jake introduces himself to him, almost blurting out his last name, which Joey stops him from saying. Joey tells Scram that he's his older brother who just started school yesterday. Scram is flattered to meet Jake and introduces himself to him. Jake almost laughs when he hears Scram's last name.

"Sorry I wasn't in school yesterday," Scram says to the five kids. "I was with my dad yesterday doing some shopping. He wanted me to come with him, so I did. At least it gave me a little time off from looking for this kid I've been looking for since Monday. Today I'm back to doing my job. After we finished shopping yesterday, I went out to do something while my dad went down to Habitation Avenue again to meet up with my mom and her friend to do some examination."

"Examination?" Joey asks.

"Forget I said that." The school bell rings. "That's the bell. It's time for me to go to class." He walks away.

Baron says, "Freaky kid, he is."

"Why do you keep calling him that?" Joey asks. "Okay, besides yourself and Scram, who's the freakiest person you have ever met?"

"Your mom!" Baron retorts.

Joey walks away from Baron and makes his way to his third-period class. Inside the locker room, Joey wants to know what Scram meant by "examination." A few seconds later, he starts looking around, wondering where Jake has gone. He notices that he isn't with them. Matt hasn't seen him, but he thinks Jake is somewhere in the building and will join them in a minute. Scram leaves the locker room and heads to the gym. This gives Joey and Matt a chance to go inside Scram's locker to see what he has inside his bag. They're only doing this to see if they can find any evidence about him. They aren't going to steal anything from Scram because then he would start to suspect things. Joey doesn't like stealing.

Joey reaches inside his book bag to take out the lock picking kit from his pencil case. He needs to get into Scram's locker to see what is inside his bag. This may give Joey and Matt more information for their mission. They take out Scram's bag and place it on the floor. Matt makes sure that the coast is clear while Joey looks through Scram's bag to see if he can find anything. Joey finds Scram's smartphone inside his pants pocket. He searches through the smartphone to see if he can find anything, but there is nothing there to be found. He opens up the notification bar and sees three active apps: a translating app, a voice app, and a gallery app. Joey opens the gallery app to look through some of the photos. While searching through them, he remembers what Scram said at lunchtime on Monday.

Joey says, "Matt, look; these are the photos Scram said he took while he was out with his friends during his free time. One little thing—I don't think these people are his friends. Scram is with a man I assume is his dad."

There are a lot of photos on Scram's smartphone. Most are of the places Scram said he visited—an apartment building and a building that Joey supposes is the S.S. Security building. That building is where they keep all the security lines, barricades, and security traffic cones. The S.S. Security building also keeps security cameras inside the building along with a monitor room.

Joey knows that the S.S Security building is located on Jenna Street; an auto repair shop is also close to that building. Joey thinks Scram has a picture of the S.S. Security building because he and his dad are trying to sneak inside there and disable all the cameras. That way, the cameras around Florida won't spot them with whatever they're carrying around. The people who work at S.S. Security have placed their own security cameras around Florida so that they can monitor certain events that take place. The videos are all shown in the monitor room.

Joey finds a photo of Village Park on Planet Avenue. It's also close to Everyday Gym. Scram said that he goes to Village Park almost every day to hang out with his friends; he also said that he goes there to plan things out so that things will go his way.

Matt says to Joey, "I'm thinking that Leonard and Rodney are the ones Scram hangs around with."

Joey finds that impossible. Leonard had that bad chemical reaction in the laboratory on the third floor of the school. He's now in the hospital, the same hospital where Dakota's cousin is. Rodney just said after school yesterday that he has to move back to Washington, DC. Joey doesn't believe Rodney.

Joey thinks whoever Scram is working with has to be at Sea Sight Elementary School or somewhere else. First Joey, Jake, Frankie, Matt, and Baron are going to look inside the school building. They need to find out who that person is. That person might know what the little wonder is. Joey hopes it will happen. He apologizes to Matt for adding another objective to their mission. Matt isn't surprised; he only wanted Joey to search through more of Scram's photos.

The next photo on Scram's smartphone is the pier located on Shore Avenue. Scram and his dad are featured in the photo, getting onto a motorboat. The motorboat is pointing toward Habitation Avenue. Joey thinks that Scram and his dad are going to Habitation Avenue to get to Haunted Mansion World. There aren't any more photos of interest left, so Joey turns off the smartphone and puts it back inside Scram's pants pocket. Then he puts his bag back inside the locker and locks the locker door.

They have a new objective: to find the person Scram is working with. Joey thinks that the male or female person is either inside the school building or somewhere in Florida. They go to the gym to have a bit of fun playing some basketball. They lose again. What else is new for them? After third period is over, they go to the hallway on the second floor. Joey makes sure Frankie knows what their new objective is.

"How are we going to find that person Scram is working with?" Frankie asks Joey.

"First we need to get the description, and second, since we are going to start in this school, we have to look for the person while the kids are in the hallway. That may be a quicker way to find him or her. Hopefully I won't get pushed to the floor again."

In Mr. H.'s class, Mr. H. is letting his students know that he is giving them an extra credit opportunity related to the essay that is due next Tuesday. The extra credit is to let the kids figure out what Captain Broach's real name is. Before he is done explaining the extra credit, Jake enters the classroom.

"Excuse me, little boy!" he yells, getting up from his seat. "Who are you?"

"You saw me yesterday. I already introduced myself to you. I'm Jake."

Mr. H. looks at his class roster. "Okay, Blake, you are on the roster. Please go have a seat before I change my mind and send you to another classroom."

"It's Jake!"

Jake sits down next to Joey and Matt. He explains to them where he was during third period. Apparently he found something on the floor when he was in the bathroom. It appears to be a sketch of three people. One of them is holding a chain, one is a person with a foot that is not facing frontward, and the last one is a girl whose hair is very long. On top of the paper, it says, "The Ghouls I Wish Were Real, by Scram Bumbleberry." Jake admits that Scram is a real artist; he has talent. But he asks Joey and Matt what all of Scram's sketches mean.

After fourth period is over, in the hallway, Matt wonders how long it's going to take them to find the person Scram is working with. Joey would like to find the person by Friday, which is tomorrow. Joey thinks that he should skip out on the trip to the history museum. If they don't find that person, it means that it was a bad decision not to go on the trip. He needs to take action on his own.

The person they are looking for could be their only chance to complete their mission. Matt is with Joey, and he is going to skip the trip as well. He has found that there are other places or ways for him to learn more about their planet. Since Matt is staying, Baron is going to stay as well, to help find this person. Frankie, on the other hand, is very sorry because he still wants to go on the trip. He asks them if they can handle finding this person by themselves while he is out having fun on the trip. Matt is optimistic that they can handle it; hopefully there won't be a problem. It would have been a real pleasure for Frankie to help his team members through the voice-to-voice radio, but the museum has metal detectors. If the security workers catch him with the device, he could get in a lot of trouble, or they could simply confiscate it. Frankie wishes the kids luck for tomorrow.

Inside the cafeteria, Scram yet again greets his five kids, asking them if they are going to the museum tomorrow. Frankie is, while Joey, Jake, Matt, and Baron will be staying at school tomorrow. Scram isn't going because he doesn't like that type of trip; it gets boring for him, so tomorrow he's staying in school.

"You should come on the trip," Frankie says to Scram, trying to encourage him. "It's going to be a fun day. Also, it's Friday."

Scram says, "Better things are going on tomorrow than going to a boring museum. I'm staying in school tomorrow. I need to get my learning on."

"Listen to this dweeb," Baron whispers to Joey.

Frankie can't stop Scram from making his decision; he wants Scram to have fun in school. Scram thinks that most of it will be fun and some of it won't. He's got loads of looking around to do tomorrow to make sure things happen. Before he goes to get lunch, he almost forgets to tell the five kids that he made a new friend yesterday. Joey doesn't want Scram to reveal the name; he simply wants a description of that person.

"He has brown hair like Baron, no earrings; he wears a blue wristband, and he also has a British accent like Baron. Hey, how come you guys are looking for him?"

"What? We didn't say anything about looking for him," Frankie says.

"Hmm, interesting," Scram says. "Hey, look—the lunch line is short. Time for me to get some food." He walks away.

"Wait a minute. Scram wasn't in school yesterday. How did he make a new friend?" Joey asks.

When lunch is over, they go to their next classes. Following the final period, Frankie goes to the bathroom. When he is about to leave, he hears someone start talking.

Frankie realizes that it's Scram, and since Frankie's voice-to-voice radio can pick up smartphone conversations, he can hear that he is talking to a woman. Scram keeps saying "Mom" while talking to the woman. Frankie notices that Scram is talking to his mom about something mission-related. He doesn't move so that Scram won't know that somebody is in the bathroom listening to his personal conversation with his mother.

Scram's mom can't believe Scram's actions; he could have foiled their plans. Scram's mom bets that the kids know what he is up to. Scram wants his mother to forgive him, so he tells her not to worry if the kids know what he is up to. At the moment, he has another plan, so there are still options in their hands.

Scram is about to get back out there and do his job. He hangs up the smartphone, and then, out of nowhere, he ends up getting shocked in his ears. What was that all about? After he gets shocked, he starts saying something completely different, making Frankie feel a bit disturbed. Frankie goes back into the hallway in complete shock.

Joey says, "That's the first time I've heard you say that. What happened?"

"I feel like Scram is not a heartless boy after all. He said, 'I can't do this anymore. I just can't. This is not who I am—I am better than this. Something is making me act like a total fool. I need some medical help.'"

Baron says, "He always needed medical help."

Frankie replies, "I think he's acting like this because of his parents. I have another feeling that his mother is controlling his mind and Scram can't break free from it. I'm starting to feel sorry for that boy. I would like to help, but he will get the idea that we've been spying on him and listening to the things that he's been doing. It's lucky that he doesn't know what we are up to."

"If he found that out, we would be dead meat. He would send all five of us to the hospital," Baron says.

The five kids walk away from their lockers. When the coast is clear, someone slowly comes out of a locker who has listened to pretty much Frankie's entire conversation. When that person comes out the locker, he goes to tell the person he is working with about what he heard from Frankie's little conversation.

The five kids have left the school building. Outside, Joey remembers that Joe isn't coming for them today. They get on the school bus and ask the driver for a ride home. He agrees, and soon they are on their way back home. Baron goes his way while Joey, Jake, Frankie, and Matt ride the bus home. Joey feels that today's school day wasn't bad; he knows that tomorrow is going to be a lot of work. They just need to find this person, and then maybe their mission will be solved.

Frankie randomly starts having anxiety, and Joey tries to calm him down. What is going on with him? Frankie has just remembered that he forgot to change the cameras' memory cards. He looks inside his string bag and notices that he didn't even pack the new disk he bought yesterday at the store. Once he steps out of that school, he cannot go back in until the next day. He feels like he's been busted.

Back at Joey and Jake's house, Jake notices that Joe isn't home. Joey reminds him that, before they left, Joe said he would be at the auto repair shop when they came home. On the bright side, they have the house to themselves. Jake makes sure that Joey doesn't forget to lock the doors and that he only cracks the windows.

While they are home by themselves, Jake goes to his bedroom to start reading the book Mr. H. has assigned to him, Joey, and the rest of the class about Captain Broach. Joey will start reading the book later. He logs into the Skybot video chat and notices that he has received another video message from Dakota. It was sent to Joey at 7:26 this morning. He starts listening to what Dakota is saying.

"Hello, Joey, Frankie, Matt, and Baron. I know it's early in the morning. I just wanted to let you guys know that my cousin is out from the hospital. He is doing fine, and he will be coming to our school on Tuesday. I will return to school on Tuesday, as well. I'm only giving you guys a quick update. I can't wait to see you all in person again next week. Take good care of yourselves. See you guys next week. Goodbye!"

Joey finds the message to be brilliant news. A few minutes later, Joey starts reading the book Mr. H. assigned to him and Jake for Tuesday's in-class essay. Later on, when Joey and Jake are done reading the book for now, Joey starts to feel bored with nothing to do for the rest of the day. While looking around the house, Joey notices that nobody has come home, which makes him remember something. He goes inside the garage and opens up the five-window garage door. He pushes the new outdoor basketball hoop outside and almost drops it, but he catches it just in time. He doesn't want to make the hoop fall to the ground. He goes back inside the bedroom to tell Jake that he has a little surprise for him.

Outside, in front of the house, Jake has on blue shorts because it is hot outside and there is a new basketball hoop in front of the garage door. He grabs his new basketball and starts a one-on-one match with Joey. During a little break, Joey finally finds a name for their team. He calls his team "Those Five Kids" because there are only five members of the team and they are all kids. Joey has a meaning for each letter in the word "those"; however, he can't explain it now. Before they go back to play some more basketball, Joey reminds Jake to have Joe, Kay-Lo, or Uncle Joseph sign his medical form. He thanks Joey for reminding him and goes inside the house for a quick moment to leave his medical form on the computer desk for later on.

Jake goes back outside to continue playing basketball. Later on, while they are still playing, Kay-Lo comes back home. It looks like she's brought some McPatty for them to eat. She goes inside the house to start making food for later in the evening.

Once Joey and Jake finish playing outside, they go back inside to eat the food that Kay-Lo has brought them from McPatty. Jake only takes the fries since he doesn't eat burgers. He doesn't like meat because of what people do to animals. Later that afternoon, Joseph comes home, but not Joe. Kay-Lo is inside the house playing music, singing and dancing again, while Jake is trying to watch some television.

Later on, back at the computer desk, Joey is about to start his homework. He gives Jake his medical form so that he can have either Kay-Lo or Uncle Joseph sign it. Jake thanks Joey for reminding him.

On this warm Thursday night, Jake is in the shower when Joe comes home. Kay-Lo wonders why he's come home so late. Joe has been out with Lance Perkins. After hearing the name, Joseph remembers who that is. Joe goes into the kitchen to talk to Joseph, explaining what's going on. He tells him that this mission they are on shouldn't be that hard for them anymore because they have Lance on their side now. He is going to be on the lookout for the person Joe described to Lance while they were at the gym earlier today. Lance gave him Sid's number, and Joe gave it to Joseph as well.

Joseph says to Joe, "It's nice to have the detective team on our side for this mission."

"You guys are on a mission, too?" Jake says to Joe and Joseph, sitting on the kitchen counter.

"How'd you get out of the shower so fast?" Joe asks.

"That's not the question I asked."

Joe says, "Don't be rude. Wait, what do you mean by 'too'?"

"Never mind that," Jake says. "I'm not going to give you any answer, and I don't feel guilty about it. Now where's my dinner?"

Sometimes Jake prevents himself from feeling guilty for a good reason. When he keeps his guilt in for too long when he does something very bad, he starts to have a panic attack, which is why he tries to prevent himself from feeling any sort of guilt.

Chapter 11

One Less

The kids are up on this sunny Friday morning. This is the last day of school for their first week. Joe is making French toast in the kitchen. Kay-Lo comes out and says good morning to Joe and Joseph. She is off for her jog before she goes to her housekeeping job at the hotel. Joey comes out of the bedroom and joins Joe in the kitchen.

"Why do you look so grouchy?" Joe asks Joey. "Did you sleep well last night?"

"No, Dad, I didn't sleep well last night," he replies rudely. "Jake kept tossing and turning in the bed like he is some kind of dead chicken roasting on one of those spinning machines."

Jake says, "It was cold and you were hogging the covers. You kept rolling around. You were probably trying to make yourself look like you were inside a cocoon, about to hatch into a butterfly, but with eyes."

"Butterflies have eyes, stupid, and your eyes look just like them."

"You look like a gremlin."

Joe says, "Please, no arguing. Just go get ready for school or something. Joey, I've noticed something about you. You're eight years old, but you call me Dad. You have yet to call me Daddy."

Joey replies, "I will never call you Daddy because it sounds outdated. Jake never called you Daddy, either."

Joey and Jake start changing into their clothes before the school bus stops in front of their house. Before they finish eating breakfast, the bus arrives. They are both ready.

"Have an awesome time in school today, Little Moth. Do any of the kids you know have a nickname?" Joe asks.

Jake answers, "I don't know anyone in school who has a nickname besides Baron. Please stop calling me Little Moth, okay?"

Joey laughs. "That's a funny nickname."

"And what are you laughing at, Booby?" Jake asks as he exits the house.

"Wow, nice comeback. I'm actually jealous."

The school bus leaves from the front of the house. They get ready for another day of school and their mission without Frankie, who is going on that trip to the history museum today. The only thing Joey, Jake, Matt, and Baron need to do today is find the person Scram is working with. If they don't find Scram's partner, there's always next week. Right now they don't have to worry about anything but finding this person with a British accent, to see what he knows about the little wonder.

When or if the five kids find out about the little wonder, they will have to find some detectives to let them go down to Haunted Mansion World and see what's happening there. For now they will have to wait. The five kids get off the school bus for the last time this week.

During first period, all the kids are in the auditorium. The ones who are going on the trip to the history museum are about to leave. First Mr. Griffin has a couple of things to do before they leave. He starts taking attendance for the kids who are going on the trip. When he is finished with the attendance, he has something to say to the kids who are staying behind.

For the kids who are staying at school, whoever has Mr. H. as their history teacher will have a substitute teacher. He warns them not to go anywhere else in the building during lunch; they must stay inside the cafeteria unless they need to use the bathroom or if there is an emergency. They must not try to sneak out of the building. Because they are elementary school kids and they are too young to walk the streets on their own, the front door will be locked. Mr. Russ is the only one who has the key to open the front door.

The security guard isn't at school again due to an illness that she's had since Tuesday. That doesn't mean that nobody is watching the kids, though; the security cameras will be recording. Mr. Russ will be on the lookout on the first floor until school is over. There is no point looking on the second floor because class won't be taking place up there today. The stairwell doors will be locked.

Now that everybody knows the rules for today, they are ready to get this show on the road. Baron is glad that Mr. Griffin is going, which means he won't have to see his enormous forehead during the day. After Mr. Griffin's little discussion with the school kids, first period is over. The people going on the trip, including Frankie and Mr. Griffin, make their way out the building. Frankie reaches inside his string bag to give Joey and Matt the new memory cards before he leaves.

Frankie doesn't give some of the memory cards to Jake and Baron because he wants both of them to be on the lookout, making sure that nobody is coming while Joey and Matt are putting the new memory cards inside the security cameras. Frankie is counting on all of them. If he hadn't forgotten to pack and install the new memory cards yesterday, the four kids wouldn't have to do it today. He wants them to accept his apology. Joey, Jake, Matt, and Baron gladly accept it.

Frankie explains to them the locations of the security cameras. The first camera is in the school monitor room. Security cameras are everywhere in the hallways on all three floors. The next security camera is located on stairwells A and B. The next ones are located in the cafeteria, gym, library, the laboratory on the third floor, school basement, and outside near the baseball field.

Once the kids retrieve all the old memory cards, Frankie wants Joey and Jake to keep the old recordings in their closet at home for safekeeping, so they don't get caught. Joey and Jake don't understand why Frankie needs them to keep the memory cards safe; they won't be useful, but Frankie wants them to keep them just in case. He wants them to make sure that nobody finds the old memory cards or they will be in big trouble.

Frankie must get going before the school bus with a different driver leaves him behind. He exits the school building and makes his way to the bus. As soon as he is gone, Jake realizes he forgot to ask him how to release the memory cards from the security cameras. Now it's going to be more difficult for them.

Before the school bell rings, the four kids are ready to search for this person. Some of the school kids are roaming around the hallway before the next class begins. Joey, Jake, Matt, and Baron start looking for the person Scram is working with. While they are in the hallway, they search hard to find this person. They ask some of the school kids their names to see if any of them has a British accent. So far, no luck.

The hallway is empty now, and they haven't found the person they are looking for. Matt starts to wonder if the person isn't inside the school building, but it is way too early in the school day to think like that. As he keeps on saying, he must think positive so that the good will happen.

A couple of minutes later, the kids are in their second-period class. Baron thinks this is all a waste of time; he does not see this person anywhere. Joey wants him to chill out; they still have the whole school day to find that person, and he is sure that Scram gave them the right description.

The hallway is completely empty. This is their chance to go inside that monitor room and remove the old memory cards from the cameras, but Joey thinks this is a bad time to go there because if they do that now, later on their teacher will wonder why they were late or didn't show up to class. The teachers know that the four kids are inside the school building. Most of the teachers they have didn't go on that trip. It is Friday, and Joey doesn't want a detention or suspension. He feels he has a great point.

When second period is over, they go back into the hallway to look for this person again. This time they are checking out the description Scram gave them yesterday during lunch. They don't have any luck there. There is still no point in giving up, though, since the school day is far from over. Baron goes to his next class by himself since Frankie is on the trip to the museum. No matter—he still has more friends to talk to while he's in class. Dale and Ian are in his class. It is lucky for Baron that he's made more friends.

Inside the locker room, Joey, Jake, and Matt are looking around, trying to see if they can find the person. They still don't have any luck. After changing into their gym clothes, they start making their way into the gym. Jake gives the gym coach his medical form and asks him if he can play some basketball. Tough news for Jake—they are all going outside to the field because it's a bright, sunny Friday. Jake wishes that it was raining outside.

Outside at the baseball field, Joey, Jake, and Matt are sitting on the bleachers. It is hot outside. Luckily, Joey and Jake are wearing shorts and T-shirts today. They've been wearing shorts all week. Matt wears jeans all the time; he doesn't like exposing his legs because they look like tree branches. For now, they are just taking their time.

Jake can't believe that he has to wait until next Monday to play a team basketball match, but he still isn't too sure if he can handle playing on teams. The training that he did with his dad doesn't seem to be enough. He thinks that once he goes home today, he will do what he used to do back at his old house in a creepy neighborhood: train by himself. He will also try to eat a bit healthier, but he has a problem doing that. He eats mostly junk food.

Matt reaches inside his leather knapsack to take out a pair of binoculars, which he thinks will be useful for this mission. He starts looking through them to see if he can find that person. There doesn't seem to be anyone out there with the description Scram gave them. Joey wants to know where he got those binoculars. Matt got them as a gift from his older brother a while back. Matt is using them just in case the person is far away. He can use the binoculars to look around without wasting time walking about. He finds that it is quicker, just in case Joey and Jake don't notice, but he is actually wrong because they don't have to find just their description; they also have to find the person's accent.

Matt doesn't think it's necessary to put the binoculars back inside his leather knapsack. Jake thinks his binoculars are very cool. He hasn't seen them in a while, so he asks Matt if he can borrow his binoculars. He promises that he will give them back to him on Monday. Matt doesn't really need the binoculars; he barely uses them, so he is going to let Jake keep them.

Before third period is over, the gym coach sends the kids back inside the building early so they won't be late for their next class. Since they cannot go to the second floor today, their class will take place on the first floor. All the stairwell doors are locked, so there is no going up to the next two floors. Baron comes out of his class and meets Joey, Jake, and Matt near the lockers. He looks mad.

"Can you believe one of those kids in class caught a cold and kept on coughing right behind me?" he yells at Joey. "I had to cover the back of my neck with two sheets of tissue paper so no germs would fly on me."

"Uh, why didn't you just give the kid the tissue paper?" Joey asks.

"Oh. That would've been the smart thing to do."

"Did you find anything that can help us with this mission while you were in class?"

Baron answers, "No. I wish I did, though."

"We've just got to keep on looking," Joey says.

They start looking for the person again, but they still can't find the person they need. Could it be that the person went on the trip to the history museum? When fourth period comes, Joey, Jake, and Matt are in Mr. H's history classroom. Mr. H. is on the trip, so the school kids have a substitute teacher who keeps spitting. How inconvenient. Later on, after fourth period is over, the four kids are in the cafeteria, about to start dealing with the school security cameras.

Joey takes out the new memory cards out from his book bag. It looks like they have enough. They quickly sneak out of the cafeteria without any of the teachers or Mr. Russ noticing that they are leaving. They can now go inside the monitor room, quickly uninstall the old memory cards, and put the new ones inside the cameras. But how are they going to remove the old memory cards from the security cameras?

Joey gives Matt half of the cards while he keeps the other half for himself. As they are making their way down the hallway to the monitor room, they make sure that the coast is clear. Matt gives a signal that it is all clear. No one is in the hallway.

When they are near the monitor room, they look again to make sure no one is around. Jake and Baron agree to stay outside to be on the lookout. Joey and Matt go inside the monitor room to see if they can find anything that will release the cameras' memory cards. They have a hard time finding anything. They start messing up the monitor room, the same thing Frankie and Baron did earlier in the week. Later on, they're still not having any luck finding anything that will release the cameras' memory cards, meaning that they've messed up the monitor room for nothing.

While they are cleaning up the room, Joey starts looking at the picture of the female security guard eating a chicken wing. It is an awkward picture; he doesn't know why someone would take a picture of herself eating. Joey touches the picture to get a closer look at it, noticing something in the background. It seems to be some kind of system. Is that the duplication system? What was she doing with it at that time?

Joey accidently pulls the tape off the controls, revealing a scratched-up blue button. The button is blue, but if it was red, Joey wouldn't have touched it. Because the scratched-up button is blue, he punches the button, releasing all the security cameras' memory cards. Jake goes inside the monitor room and tells them that the memory card came out of the camera. He sees Joey holding the picture of the security guard. Jake takes it from him and looks at it. For some strange reason Jake wants to keep the picture, but if he does, the security guard will notice that it's gone. Joey leaves it inside the monitor room so that there will be no trouble.

When Joey puts the picture back, they step out from the monitor room to go into the hallway and replace the old memory card with the new one. The camera is too high for them to reach. Baron remembers something and goes inside the monitor room to take out that step stool. Joey can now reach the camera with ease. While Joey is up on the step stool changing the memory cards, Jake goes to one side of the hallway while Baron goes to the other, making sure that no one is around.

Near the camera, Joey takes out the old memory card to replace it with a new one. He does the same to every camera on the floor except the one outside; they can't go outside because the front door is locked and only Mr. Russ has the keys to unlock it. They decide to go to the school gym next.

No one is in the gym. The camera there isn't that high up, but Joey still can't reach it and neither can Matt, even though they are both using the step stool. What are they going to do now?

Joey, Matt, and Baron decide to step on the bleachers and reach toward the camera. They still can't reach it, but Matt has an idea. He moves closer to the security camera, reaches it, and takes out the old memory card using his index finger and thumb. He takes one of the new memory cards out of his pocket. This time he has trouble putting it inside the camera's slot because he has to reach a bit farther this time.

Matt makes one of the gutsiest moves of his life: he stands on the bleacher railings with no grip on the wall. Just in case he falls, he has Joey, Jake, and Baron to catch him. While standing on the bleacher railing, Matt slowly stretches out his right arm to reach the camera. He starts to lose his balance on the railing, but he sticks it out. Again he slowly stretches out his right arm, trying to place the new memory card inside the camera. One more reach and he places the new card inside the slot.

Matt falls off the bleacher railing, and Jake ends up catching him. Matt thanks Jake for saving his life; it was lucky that he was standing there. Jake appreciates Matt and would do anything to help out a friend.

As Joey and Baron are about to step off the bleachers, one of the gym doors opens. Joey notices that it is the gym coach. He and Baron quickly jump off of the bleachers and hide underneath them. So do Jake and Matt. Jake starts to peek out from underneath the bleachers, seeing the gym coach resting a few file papers on a little brown, square table.

Jake turns his head, about to speak to Joey, Matt, and Baron, but he accidently bumps his head into Matt's head, making him move back a little, which then makes his left ankle hit a hundred-pound dumbbell, which then causes him to fall to the floor. Matt feels a lot of pain. His left foot hurts a lot; he almost can't move it.

The gym coach is still inside the gym packing up a few papers when he hears a little scream that catches his attention. He starts looking around the gym, making sure that nobody is there. Why does the gym coach look so suspicious? The coach goes back to his table and puts files inside the file holder; it looks like papers that have been graded. The gym coach has only come to the gym to put away his papers. That doesn't seem too suspicious to Jake, who is watching what the coach is doing. The gym coach then leaves the gym to head back to the cafeteria.

It is lucky that the four kids didn't get caught. Joey drags Matt from underneath the bleachers, wondering if he is okay, while Jake has to be nosy and see the papers the gym coach put inside the file holder. Matt's ankle is in a lot of pain, but at least he has put the new memory card inside the camera slot. Joey notices that, when Matt fell, he seemed to have grabbed the beam of the camera off. There is no need to worry; nobody will notice that they were the ones who did that.

Jake is over at the gym coach's desk looking through some of the files. He only wants to see what kind of grade the teacher gave him for today's class. So far it is looking good, but that isn't the only file he is going to look at. He looks at Joey, Frankie, Matt, and Baron's files to see if their grades are good, as well. Jake starts searching for Scram's file but can't find it anywhere. That seems odd to him because he knows that Scram has gym with him. Jake is starting to wonder about something, but he can't put his finger on what.

Jake goes to Matt to help him up and takes him to the school infirmary to get his ankle checked out. He apologizes deeply to Matt; he didn't mean to make him bump his head, which then caused his left ankle to hit the dumbbells. Matt doesn't care; he knows that it was an accident.

A short time later, Jake and Matt learn that Matt has a fractured ankle, and the ambulance is on its way to take him to the hospital. Jake feels really upset, but Matt doesn't want him to feel that way; he will be okay after his ankle gets better. He gives Jake the rest of the memory cards so they can get the job done. Jake thanks him and leaves the infirmary.

Joey, Jake, and Baron make their way up to the second floor of the school building, but then they remember that the doors to stairwells A and B are locked. They have no idea where they are going to get a key until they remember that Mr. Russ has the keys. How are they going to get the keys from him? It will be impossible to get the keys from Mr. Russ. There has to be another way. They start to think of something. After a few seconds of thinking, Joey remembers that Frankie gave him a lock picking kit. He reaches inside his book bag to get it from his pencil case. He uses the kit to pick the lock, but he can't get it open. After a few tries he realizes that there is no way to open that door without a key.

Baron sighs, grabbing the lock picking kit and lightly pushing Joey out of the way. He uses the lock picking kit to pick the door lock. Surprisingly, he gets it open, and then he calls Joey a bumbling idiot. Joey is not surprised. On the second floor, after unlocking the door to stairwell A, they do the same thing with the security cameras until they reach the third floor.

On the third floor, they go through two double doors that look quite familiar to Baron. The doors lead them into the laboratory. Inside the lab is a beaker and some spilt chemical on the table. It looks like the same matter that's been lying on the table since Tuesday, before Frankie and Baron went into the lab.

Over near the lab windows, Joey places the step stool underneath the security camera so that he can change the memory card. He accidently drops the old memory card, which Baron picks up. Once Joey installs the new memory card, someone slams the lab door, making Joey, Jake, and Baron turn around quickly. It is Leonard, whom Baron hasn't seen since Tuesday, who has closed the lab door. Baron goes up to Leonard to find out how his right hand looks after the chemical reaction. Leonard grabs Baron by the arm, opens the lab door, and pushes him out, locking the door from the inside.

Leonard reached inside his left pants pocket while he looks at Joey and Jake. He takes out a Taser and starts to go after Joey and Jake. Joey hides underneath a lab table as Jake is about to get attacked by Leonard. Jake wants to hide, but he is tired of running away. This time he is not going to flee; this time he wants to fight. He believes in the strength training that Joe has done with him in the past few days, so he goes up to Leonard and looks him in the eye. Jake is about to see who the tough kid is.

Leonard fires a Taser at Jake but misses, and Jake has the advantage to attack him. Leonard blocks the attack and punches Jake in the jaw. After Leonard punches Jake, he kicks him in both legs, which causes Jake to drop to the floor. While Jake is on the floor, Leonard walks up to him and aims the Taser at Jake, but Joey comes out from underneath a lab table and jumps on Leonard's back. This gives Jake a chance to get up off the floor.

As Joey is holding on to Leonard, Jake tries to take the Taser away from him. There is no explanation as to why Leonard brought a Taser to school or where he got one. While Jake is trying to take away the Taser, Leonard overpowers Joey and drops him to the floor on his back. Then he gives Jake a head butt. Leonard fires the Taser at Jake again, but he misses. Jake can dodge things very easily. It must be the training he did with Joe, when Joe taught him how to block attacks.

Leonard is going to do what it takes to stun Joey and Jake. Why is he attacking them? There's got to be some sort of solution. While Joey is on the floor, he crawls up to Leonard's right leg, grabs it, and bites it, making Leonard scream in pain. When Leonard looks up, Jake comes out of nowhere and spin-kicks him in the stomach, making his Taser fly out of his right hand and land on a lab table near the spilt chemical.

Jake pushes Leonard down to the floor, grabbing his shirt and making a fist, about to punch him in the face. Before he does that, the lab table with the spilt chemical catches on fire due to the electricity of the Taser. Jake feels terrified, and this gives Leonard a chance to push him off and try to escape the lab. But Jake stops and continues fighting with Leonard with the table on fire.

Joey wants Jake to stop attacking Leonard and leave the lab before the fire starts to spread. Jake looks at the lab table, and it does look like the flames are about to spread. The flames distract Jake, so Leonard knees him and escapes the laboratory. Joey helps Jake up and quickly runs out of the lab before the fire starts to spread.

"What is that kid's problem?" Joey asks Jake. "Did you see how fast he tried to stun us with that Taser?"

Jake says, "Joey, you are so lucky that I got accepted to this school so quickly. If you had been in there by yourself getting attacked, who knows what would have happened to you? I still don't understand why Leonard tried using that Taser on us, and thanks for making me let him get away. Now I won't be able to show him who the tough kid is. At least I gave him a good spin kick to the stomach. I didn't want to hit him in the chin because I got nervous for some reason."

"Does it matter?" Baron asks. "But one question—how come he decided to attack you guys but not me?"

Part of the school laboratory is on fire, setting off the alarm and fire sprinklers. School kids run toward the front door and try to open it, but the door is locked. They are trying hard to get out before the smoke reaches them. Before it does, Mr. Russ comes quickly to unlock the front door. The kids run out of the building to safety. Joey, Jake, and Baron are still on the third floor, right there near the fire. They start to run away from it because the smoke is flying toward them pretty fast.

One of the double laboratory doors is open, making the smoke escape the lab more quickly. The smoke starts to turn black as the oxygen starts to dissolve. Luckily, all the school kids, staff, and Mr. Russ have escaped the building. They all are safe, but some of the kids are scared, crying and shaking. This is not how Joey wants to spend his Friday. On the other hand, Jake tells him that at least everybody got out safe. Jake hugs Joey, glad that he is okay.

When Joey first saw the laboratory on fire, something started weighing on his mind. Now he goes up to Mr. Russ and tells him the truth about what happened, and also blames Scram for sending a kid to school with a Taser. Mr. Russ denies what Joey is saying; he can't believe that a student would bring a Taser to school to attack Joey and Jake and then end up setting the lab on fire. Besides, he knows that the stairwell doors were locked. Mr. Russ starts to think that Joey isn't feeling too well after what just happened.

Joey can't believe that Mr. Russ thinks he wasn't telling the truth. Joey decides to go home. Jake talks to Joey in a soft voice so that no one will find out about what they were doing all day. Jake tells Joey that he can't leave now. They have just three more cameras to change—one in the cafeteria, one in the school basement, and one near the baseball field on the side of the building. Joey wants Jake and Baron to do it themselves, so he gives Jake the memory cards. Then he makes his way home.

Joey isn't upset; he is only going home to ease his pain away after the event that just took place in the school building that involved him, Jake, and Baron. Because people are in front of the school building, this gives Jake and Baron enough time to install the new memory card in the camera near the baseball field. Outside, near the baseball field, Jake finds the camera, which is high above him. They don't have the step stool with them; they left it inside the burning laboratory. How are they going to reach the baseball field security camera?

Jake remembers something from his past. He asks Baron to spring him toward the camera. Baron is glad to do that; he used to catapult his two sisters all the time. When Baron springs Jake in the air, Jake grabs the camera with both hands, trying to control his strength. When he grabs it, he takes his left hand off the camera and reaches into his right pants pocket to take out the new memory card. He accidently drops one, so Baron picks it up and puts it in his pocket.

Jake takes out the old memory card from the security camera and installs the new one. He is all good. All he needs to do is make sure Baron catches him when he lets go of the camera and try to install the next two memory cards in the security cameras in the cafeteria and in the school basement. Surprisingly, when Jake lets go of the camera, Baron catches Jake and holds him like a baby. Jake thanks Baron for catching him. Baron purposely drops Jake on the grass and walks away from him.

News reporters arrive in front of the school to report on the fire. A fireman comes out of the building. There is still smoke inside, and there is still a fire on the third floor. The fireman tells everybody that the school building will remain closed until further notice.

"Excuse me!" Mr. Russ says to the fireman. "Did any of you guys find out what caused the fire in the lab?"

The fireman replies, "The only evidence that we found is this Taser, which may have caused the fire. We are going to examine everything inside that building. If the building is not safe anymore, this school will have to be shut down."

"What about these school kids? What about my job?"

"The commissioner will sort things out."

More fire trucks arrive in front the school. Mr. Russ starts to realize something about Joey. He looks around for Jake to see if he knows anything about what Joey said. In the back of the school building, Jake and Baron notice that the smoke has yet to reach the first floor. They need to hurry and install the new memory card inside the cafeteria and in the school basement. To do this quickly, they are going to split up. Jake gives Baron a new memory card and keeps one for himself.

At the back of the school building, in the parking lot, Jake and Baron make their way through the back door. They can't go out through the front because everybody is in front of the school. On the first floor, near the basement staircase, Baron goes down to the basement and looks for the security camera. The basement is a little dark; he wishes that he had a flashlight with him. As Baron is searching around for the security camera, someone comes down the basement staircase. Baron hides behind a boiler tank to make sure he isn't caught.

Three firefighters come down to the basement to see if any damage has been done to the pipes. They need some tools, so they go back outside to get them from the fire truck. This is Baron's chance to continue searching for the security camera. The firefighters retrieve their tools and are about to head back to the basement. At that same time, Baron has found the security camera. There are no step stools, so the only plan Baron can think of is to climb the boiler tank and install the new memory card.

Once he has reached the top of the boiler tank, Baron hopes that it won't explode for any reason. He takes the old memory card out of the security camera and replaces it with the new one. When he is done, he quickly jumps off the boiler tank and runs out of the basement. He is just in time; the firefighters are returning to the basement. The next thing Baron needs to do is go to the cafeteria to see how Jake is doing.

The smoke has reached the first floor of the building. Baron is inside the cafeteria looking for Jake, but he can't find him. Finally he spots Jake hiding underneath a lunch table on the other side of the cafeteria. Baron tells Jake that this isn't a good hiding spot; the firefighters can still see them. Jake knows. When Baron comes over to this side of the cafeteria, he spots the security camera, which is right near the kitchen, but firefighters are there inspecting the appliance.

More smoke starts spreading on the first floor. On the other side of the cafeteria, Jake and Baron are still hiding underneath the lunch table. There are six firefighters inside the kitchen inspecting the appliances. This is wasting Jake and Baron's time. Baron comes up with an idea; to get the firefighters out of the kitchen, he will yell and pretend that he is in trouble. This plan will allow Jake to be alone, and Baron knows that it will work.

Baron gets out from underneath the lunch table, goes farther across in the cafeteria, lies down on the floor on his back, gives Jake a thumbs up, and starts to scream, pretending he is hurt. All six firefighters hear the scream and see Baron on the floor begging for help. All six of them go up to him, and Baron explains that he is having trouble breathing; he was trapped on the second floor and managed to escape. The six firefighters take him out of the building.

Jake comes out from underneath the lunch table, climbs on top of it, and replaces the old security camera memory card with a new one. This is the last security camera. All the security cameras have new memory cards now. All he needs to do is go inside the monitor room and hit the record button. When that is done, Jake sneakily escapes the school building by going through the back door. The first floor is already covered in smoke.

By the time Jake reaches the front of the building, firefighters are already putting the fire out. Baron is okay in the front; he tells the firefighters that it was only a stomach cramp. He sees Jake smiling at him; he is so glad that he is okay. Jake and Baron are relieved that all the security cameras' memory cards have been changed. Baron feels that it wasn't necessary; he and Frankie could've taken the punishment for when he and Frankie were chased down the school hallway on Tuesday.

"There you are!" Mr. Russ says to Jake. "I want to tell you something. A fireman told me that the fire was caused by a Taser, and it's funny that Joey mentioned a Taser. I don't remember seeing a Taser inside the lab before I locked up the stairwell doors. Joey said that a student came into the school to attack you and him. Is that true?"

"No!" Jake lies.

"Since you said no, I don't know who to believe—you or Joey. Hmm, do you guys know this kid named Scram? Joey told me about him a few minutes ago and said he is responsible for sending a student to school with a Taser. But on Wednesday, I was in my office going through student files, and I just now realized that there is no student named Scram at this school. We don't have any files on him."

"No wonder I didn't see his name when I was going through the gym teacher's files," Jake accidently blurts out. "Umm, I'm just kidding, Principal Russ, just kidding. But yeah, we know who he is, and I know who else is responsible. I just can't get the name."

"All right. Thank you! Be safe!" Mr. Russ walks away.

"Who else do you think is responsible?" Baron asks Jake.

"His partner."

Jake figures out that Scram was never supposed to be inside this school; he's been trespassing all along. He is surprised nobody noticed. Jake gives Scram a lot of credit for being such a sneaky boy. All they need to do now is find the person he's working with. Jake guesses that they can't do that now because of the fire. It looks like they will have to wait.

Baron says, "If we can't come to this school on Monday, how else are we going to find this person, and what about my Saturday morning program?" He looks at Jake. "One last question—what is that you are holding?"

"Oh, I took the picture of the female security guard eating a chicken wing from the monitor room before I escaped the building. I couldn't resist because it's a funny picture. I want to show Mom, Dad, and Uncle Joseph, if I can remember. I will also keep the old memory cards. You keep the extra ones," Jake says.

"Thanks a lot, kid!" Baron exclaims. "Are you going to take the local bus home?"

"No, I'm walking home by myself. I'm getting to know the area quite well thanks to Dad, who took me around the area before I had found a school."

"I should thank you for making me have the best school day ever. Today was amazing! For being such a great friend—" Baron reaches inside his knapsack, "I'm going to let you keep this picture of Haunted Mansion World, featuring this random portrait frame."

"Wow, you're so kind. To be honest with you, you have become very helpful lately. I thought you were only meant to be dumb."

"Anyway, have a good weekend. I know I will. Get home safe, kid. You still look a bit familiar to me."

Jake starts to make his way home on foot. When he arrives home, he sees Joey playing some outdoor basketball. He asks Joey how he is doing.

"I'm doing great," Joey answers. "I just took a nap, and I feel like a new kid. Don't you love being a kid?"

"Sometimes no, because your parents always tell you to go to bed when the time comes. Kids should never have a bedtime. We should tell adults to go to bed. Anyway, we succeeded in putting all the new memory cards inside the security cameras. It's surprising that we didn't get caught. To be honest with you, it's been a really fun and scary Friday. I only wish that Matt wasn't in the hospital," Jake says.

"At least he wasn't with us when we were getting attacked by Leonard. We still need to find out why he only attacked you and me but not Baron."

Later that afternoon Joe and Kay-Lo barge into the house to see if Joey and Jake are home. Yes, they are. Jake is lying on the living room couch, watching a middle school movie, and Joey is at the computer desk coloring some pictures.

Kay-Lo wants to know if they are all right. She had been afraid that they were hurt. Joe had been watching television by himself while he was on break at the day care center when the school fire came on as breaking news. Jake tells them that they are okay and that the fire didn't harm anyone. But he doesn't want to tell them what caused the fire or that they got attacked by a student with a Taser. He doesn't want his parents to worry.

"Listen!" Joe says to Joey and Jake. "Any time you guys see unusual fire, wherever you are, I want you guys to run."

"Like I've never heard that before!" Jake says.

"I'm just saying!"

As soon as Joe mentions the word "unusual," Joey explained when he was home earlier today he heard a noise coming from the basement, and decides to check it out. He thinks that it is the basement boiler. Later, he goes outside to play basketball, but the outdoor basketball hoop isn't outside. Before he turns back around, he hears the front door randomly close. He tries opening it, but it won't open. He peeps through the window and doesn't see anyone.

While Joey is trapped outside his house, he starts hearing footsteps inside the house and a creaking noise. It sounds like the attic staircase has opened. Because he can't open the front door, he goes to the back door, but it is locked. When he comes back to the front, he sits down to wait until he can enter the house. Then he hears a noise from the back of the house and sees the back door open. He looks around but doesn't find anyone.

"Hold on!" Joe says to Joey. "Where was Jake?"

Joey looks at Jake. "He was . . . in the shower at that time, so he didn't hear anything," he lies.

Joe and Kay-Lo start searching the house to make sure nothing that Joey was talking about is in there. They don't find anything; everything looks normal. Jake thanks Joey for not letting him get in trouble, because he knows that he has to be with Joey while they are home by themselves.

At 6:27 in the evening, Jake is in the kitchen with Joe eating some yogurt. Before Jake goes outside to play with his neighborhood friends, there is something he wants to say to Joe.

"I'm loving Sea Sight Elementary School. So far, I'm not being bullied."

"That's because you've got Joey, and his friends will protect both of you," Joe says.

"I'm not leaving that school until fifth grade is over, which is next year. The year after that, we all will be going to middle school. I hope we can see some of our old friends when we go there. We will just have to wait and see in two years. So, Dad, have you ever been to that Haunted Mansion World on Habitation Avenue?"

"Near that creepy graveyard? No way! Why did you ask?"

"Oh, nothing. It's not that serious," Jake says.

Jake isn't ready to explain why he asked Joe that question. He should've left it for another time. At the moment, Jake is thinking about going inside Haunted Mansion World to see what Scram's dad is doing there with that duplication system, but he is afraid to go because, since the mansion is called the "Haunted Mansion World," he believes that something scary will attack him.

Later that evening, when it is dark outside, Joey and Jake come back inside the house to log in to Skybot. Once they log in, they start talking to Frankie, Dakota, and Baron.

"Boy, I'm I glad to see you guys online," says Baron. "I spoke to Matt on the phone, and he had his leg surgically repaired.

It's in a cast, so he won't be back at school for the next two weeks. That's if we are back at school during that time. Matt's not leaving the hospital until Sunday night."

"Thank goodness he's all right. Hey, Frankie, how was your trip to the history museum?" Jake asks.

"It was awesome. I learned a lot. Mr. H. kept making these jokes that weren't funny, and he kept saying 'Quiet in the class' every time the school kids talked while he was touring. We weren't inside a classroom. What was he talking about? He must be Baron's dad or something."

"Hey, watch it, mate!" Baron warns.

"At least you had fun, Frankie!" Joey says.

When nighttime comes, Frankie asks whether or not Joey, Jake, and Baron have succeeded in putting all the new memory cards inside the security cameras. Jake tells him that everything is okay. All the cameras in the building have new memory cards now. All five kids are hoping to get this mission over with, but the school fire earlier today may affect that. Jake is hoping that some day they will be able to find out what the little wonder is.

Chapter 12

Mysterious Weekend

Another weekend arrives, making it one week since Joseph and Jake moved to Florida. This Saturday morning, Kay-Lo goes for her jog and leaves the front door open yet again. Later on, Joe sees the door open, so he closes it. He really wants Kay-Lo to stop leaving the front door open; it's annoying him. Joe makes sure that the back door is locked. An hour later, Kay-Lo comes back, checking the security tape because of the school fire from yesterday. In the kitchen, Joseph is telling Joe how nice it is to have been at his new house for a week. Before he can say anything else, Jake rushes into the kitchen and wildly opens the refrigerator, almost spilling the milk on the floor.

"Whoa! Hold on a second, Jake. What is going on with you?" Joe asks.

"Nothing is wrong with me," he quickly answers. "I'm just watching one of those Saturday morning shows. It's on a commercial break right now, so I came to the kitchen to get some food for Joey because he is annoying the heck out me to get him some breakfast. That lazy bum can't even get out of bed." He takes out two bags of Doritos. "See you two later." He runs back inside the bedroom.

Joseph asks, "Why do you keep chips in the fridge?"

Joe replies, "I don't know. Don't ask me any more questions."

"Joe, the house security camera isn't working," Kay-Lo says. "Do you mind fixing it for me?"

"You know, Kay-Lo, you seriously need to start fixing things yourself around here. Whatever happened to 'when you do things yourself, you build up more experience'?"

"It's different with me!" she protests.

Joseph leaves the house to go to Everyday Gym. He wants to see if he can get a job there. Then he will stop by the auto repair shop for the last time. Joe goes to the living room to see what is wrong with the house security camera that Kay-Lo cannot fix.

Then Joe goes up to the attic to get the red toolbox himself. Kay-Lo turns on the television to see if it will show live security footage. Apparently no picture is available; the television is totally blank. Joe comes back downstairs with the red toolbox and grabs the stepladder from the kitchen so that he can see what is wrong with the house security camera.

Later on, Kay-Lo goes to take a nice, hot bubble bath while Joe is still trying to fix the security camera. He starts to get frustrated because he doesn't know what is wrong with it. He checks the white wire connected to the camera, and everything seems to be okay. He wonders why the camera footage isn't showing up on the television screen.

Joe grabs a ladder from the garage and goes up on the roof to check the antenna. Everything seems to be in order. Joe has no clue what happened to the signal. Before Joe comes down from the rooftop, the ladder mysteriously starts to move, and then it falls to the ground. Joe thinks he must be seeing things. He rubs both of his eyes; then, when he looks down at the ground, the ladder is gone. Joe is now stranded on the rooftop.

Joe calls for Joey or Jake. Jake comes out of the house. Not knowing where his dad is calling him from, he looks up to see him stuck on the rooftop. Jake nearly dies of laughter. Tears come out of his eyes as he tells Joe not to get hit with raw eggs by teenagers. Joe doesn't listen to what Jake just said; he just asks him to find a ladder that can help him get off the roof.

Jake goes to the garage, still laughing hard, to find another ladder so that he can help Joe get off the rooftop. He opens the inside garage door. It is pretty dark inside the garage. He starts exploring, trying to find a ladder, but he can't find one. He tries turning on the light, but thanks to his bad luck, the light bulb blows out. He will have to look for the ladder without any light.

While he's in the garage looking for a ladder, the inside garage door closes, making the garage slightly darker. Jake tries to open the door, but it won't open. He thinks that Joey must have closed the door, so he asks him repeatedly to open the door. Joey opens the inside garage door and asks Jake why he's locked himself in the garage.

"I didn't lock myself in the garage!" he yells at Joey. "You closed the door on purpose so that I would get scared in the dark."

Joey says innocently, "I didn't close the door. You must be seeing things. Why are you in here, anyway?"

"I'm trying to find a ladder because Dad is stuck on the rooftop, which is hysterical, but now you're wasting my time by closing the door. Don't do that again."

"Look, I don't know what you are talking about. I did not close the door, and there's an extra ladder up in the attic. Use your mind." Joey walks away.

Jake closes the inside garage door and goes up to the attic to get a ladder. When he finds one, he grabs it and makes his way back to the front of the house. He places the ladder against the house so that Joe can come down from the rooftop. Jake looks at Joe with a grin on his face. He is about to laugh, but Joe tapes his mouth with clear tape, grabs the ladder, and heads back into the house.

Jake closes the front door, about to go watch the rest of his Saturday morning program. When the clock strikes noon, all of Joey and Jake's shows are over. Now they have nothing else to do. Later on, Joe is at the front door, still unable to figure out what's wrong with the house security camera. Everything looks normal, so he can't understand why he can't see any picture on the television screen. He thinks that it isn't the camera that's acting up; it must be the television. He goes over to the television to see what's up.

In the bedroom Joey keeps the old recordings of the school building hidden deep inside his and Jake's closet, along with other personal items. He will store them in there until Frankie gets the picture that they are not useful for anything. The old memory card from the lab's security camera hadn't caught what happened there because it was already out of the security camera then. This is a lucky break for Joey, Jake, and Baron.

Joe is still trying to figure out why the television isn't showing the house security camera footage. There is nothing else he can do, but he is getting tired of trying to see what's wrong. He is going stop for now and will continue some other time. He goes back up to the attic and puts away his red toolbox. When he exits the attic, he raises the staircase so it will close, but it won't work. Joe tries to close it many times, but the staircase still isn't closing. Joe gets mad and forgets about it. He goes to the living room to watch some television.

On this slow Saturday afternoon, Kay-Lo leaves the house to do some shopping. Later on, Joseph comes back inside the house to talk to Joe in the kitchen. He tells him that he just cashed in the rest of the money for the car, and they are all set to get it back tomorrow. This is great news for Joe; he will never do anything like that to the car again. He's learned his lesson. He will never again have another car chase for the rest of his life. He still wants to know who that guy was, and if it was he who kidnapped Joe and Joseph's parents.

Joe is satisfied that his parents weren't killed, and he hopes they are still alive. He wants to know where they are so he can find them and save them from any harm. He hopes that they are safe and sound. Joe and Joseph's life will change if they find their parents. Joe wants that to happen badly.

Jake comes out of the bedroom and goes into the refrigerator, taking out a bagel with eggs and cheese and warming it up in the microwave while Joey goes on Skybot to talk to Baron.

"Hold on a second, Jake. You ate Doritos for breakfast, and now you're eating a bagel with bacon, eggs, and cheese for lunch?" Joe asks.

"I sure am! At least the egg wasn't made on that ugly, burnt-up stove in this kitchen. I wish you guys would replace it. And I don't eat bacon. Never feed me meaty food! I still can't get over the fact that you got stuck on the rooftop."

Joe asks, "Was it you who moved the ladder? You moved it pretty quickly."

"I didn't touch the ladder," Jake says. "How could I touch it if I was in the bedroom watching fantasy cartoons?"

"Good point, but I find it odd that the ladder just disappeared like that. Now I'm going to have that stuck in my head. Well, before that thought starts bothering me, I might as well take a walkabout outside." Joe exits the house.

Several minutes after Joe has left the house, someone knocks on the front door. Jake answers it and does not recognize the man and kid standing there. Their names are Gerald and Brunson. They greet Jake. Jake hears their accent and asks them if they are from the United Kingdom.

"We sure are," Gerald answers. "We moved here only a year ago."

"Uh huh. Do you happen to be working with someone named Scram?"

"Who's that?" Gerald asks.

"Don't play games with me!" Jake yells. "Tell me if you're working with him. I know for sure you are up to something, and that's why you're at my house. You're another person who is responsible for sending a Sea Sight Elementary School student to school with a Taser, which then happened to cause a fire in the lab."

Gerald asks, "You heard about that too?"

"I go to that school. I was in there when it happened."

"To be honest with you, I am not working with anyone."

"Oh really?" Jake asks. "What about your son, Brendon?"

"It's Brunson, and I'm not working with anyone," the kid says.

"Yeah, right! Don't lie to me! I know for sure that one of you is working with Scram and his dad. Speak up now!"

Joseph comes out from the kitchen, wondering why Jake is yelling. Gerald does not like Jake's attitude; he doesn't even want to talk to Joseph because of Jake's rude mouth. Gerald leaves the house with Brunson. Joseph closes the front door and asks why Jake just did that. He wants to know what is going on inside his head. Jake is afraid to tell him the truth, but Joseph believes in him. He simply wants him to take his time. Jake takes a deep breath, about to tell Joseph the truth, but he doesn't know the whole story. Joey comes over from the computer desk to back him up.

After the explanation, Joseph figures out what Joey, Jake, and their friends have been doing this whole week in school. He can't believe that they've been on a mission as well, but he advises them not to continue with it because of their age and safety. Joseph will see if he, Lance Perkins, and Sid Vale can handle the mission without Joe noticing. For now, Joseph wants Joey and Jake to stay put inside the house while he tries to catch up with Gerald and Brunson, to tell them the truth about why Jake was talking to them with a bad attitude.

That evening, Kay-Lo comes back home. Joseph didn't even realize that she had left the house. He wants to know where she went. Kay-Lo went to the App Emporium to buy a new laptop computer. She takes the laptop out of her blue shopping bag and shows it to everyone. The computer cost $380.

Kay-Lo did not buy it for Joe, Joseph, or herself; she actually bought it for Joey and Jake to use because she trusts them with their responsibilities. And the laptop is also to be used for their schoolwork. She is still going to allow the desktop computer to stay in its current location.

The best features of the laptop are that it can hold seven hundred gigabytes of memory (tons of security recordings), and it is waterproof, so if any rain falls on it or if it's underwater, the circuits won't short out. The laptop also contains a built-in microphone so they can talk to anyone online, but a webcam is required to see that person. Kay-Lo stores the laptop up in the attic so that it will be safe to use when Joey and Jake reach middle school.

That night, a few of Joey and Jake's cousins and neighborhood friends come over for a video game night. Later on, Joe comes home feeling very exhausted after a long meeting at work. He sees Kay-Lo in the living room, still trying to figure out what is wrong with the security camera. Joe wants Kay-Lo to stop trying to see what's wrong with the camera; he will handle it.

Kay-Lo doesn't know what is going on. The house security camera has randomly stopped working, the attic staircase isn't closing, and Joe's ladder mysteriously disappeared. She finds it weird that these three events happened in one day. There has to be a strange reason for all these random events that occurred today.

Chapter 13

House Terror

Jake is the last one in the house to wake up on this boring Sunday morning. He sees that the bedroom is a mess from the game night they had last night. He has a little headache, so he gets out of bed to take some liquid medicine when he notices something wrong. He comes out of the bedroom screaming out to everyone that he can't find the clown doll he got as a present from Baron last Saturday night during the reunion party. He actually loves that doll. He doesn't like when he receives things and they disappear. He wants someone to owe him a new clown doll.

After taking some liquid medicine, Jake sits down at the kitchen counter next to Joe. There is something on his mind. He is afraid to tell Joe, but he's going to tell him anyway. This has something to do with the conversation they were going to have on Friday evening, but Jake canceled it. This time the conversation is going to happen.

"Dad, I think ghouls exist inside Haunted Mansion World. I asked you on Friday night if you've ever been there because I wanted to know if you've ever witnessed a ghoul there."

Joe laughs. "Little Moth, ghouls don't exist, and like I said, I've never been to that abandoned Haunted Mansion World."

"Would you please stop calling me Little Moth? Look, in my opinion, I think they do exist because of this kid who goes to my school named Scram Bumbleberry. I found his drawing about the ghouls he wishes were real. I think he means that he wants them to exist and make them appear inside that mansion since it's the only place that's haunted."

"It's not haunted! They call it Haunted Mansion World because it's been abandoned since the seventies. By the way, what kind of last name is Bumbleberry?" Joe asks.

"Nobody knows! Anyway, that's all I wanted to talk to you about."

Jake exits the kitchen and goes back into the bedroom to change because he and Joey are heading over to Frankie's house very soon. When they are leaving, they go into the garage and take out their bikes. They make sure that the five-windowed garage door is closed before they leave; then they make their way toward Frankie's house.

Over at Frankie's house, Frankie is home alone. Joey asks him where his parents have gone. Frankie has no idea; when he woke up they were gone. Frankie doesn't like it when he's sleeping and his parents don't tell him anything. Even when his parents call him and he does answer, neither of them answers him. Frankie figures what's the point of calling? Frankie really wants to stay at Joey and Jake's house, and he admits to them that he doesn't like living with his parents. Joey is going to see what he can do. He feels sorry for his cousin Frankie and wants to help him.

Sunday afternoon has arrived. Joe is at the auto repair shop to get the car back after a week and a half without it. The mechanical worker kindly returns Joe's car to him. The vehicle is all fixed and ready to do more driving. They have changed the wheels, motor, and fuel tank, and they have fixed the scratched-up spot. Joe gets into the black car and takes off with it releasing exhaust, making the engineer cough.

Back at the house, Joe parks the car in front of the garage door. Kay-Lo comes out to look at it. She admits that the car is looking better than ever.

Before nighttime hits, Joey and Jake leave the house with Frankie because, apparently, Frankie's parents have not returned to the house. He can't stay there all by himself. Frankie starts thinking negative thoughts—that his parents don't love him and that's why they left him in the house all alone. They arrive in front of the house, and Jake opens the garage door, allowing him, Joey, and Frankie to place their bikes inside. Once that is done, Jake closes the garage door.

When nighttime comes, Kay-Lo is yet again singing and dancing to music while Jake tries to finish reading the book Mr. H. assigned this past Tuesday. It might not be necessary anymore. After Kay-Lo finishes dancing, she asks Frankie what he is doing at their house at this time. Frankie explains to her that his parents haven't been home since this morning, so he is hoping that Kay-Lo will let him stay at her house for now. Kay-Lo tries calling his house to see if his parents are back yet. After a few calls, no one has answered, so Kay-Lo thinks that they must be running late. When she calls again later on and nobody picks up, she allows Frankie to sleep over with his two cousins. Kay-Lo wonders what has happened to his parents.

At dinnertime, everyone is eating salad and rolls in the living room and watching their favorite sitcom, *4 Rich Girls*. The show is eventually interrupted with breaking news, making Jake mad because he loves seeing girls fight. Kay-Lo flips the channel and sees that CC7 has the breaking news as well. The breaking news is about the fire that broke out at Sea Sight Elementary School this past Friday. What kind of new information do they have about the school building?

The commissioner reveals that the school fire was minor. Firefighters have determined that there is no faulty electrical wiring, and the pipes in the basement that lead everywhere in the building look normal. The good news is that there has been no damage to the boiler tank in the basement, and there is nothing wrong with the school building. The commissioner announces that it is safe for all staff and students of Sea Sight Elementary School to reenter the school building.

On Saturday evening, inside the school laboratory, firefighters found the cause of the fire: a spilt chemical substance and a Taser on the same table. On Sunday morning, the principal of Sea Sight Elementary School called security and firefighters, wanting to show them something.

According to the breaking news, Mr. Russ was going to show them the camera footage inside the school's new monitor room to see if they could spot anything suspicious on the recording. Mysteriously, the school security camera never picked up the moments when the fire started. The recording doesn't start until the fire was already happening and the whole school building was filled with smoke.

One last announcement is that the second and third floors of Sea Sight Elementary School will be on lockdown. The school is safe to reenter and classes will continue. That is the end of the breaking news.

Joey and Jake look at each other, smiling. They are relieved that they changed the camera memory cards just in time, before Mr. Russ tried to reveal what might have happened. Baron must be relieved as well.

By midnight, almost everyone in the house is in their bed, resting up for a new day. Kay-Lo calls Frankie's parents again, but no one answers. Frankie might as well stay for the night; he is going to sleep on the floor next to Joey and Jake's bed.

When everyone is in bed, the house lights start flickering on and off repeatedly. Joe thinks that he has been wasting power, so he turns off all the lights in the house and then lies down on his foam mattress next to Kay-Lo. As soon as he puts his left foot underneath the covers, the lights started flickering again. This seems impossible; he just turned off all the lights.

Joe goes to Joey and Jake's bedroom to see if one of them is messing around with the light switch. Apparently they aren't doing anything—Joey and Frankie are sleeping and Jake is still up reading *The Mysteries of Captain Broach* for Mr. H.'s class.

"Was it you messing with the light switch?" Joe asks Jake while standing at the bedroom door.

"I thought I was the only one that noticed it," Jake replies, shocked. "That light was driving me crazy. I can't even read properly with the lights flickering, and then there's Mom with her annoying singing and dancing. Besides, I don't even know why Mr. H. is making us read about pirates and having us write an essay about it in history class this Tuesday. The worst part is that Mr. H. is always calling me Blake."

Joe laughs. "Okay, but go to sleep. It's late. I will see what's going on with the lights when I get home from work later."

"I think you guys have an electrical fault in the house," Jake says, and then he hears something in the basement. "Did you hear that?"

Joe picks up the mini flashlight from the computer desk and goes down to the basement with Jake to see what that noise is. They look around a few containers and behind the boiler. No one is there. They check the basement window to make sure that it isn't broken. It is locked tight, and no glass has shattered.

Joe and Jake are sure that nobody is in the basement. They are making their way back upstairs when Joe's flashlight shuts off unexpectedly, and the basement door slams shut in their faces.

Jake almost falls down the basement stairs, but Joe catches him. Jake wonders if the door just closed by itself.

Kay-Lo hears the door slam and runs out of the bedroom. She tries to open the basement door, but it won't open. Joe and Jake are knocking and pushing on the door, trying to open it. Kay-Lo pulls and pulls until the basement door opens, making Joe and Jake land on top of her.

After Joe closes the basement door, there is a loud bang that creates a huge white light behind the door. Joe doesn't know what is going on in the house, but he is going to investigate it. Right now he wants everyone to stay in a safe place. Jake would rather leave the house now that something like this has happened. He rejoins Joey and Frankie in the bedroom and closes the bedroom door before another creepy thing can happen. Joey and Frankie can't hear what happened because Jake has closed the bedroom door so that they don't get nervous.

At two a.m., the house lights started flickering on and off again. This time it's because one of the light bulbs has blown out. Everybody is asleep, so they don't see the lights flickering. After more light bulbs blow out, the flickering stops.

A few minutes after the flickering lights have stopped, a noise comes from somewhere in the house. It starts to wake Joey up, but he isn't awake just yet. Joe, Joseph, Kay-Lo, and Jake don't hear it because they are heavy sleepers. Frankie isn't a heavy sleeper, but he can manage to sleep the whole night without waking up even if there is some noise coming from outside the bedroom. Joey is not a heavy sleeper due to lack of sleep when he was a baby. Jake, on the other hand, will sleep throughout the day.

There is another noise, and this time it fully wakes Joey up from his sleep. He lies in bed with his eyes open, looking at the ceiling. Something falls on the floor outside the bedroom; it sounds like pots and pans. Joey gets out of bed to see what's making all that noise. When he leaves the bedroom, the door slowly closes behind him, but he is unaware of it.

Since it sounded like pots and pans, Joey goes into the kitchen and notices that nothing is on the floor. While Joey is taking his time walking in the slightly dark kitchen, every single cabinet door starts to move. They keep opening and closing, creating a lot of soft noise. Joey still has no clue what's going on.

While Joey is searching the house, the cabinet doors are still opening and closing repeatedly. He slowly opened up the inside garage door taking a look in there. The garage is so dark that Joey couldn't see a thing; he tried turning on the garage light, but the light bulb blew out when Jake went into the garage on Saturday morning.

Joey goes back to the bedroom and takes out a mega flashlight from the dressing table drawer. He makes sure that it is working. Yes! He goes back to the garage, noticing a shadow in the light that is shining on the wall. That isn't Joey's shadow. Joey looks at it for a few seconds, and then the shadow runs away from the light.

Joey turns around to make sure that nobody is behind him. Joey is still looking around in the garage. The five-windowed garage door slowly starts to open. While it is opening, Joey checks the door switch, and it is down. Joey thought the switch was supposed to be up when the garage door opened. He starts to wonder if the house is haunted. It almost feels like he is inside that Haunted Mansion World. Right now, Joey believes that he is in a dream; all of this isn't real, which is probably why he is exploring the slightly dark house.

As the garage door goes up, Joey goes outside. As he sets foot outside the garage, the outdoor basketball hoop happens to fall all the way down, creating a loud noise that scares Joey and makes him turn around quickly. He starts breathing hard, staring at the outdoor basketball hoop that just fell on the ground and shining the flashlight on it. He is about to go back into the garage to make the hoop stand again, but the garage door closes really fast, slamming hard on the ground and shattering one of the door's five windows. Joey moves back fast. He lands on the ground and drops his mega flashlight.

Joey picks up the flashlight and brings himself off the ground. He starts shining the flashlight on the garage door, trying to see if he can find anything on it besides the glass windows. He moves away from the garage and looks around in front of the house. He tries to open the front door, but it's locked, so he goes to the back of the house to see if the back door is open. It is locked too.

Joey starts looking at the trampoline, noticing that the net has fallen down. He starts to examine it and realizes that the net has been cut open. After exploring near the trampoline, Joey goes back to the front of the house to see if he can enter. He is locked out in the middle of the morning, all alone outside his house. He tries to open the basement window on the side of the house.

After struggling a few times with it, Joey finally opens the basement window. How did the basement window get unlocked? The basement window doesn't open wide. While Joey is trying to crawl through the window to enter the basement, something grabs his ankle and pulls him away from the basement window, making him drop the flashlight in the basement. He turns around, wondering what just pulled him. Nothing is around him. The basement window has closed.

Joey goes back to the basement window and tries to open it again. This time it won't open; it seems to be locked again. Joey doesn't know how the window has become locked again. Joey looks at the basement from the outside and realizes that he dropped the mega flashlight while it was still on. While Joey is looking at the flashlight, it moves by itself. Joey wonders if he is seeing things. He looks behind him again, making sure that nobody is sneaking up on him.

Joey looks at the flashlight again. This time it doesn't only move; it disappears suddenly. It looks like someone has pulled it away. Joey's eyes open wide, and he starts to feel terrified. He runs to the front door and bangs on it, but no one in the house can hear him. Joey is starting not to like people who are heavy sleepers.

Joey goes to the back door and does the same, but nobody in the house can hear his knocking on the back door. A minute later, Joey starts wandering around the outside of the house until he notices something else. He sees a message near the hose faucet connected to the house that reads, "I'm going to get you. Those five kids won't be returning to school tomorrow." Joey has no clue what that means.

As Joey is trying to figure out the message, he sees the front door slowly opening. Someone must have heard the knocking. Joey enters the house, and the front door slams shut. He falls to the floor, suddenly being dragged into the basement. He falls down the basement stairs. He is screaming loudly because he can't see what is dragging him. The basement door slams shut. Joey is still screaming when he sees something right near his face.

Joe hears the scream coming from the basement. He wakes up Kay-Lo, and both of them rush to the basement door. They open it, and they can still hear screaming. The light still won't come on after Kay-Lo hits the switch. When they go down into the basement, Joe picks up the mega flashlight and sees Joey on the floor, shaking.

"Joey, Joey, talk to me. What's wrong?"

Joey can't talk. His mouth is trembling, and both of his shoulders are shaking. Joe and Kay-Lo try to calm him down. Kay-Lo can't take it anymore; she goes back upstairs to wake up Joseph, Jake, and Frankie. Then she goes to the house phone to call the ambulance. While Kay-Lo is doing that, Joe is still in the basement with Joey wrapped in his arms.

"Calm down, just calm down," Joe says to him, trying to quiet him. "Tell me what happened if you can. How did you end up in the basement?"

"C-c-clown. Clown doll!"

"Clown doll?" Joe asks.

Joe knows that Jake owns a clown doll, but then Jake complained that it was missing when he woke up Sunday morning. Joe starts to think that the clown doll is really alive. He lifts Joey and brings him up to the living room. He places Joey on the couch and tells him that everything is going to be okay. Nothing will attack him again.

Joe remembers something. The event that just happened to Joey feels familiar to him. The day before Joseph and Jake moved into the house, he had a dream that something strange happened to Joey. Then, when he came out of his bedroom with his eyes red, not knowing that he had fallen asleep, he couldn't get over what he saw. This means that it wasn't a dream he had; it was actually a vision. That vision came first, before the flipped-over bus vision. The vision probably happened after Joe first put the future sighting Crystal of Power around his neck before fixing the broken air conditioner. Joe doesn't understand why his first vision took so long to occur.

The paramedics come inside the house to check on Joey. They have to bring him to the hospital. A little while later, Joe, Joseph, Kay-Lo, Jake, and Frankie are all in the hospital room with Joey.

"Sorry about the accident," Kay-Lo says softly to Joey. "How are you feeling?"

"I can't get the clown doll out of my head. I think the doll was the one who kept locking and unlocking the basement window. It's alive, but how?"

"That probably explains why it was missing when I got out of bed Sunday morning. Joey, don't worry about that clown doll again. It's not inside the house anymore," Jake says.

"How is that?" Joe asks.

"While Mom was on the phone with the paramedics and you had Joey lie down on the couch, I went down to the basement and looked through some of the containers and a few plastic bags. There was no clown doll to be found. I looked everywhere in the house, including the attic, and still no clown doll. If the clown doll was alive, don't you think it might have escaped through the basement window or the front door and is somewhere on the streets right now?"

Joe is going to think about what Jake has just said later on. Right now he is going to make sure nothing else happens to Joey. They all stay in the hospital room with Joey for the rest of night, to keep him company and to keep him safe.

Chapter 14

High Production

Joe wakes up in the hospital room, seeing that the sun has come up on this Monday morning. While he is looking out the hospital window at the beautiful sunrise, he thinks that there might be a chance to bring Jake to the Star-Bright coffeehouse tonight.

Joe looks at his watch and realizes that it's time for him to head home and get ready for work at the day care center. Before they make their way out, Joe starts talking to the nurse. Joey wants to talk to Jake in private after Joe finishes talking to the nurse. Joe asks the nurse if Joey is going to be all right.

"He sure is," she answers Joe. "He should be out by sometime tomorrow. For now he will have to stay in the emergency room for the whole day. I will do some testing on him, and before he leaves, I will give him some medication. Don't worry—he will be back with you by tomorrow. If you need me, my name is Abigail Stern, and this is the number to reach this emergency room." She exits the emergency room.

Joe says, "Joey, please get better. I hope to see you back home where you belong tomorrow. Jake, I'm going to give you a couple of minutes to talk to your brother. I'll be in the hallway waiting for you. Don't take too long." He leaves the emergency room.

Jake asks, "What's up, little brother? Are you feeling okay?"

"I'm feeling a bit better." Joey coughs. "I . . . I should be out very soon, I hope. Not to waste your time, but can you do me a favor? Can you keep trying to find this person Scram is working with? Do this for me and Matt."

"I've got all your words in my head. See you soon."

Jake gives Joey a hug and then leaves the emergency room. When Jake is gone, Joey puts his head down. Later he hears a little noise, like something is moving. Any time he lifts his head up, the noise stops, and when he puts his head down, the noise continues. When the item falls on the floor, it makes a huge noise. Joey hides underneath the covers. He peeks over the bedcovers, looking at the white ceiling. Then he looks at the floor to see what dropped. He sees an oxygen tank lying on the floor. The window is open, so Joey figures it was just the wind until he realizes that the wind couldn't have made the oxygen tank fall to the floor. The oxygen tank weighs a lot.

Back at home, Joe gets ready for work. When he comes home later, he is going to see if he can find out more about what Jake said while they were in the emergency room. Then he will see if he can bring Jake to the Star-Bright coffeehouse. Speaking of Jake, Joe sees that the school bus has arrived in front of the house. Jake and Frankie go out of the house. Joe had forgotten that Frankie stayed for the night.

Only Jake, Frankie, and Baron are on the school bus, while Joey is in the hospital and Matt is home recovering from his left ankle injury after accidently hitting the dumbbell on Friday.

Jake and Frankie are sitting next to each other, wondering what's going to happen in school today since Joey and Matt aren't with them. They will try their best to complete this mission for them. While they are on the school bus, Baron explains to Jake and Frankie that, before they got on the bus, he noticed that Scram wasn't on the bus. Jake wonders where he is; none of them have seen that kid since Thursday, the day before Leonard entered the school with a Taser and attacked Joey and Jake. Jake is sure that Scram and his partner are responsible for sending Leonard to school with a Taser.

The school bus arrives in front the school building and the kids exit the school bus for another week of school.

"Guys, wait!" Uriah says to Jake, Frankie, and Baron as he runs toward them. "Frankie, while we were on our way home from the history museum, this thing fell out from this kid's ear. Since you're so good with electronics, would you mind explaining what it is?"

Frankie takes the item from Uriah. "This must be the device that had a flashing green light along with that beeping sound, but I have no clue what it is. Do you know who the kid was?"

"No clue, but I can give you guys a description of the kid. He has short brown hair, no earrings, and most of the time he wears these cool black and yellow sneakers with gray shoelaces. I want one of those. Well, have fun in school today. See you guys later in gym." Uriah walks away.

"Why does everyone have brown hair nowadays?" Baron asks. "I know my brown hair is awesome, but you don't have to imitate me."

Frankie replies, "What are you talking about, and who are you talking to?"

Baron walks away without responding.

The kid Uriah mentioned isn't the person Jake, Frankie, and Baron are looking for. Jake takes the device from Frankie and looks at it. He wants to know what the device is. This tells him that they have to look for two people now while at school. They need to find the person Uriah mentioned to find out what the device is.

Before first period starts, Jake, Frankie, and Baron search the hallway for these two people. They still aren't having any luck. Later, when they are done searching, they wait for the bell to ring so they can head over to their first-period class. They notice that the door in the hallway that leads to stairwell A has a fire hazard sign that says, "Do Not Enter. Fire Hazard." Stairwell B has one as well.

"See you guys after class," Frankie says to Jake and Baron. He heads over to his first-period class.

"C'mon, kid, another boring school day is ahead of us," Baron says.

Mr. Russ says, "Jake, can you come over here for a minute, please?"

"Go to class, Baron," Jake tells him. "You don't have to do anything for me, just in case this turns out badly."

"Okay. Have fun!" Baron replies.

Jake goes over to meet Mr. Russ near the monitor room with a nervous look on his face. His mouth starts to dry up, but Mr. Russ isn't going to do anything to him. He only wants to ask Jake if he and Joey were in the school lab on Friday. Jake gives him a false answer, and Mr. Russ believes him. He wants Jake to come into the monitor room with him and show him something. Mr. Russ goes to the monitor and shows Jake a recording from Friday. Earlier this morning, Mr. Russ discovered someone on the recording moving in the school basement. It isn't a fireman; the person in the recording has long hair and seems to be holding something. The person's face isn't clearly visible.

Because there was too much smoke in the basement at that time, it isn't clear who was in there. Seeing that there was a lot of smoke in the school basement on Friday, Mr. Russ wants to inspect Jake's hair to see if there is any ash still in his hair. Mr. Russ starts inspecting Jake's hair. This is the creepiest thing that has ever happened to Jake. Mr. Russ sees that Jake's hair is very clean.

Jake understands why Mr. Russ just examined his hair. Jake's hair is long, so even after cleaning it, some of the ash could have remained. Jake insists that he had nothing to do with the fire, and neither did Joey. He has another thing to explain, too.

The female security guard enters the monitor room. "Whoa, I didn't know this room was occupied." She starts to walk away.

Mr. Russ says, "Wait a minute, come back here."

"Oh, geez. Yes, can I help you with something?" she asks.

"Jake, hold your explanation. I want to have a word with this security guard." He turns to her. "There is something suspicious about you. You weren't in school last week except for on Monday, and now you return? May I ask where you were when you were sick?"

"Home, of course. I've been sick since last Tuesday. I didn't return to school until Friday morning. While I was out sick, I was testing out a machine that I had the technology to make."

Jake asks, "So you were too sick to come to school, but you stayed home while you were sick to handle a machine? Woman, you must be messed up in the head."

"Watch your mouth, Jake—I mean, kid."

"Wait, how did she know my—" Jake begins.

Mr. Russ interrupts, "Jake, I want you to leave the monitor room. I'm sorry for thinking of you as a suspect in the fire. Go to class, and I will give you an apology gift before school ends."

Jake thanks Mr. Russ and exits the monitor room, but he doesn't head over to class; instead, he eavesdrops on the conversation between Mr. Russ and the security guard. Inside the monitor room, Mr. Russ shows the security guard footage that the camera caught in the school basement some time Friday afternoon. Mr. Russ inspects the security guard's long hair, and he finds ash there. She has been caught!

The security guard asks, "Why do you think I am suspicious? How do you even know if that's me inside the basement? When was the footage recorded?"

Mr. Russ replies, "It was recorded at 2:38 in the afternoon, and that is usually when school ends for the day. No one was inside the school building at that time—the fire was already gone. Why did you decide to come back to this school on the day of the fire?"

The security guard wants Mr. Russ to shut his mouth. She admits that it was her, and that she was the one who sent a kid into this school with a Taser. Her husband told her to give the kid a Taser, and then she sent him to school with it to capture and kidnap three specific kids. "Before you ask me for their names, I have no idea," she tells Mr. Russ. "Now get out of my face, you old coot. I'm never coming back to this school, and you will never find me. The police are on strike, and there is nothing you can do about it." She pushes Mr. Russ into the monitors and then leaves the building.

Mr. Russ is going to see if he can get more real security guards for the school. He realizes now that the security guard he just spoke to is a fake. He notices that she was trying to prove it wasn't her in the school basement. It was lucky that Mr. Russ had thought to check people with long hair for ash. Jake is the only school kid he checked for ash, and he regrets it. He should never have done that to such a little kid.

After first period is over, Jake explains to Frankie and Baron in the hallway that the fake security guard had made Leonard enter the school with a Taser. This whole time he thought Scram and his partner had done it. He still doesn't get why Leonard agreed to do it. Frankie asks the security guard's name. Jake wants to know too, but now that she's gone, they will never know who she is.

"At least she's out of the school," Baron says to Jake and Frankie.

Frankie replies, "One thing she forgot—detectives are still around. I hope they find her."

"Principal Russ could've caught her right there in the monitor room. I swear, people in this world get dumber and dumber."

"Like you?" Frankie asks Baron.

Jake says, "Something is bothering me, though. She said that she sent Leonard to school with a Taser because she and her husband wanted to capture and kidnap three specific kids. Hmm, three kids. Baron, if Leonard was only attacking Joey and me, and not you, then who do you think is the third kid that Leonard was supposed to attack?"

"No clue!" Baron answers.

"Well, Principal Russ just said that the security guard was an imposter. By the way, she never explained why she was in the basement. One last thing, how did she know my first name?"

When third period comes, Frankie and Baron go to their class while Jake heads to the gym to play a basketball match. The gym coach removed the dumbbells after he was told about Matt's accident. He wants to make sure that no more accidents happen.

Jake joins up with Uriah, Dale, Ian, and the rest of the team. Once the gym coach blows the whistle, they start the game. Jake's team doesn't have the ball; the other team does. One of the kids on the other team throws the ball, which hits the rim of the basketball hoop and misses. The ball bounces back to their team. Another kid throws the ball and makes the shot.

Jake's team has the ball now. Dale passes the ball to Uriah, and then he passes the ball to Jake. Jake checks the shot and makes the ball go through the net. This was his first throw of the team match, and he made it in. Half an hour later, the score is tied. Who is going to make the winning shot? Jake realizes that he is playing in a team match, and so far he hasn't gotten into an accident. He feels positive that he can play in a team match any time. He doesn't feel afraid anymore; that fear is gone.

Gym class is a short period, so the game ends a little early. The score is still tied up. Jake has the ball; if he makes one more basket, his team wins the game. Before Jake is about to make a shot, he starts to hear voices in his head. They sounded like whispers. Jake believes that it is Joey saying something evil to him. He snaps out of it and notices that he still has the basketball in his hands. He checks the shot, hoping the ball will go in, and . . . it doesn't. The kid on the other team takes the basketball, but then he accidently loses it. Jake runs to the basketball and quickly checks the shot, scoring the winning points. Jake's team starts praising Jake.

"Way to go!" Uriah says to Jake, high-fiving him.

"Yeah, what he said. You have what it takes to become a really great basketball player," says Dale.

Ian adds, "Superb skills, Jake. I like it."

"Well, I did it for Joey and Matt, who aren't in school today. Thanks for the compliments."

After third and fourth period are over, it is lunchtime in the cafeteria. Jake, Frankie, and Baron are having a normal lunch period without having to do anything mission-related. Jake starts to explain how much he misses Joey. Too much bad stuff happened last week and over the weekend.

"Now that you mention Joey," Baron says to Jake, putting down his cheese sandwich, "I haven't seen him all day. Is he okay?"

"I really hope so," Jake replies. "But I heard his voice in my head while I was playing basketball during gym, and he said something mean. He said, 'Join me or I will make you suffer.' What do you guys think that means?"

"I think you're just mentally stupid!" Baron says.

Frankie says, "I think it means that something bad is going to happen to you if you don't do what Joey tells you. I don't know; it sounds confusing."

After lunch is over, there is a little violence in the hallway before fifth period. Some kid is fighting with another kid. One kid has the other in a headlock. A huge crowd of school kids forms to watch the fight. Mr. Russ and Mr. H. both come at the right time to break it up. The two kids are sent to Mr. Russ's office. Frankie notices something; he points at one fighting kid's sneakers. The sneakers are black and yellow with gray shoelaces. They look like the same sneakers Uriah described earlier, before first period.

When one of the fighting kids is released from Mr. Russ's office during fifth period, Jake, Frankie, and Baron stop him. It's the kid wearing the black and yellow sneakers with gray shoelaces. Jake only wants to have a little word with the kid. The kid thinks that he is going to make fun of his sneakers. Jake isn't going to make fun of the kid's sneakers; why would he think that? Jake wants to ask the kid a few questions, including his name. The kid tells him that his name is Laurence.

"It's nice to meet you, Laurence," Jake says. "How come you were fighting with that kid?"

"The kid was fighting me because of my sneakers. He kept making fun of them. I told him to knock it off, and then he randomly attacked me for no reason. I guess he was jealous of my sneakers—maybe that's why he attacked me. People from the United Kingdom are so mean."

Baron says, "Hey, watch it, buddy. Not all of us British people are mean."

"That wasn't nice of the kid to attack you. Look, my name is Jake, and these two here are Frankie and Baron. I stopped you because of this." He takes the device out of his right pants pocket. "Do you have any idea what this is?"

Laurence knows what the device is. It's called the HC Mind Chip. The mind chip needs to be taken back to the High Production factory right away. It isn't supposed to be released into the world. There are a total of eleven HC Mind Chips. The HC Mind Chip controls people's brains and makes them act heartless. People know what they are doing, but they don't care, and they won't feel sorry for anyone. Originally, the chips were supposed to help people improve their brains, but the experiment failed. Months later, after the failed experiment, all eleven HC Mind Chips went missing, along with a blue and white cyborg that also went missing on the same day. Factory workers still don't know why they went missing.

Laurence knows all of this because his dad works at the High Production factory. Laurence will finally be able to see him again when he returns to Florida this upcoming spring break. Laurence has overheard a rumor from his dad: the HC Mind Chips can bring statues and other objects to life and make them evil. Laurence isn't too sure about that rumor.

A kid attacked Laurence last Wednesday, putting an HC Mind Chip inside his left ear because Laurence refused to become his friend. It's the same kid with the ridiculous last name.

"We know who you're talking about," Jake says to Laurence. "What's the kid's name who just attacked you? You said that he is from the United Kingdom."

"His name is Dennis."

Jake freezes for a second, then asks him what Dennis's last name is. Laurence tells him that it's Bloomingburg. Jake can't believe it; that's the same kid who bullied him back in New York at Volotont Elementary. There is no way that Dennis is attending the same school as Jake. Jake realizes that his dad wasn't joking when he said that people he knew years ago can pop out of nowhere.

If Laurence isn't mistaken, he believes that Dennis has an HC Mind Chip inside one of his ears, because, while he was in a headlock, Laurence kept hearing a beeping noise coming from Dennis. Laurence wants Jake, Frankie, or Baron to talk to Dennis and see if he has an HC Mind Chip inside one of his ears.

"Thanks for telling us loads about the HC Mind Chips," Jake says to Laurence.

"You're very welcome!" Laurence says. "We are going to try our best to find all the missing HC Mind Chips. If you guys want my help finding them, I will be most honored. That will make this search a bit easier. Nice talking to you guys." He walks away.

"Nice meeting you, Laurence. Okay, Frankie, let's go to class. See you later, Baron," Jake says.

Baron replies, "I always have to be by myself. Consider me lucky? No way!"

Baron makes his way to class by himself until he accidently bumps into a kid who came out of Mr. Russ's office. Baron remembers the description Scram gave last week of the kid while in the cafeteria. That kid is Dennis. Baron stops Dennis to make sure he is talking to the right person. Dennis wants to know what this clown wants. Baron asks to look inside Dennis's ears. As weird as it sounds, Baron holds Dennis so he won't go anywhere while he looks inside his ears.

Baron looks inside Dennis's ears and hears a beeping noise. There is actually an HC Mind Chip inside his right ear. Baron wants to know how long Dennis has had that device there. Dennis explains that he's had it since last Wednesday. Some weird kid gave it to him and told him to put it inside one of his ears. Baron wants Dennis to explain why Scram gave him the HC Mind Chip. He knows who the weird kid is that Dennis was talking about.

Dennis didn't know what it was at first. When Scram gave him the HC Mind Chip and put it inside his ear, he mentioned something about a little wonder. Scram wanted Dennis to help him find a gold and black jewelry box that holds something called the Crystals of Power. If he doesn't find it, Scram said that he won't care about Dennis's life anymore—meaning that if Dennis died, Scram wouldn't care, which is very heartless for a kid his age.

"Are the Crystals of Power the little wonder?" Baron asks Dennis, holding him to make sure he won't escape.

"No, the little wonder he is looking for is a pendant that was made a long time ago."

"What kind of pendant is it?"

Dennis replies, "I don't know. Scram didn't give me specific details. I don't think he knows the description of the pendant. Maybe that's why."

Baron doesn't want to do this, but he sticks his pinky inside Dennis's right ear to take the HC Mind Chip out. Baron then lets go of Dennis. When the Mind Chip is out, the beeping sound coming from the HC Mind Chip stops. Dennis's common sense starts to come back, and he feels a headache coming on. Baron asks him if he knows anything about the Crystals of Power.

Apparently Dennis doesn't know, but he noticed when he was wearing that mind chip that he felt different, like he didn't care what happens to people. Since that happened, he started believing that Scram may have a mind chip inside one of his ears, which would explain why he is such a heartless and strange kid. That is all Dennis has to say. He leaves to see if the infirmary has any aspirin.

Baron can't figure out whether Scram has an HC Mind Chip because he never heard a beeping noise coming from either of his ears. The only way to find out is to find Scram and try to capture him before he ends up leaving Florida. This could be a chance to see if he has an HC Mind Chip inside one of his ears.

When school is over Jake, Frankie, and Baron are still inside the school building. Baron tells Jake what the little wonder is. Jake can't believe that Baron has figured out what the little wonder is. Very shocking! It is very lucky that they found Scram's partner, Dennis, and learned that the secret item is a pendant. Frankie figured that the pendent was the secret Joey was originally suppose to expose to Scram once Scram finds out where he lived. Another thing he figured is that Scram decided to only find out where Joey lived just in case Joey suspected that Scram was trying to be sneaky and trick Joey into revealing his secret after asking him some weird questions. But there is a question that Frankie has right now; did Joey really know about the secret?

Baron gives the HC Mind Chip to Jake. "Here, I took the mind chip out from Dennis's right ear."

Frankie says, "You should have used tweezers to take it out. I have some inside my string bag."

"So I stuck my pinky finger inside his waxy ear when you had tweezers? Frankie, don't talk to me."

"Since we found out what the little wonder is, it is time for us to find some detectives who can go down to Haunted Mansion World to see what Scram's dad is doing in there. But where are we going to find detectives?"

"Look around and we may find some. Duh!" Baron says.

Dennis walks out of the school building and notices Jake. The last time he saw him in person was back in New York, where they used to go to school together. He also remembers him from

Sandy Beach; he just didn't recognize him then. He apologizes for kicking sand in his face and messing with his friend. That friend is actually his brother, Joey.

Jake greets Dennis nervously. He never knew that he goes to this school. Dennis has been at this school since last year. Dennis wants Jake to listen to him; he would like to apologize for torturing him every day in school. Dennis isn't a bully anymore because he wants to become more mature as he gets older. He doesn't want to have the same personality forever. Dennis wants for them to become friends and to forget about the past.

Jake starts to smile a little smile and accepts Dennis's friend request. Jake has one question for Dennis: why did he bully him back at their old school in New York?

Dennis is proud to explain this to Jake. Before bullying Jake at Volotont Elementary, Dennis himself was bullied by older kids at another school. They picked on him, said some bad words to him, knocked his lunch tray out of his hands and ruined his good shirt, and ripped up his completed homework pages. Once, it was freezing outside and he wore a hooded jacket that had a little string to pull in his hood. The older kids came out of nowhere and pulled the hood over Dennis's face, also pulling the strings to cover up his whole head.

After that, Dennis felt a kick on his bum, which made him land near a garbage can. The garbage then fell on him, and the school kids started to laugh. The bullies laughed at him as well. They were calling him short stuff, a midget, and also an ant. After this incident, Dennis's mother heard the news from the principal. His mother knew that the school wasn't safe for him, so she ended up sending him to Volotont Elementary, the same school Baron and Jake used to go to.

Once Dennis moved to Volotont Elementary, he wanted to start fresh. If people wanted to bully him, he wanted to see how they liked it when he bullied them. But the only person he bullied was Jake because Jake was short and puny-looking, and also because of the way he dressed. Dennis used to make fun of every outfit Jake wore, calling him a raggedy nerd.

When Jake came back to school with really cool clothes, Dennis became jealous. Not even his parents would buy him cool clothes like the ones Jake was wearing then. But Dennis still bullied Jake because he was still short and looked like a weakling. At the time, Dennis thought that bigger guys beat up smaller guys. Now he realized that this isn't true; smaller guys can beat up bigger guys as well. Dennis learned his lesson: never again in his life would he be a bully.

Dennis says, "Oh, and Jake, tell your little brother that I apologize for being pushy earlier last week. I've felt like bothering him since I noticed him back at Sandy Beach. It was pretty funny when he kept falling on the floor every time I pushed him. Well, best be going home now. See you guys tomorrow. It feels good to be back. Oh, by the way, Baron, if that's your name—you have a ladybug on your head. Cheers!" He walks away.

Baron takes the ladybug off his head. "Well, at least it's better than dandruff."

Mr. Russ comes over. "Ah, there you are, Jake. Here's the apology gift I promised earlier."

Jake smiles. "You got me a gargoyle figurine? Thanks, Principal Russ."

"Don't forget to believe in yourself." He walks away.

Jake loves his new figurine; he is going to keep it safe with the rest of his figurine collection. Now that they've found out what the little wonder is, Jake asks Frankie and Baron if they want to come over to his house to play some video games. Baron has nothing better to do when he gets home, so he might as well have some fun at Jake's house.

When Frankie and Baron get to Jake's house, they see Joe in the kitchen looking at the black and gold jewelry box. The future sighting Crystal of Power is missing. Joe has no clue how the crystal disappeared. He thought that the attic was a safe place to hide the Crystals of Power. He called Kay-Lo and Joseph earlier, but neither of them had a clue how the crystal necklace went missing. None of them, including Joe, has mentioned the Crystals of Power since the Saturday when Joseph and Jake arrived at the house for the reunion party. Joe is sure that Joey and Jake still don't know about the Crystals of Power, so he doesn't ask them anything about the missing future sighting crystal. Besides, Joey is still in the hospital.

Joe decides to look at the Crystals of Power on this particular day because he wants to find out if any of them has something to do with Joey getting attacked. Joe believes Jake's words from the hospital about the clown doll being alive, but he doesn't know how. He is starting to believe that it was the clown doll that stole the future sighting crystal. He wonders how the clown doll found it.

Nighttime has come, and there is a bright full moon. Baron has already gone home, but Frankie is still there without a word from his parents. Joseph comes home spreading the news that he got hired at Everyday Gym. He is not going to start until next Monday. He can't wait to make people's lives healthier. Joe is very happy for him. Now that three adults in the house are working, Kay-Lo thinks that more moneymaking equals more spending.

It isn't too late at night, so Joe decides to take Jake to the Star-Bright coffeehouse. Jake is excited and quickly gets dressed. He puts on some cologne so that he will feel fresh when he enters the coffeehouse. He leaves the house, about to have a fun night with Joe. Jake brings along his backpack just in case he needs to carry something later.

Joe was going to bring Frankie, but apparently he's sleeping, and Jake probably won't want him to come anyway because the night is only for him and Joe. Joe is about to get in the car until he remembers that Jake won't want to go in there because of a past incident he can't remember. Before they leave, Joe parks the car in the garage. He wants to know what happened to one of the door windows. It's broken, and Jake has no idea how that happened.

Joe tells Joseph to tell Kay-Lo that he and Jake are going out for a bit. Kay-Lo is in the shower, so Joseph decides to wait for her to get out so he can tell her. Joe meets up with Jake in front of the house, and they start walking to the Star-Bright coffeehouse. They soon arrive and set foot inside the coffeehouse.

Jake admires the place and thinks that it's amazing, better than the one back in New York. He sits down and takes in his surroundings while Joe goes to buy some coffee for them. A few minutes later, their coffees arrive. Jake has a special new one called the Cherryginated Silk. Jake loves it. It's made out of coffee, cherry juice, and a hint of soy milk.

"Love this coffee," Jake says to Joe. "Uncle Joseph should make one like this."

"What was it like living with your Uncle Joseph back in New York?"

"Not bad. Most of the time he wasn't home, so he left me at Grandma Alexis's house. She never stops talking. Isn't she Mom's mother?"

"Yeah, she is, and she does have an annoying, yappy mouth. I agree with you."

Jake says, "Mom is the same way. The worst part is when she sings and dances around the house. She was doing it almost all of last week! She can't even move her body correctly when she dances. She looks like she's about to fall apart. She's old!"

"No, she's not," Joe says. "She's still in her twenties, and it would be nice if you worked on your rude mouth."

"Sorry, sometimes I can't help it. But I promise you, I will work on it."

"Speaking of work, was it necessary to bring your backpack with your schoolwork in here?"

Jake has brought along his backpack in case he finds something cool while he's out. He's got loads of stuff in there. He reaches inside his backpack and takes out the awesome old binoculars that Matt let him keep this past Friday. Jake doesn't know when he is going to use them. He also has this mega flashlight that was in the basement the day Joey was attacked. He also has tweezers, but he has no idea how they got there.

Most of the things inside Jake's backpack are books, papers, and a picture Baron gave him this past Friday at school because Jake is such a great friend to him. Jake feels guilty that he forgot he had the picture.

"Are you okay there?" Joe asks Jake. "It looks like you need to lie down."

Jake can't take it anymore. Any time he starts to feel guilty, he feels like he is going to have a panic attack. He and Joey have been afraid to tell Joe this, but if Jake wants to get rid of his guilt, he might as well explain to Joe what happened in school this past week.

Once Jake finishes explaining everything to Joe—from Dakota's message to Joey on Sunday before the first day of school all the way to what the little wonder was revealed to be—Joe starts to understand how the five kids ended up being on a mission. He revealed to the random guy he chased down a couple Fridays ago where Joey and Jake go to school. He apologizes to Jake for causing trouble for him and his friends. Joe made a mistake when he revealed their school; he will try his best not to do it again. He wants the five kids never to be on a secret mission again.

"So let me make sure that my mind is clear," Joe says to Jake. "You said that the little wonder happens to be a pendant."

"Yes, and I believe that it happens to be in Haunted Mansion World!"

"That's probably where the future sighting crystal is, too," Joe sighs. "I can't believe I'm about to reveal this to you. Even though I tried my best to hide these crystals from you and Joey, I think today you are going to see a Crystal of Power for the first time."

"If you were trying to hide them from us, you shouldn't have mentioned them just now."

"I said it on purpose because there's a possibility of you seeing it," Joe replies.

Jake thinks it's funny that they both had something to hide. Jake isn't afraid to explain this to Joe now. He and Joey have been trying to hide this from Joe. Jake explains that he and Joey got attacked by a kid with a Taser. Scram's mom was responsible for giving the kid the Taser and sending him to school with it. Jake doesn't want to mention the kid's name to Joe. The kid used the Taser to attack him and Joey, but he was only after them and not Baron, who was with them at that time. The kid was supposed to attack three specific kids at that school, but they don't know who the third one is.

Joe looks at the picture of Haunted Mansion World featuring a portrait frame. Because Haunted Mansion World is included in this, it is best for him and Jake to go down there and see if they can find the missing future sighting crystal. If they're lucky, they might be able to find some answers about this pendant and find out the purpose of this random portrait frame.

Jake doesn't want to go because Haunted Mansion World is too dangerous and scary. He was planning to leave it to a detective, if he could find one. Joe still wants Jake to come with him because this has something to do with him as well, and he also has almost all the information. They finish up their coffee and leave the coffeehouse. Jake really doesn't want to go down to Haunted Mansion World. He wishes that it was his bedtime.

After leaving Star-Bright, Joe and Jake make their way over to Habitation Avenue. It takes them almost half an hour to get there. When they arrive, they are about to sneak into the closed graveyard while the gates are closed. The gate is locked from the other side and the bars are way too close to each other, so Joe and Jake can't fit their hands through them.

Jake has an idea. He asks Joe to spring him over the gate, so he does. When he reaches the other side, Jake opens the gate for Joe. It appears that Jake was telling the truth when he told Joseph about the cheerleader springing him up into the air and landing safely on his feet. Joe is proud to know that Jake is athletic like he is.

Joe closes and locks the graveyard gate. They start looking around the area to make sure that there aren't any security cameras. The coast is clear, so they make their way to Haunted Mansion World.

Chapter 15

Haunted Existence

On the trail to Haunted Mansion World in the closed graveyard, Joe starts to feel like something or someone strange is following him and Jake. He turns around and sees that nothing is following them. It's just a dark graveyard with no lights on. They continue to the mansion to find the future sighting Crystal of Power and to find information about the pendant. When they arrive, Joe is just about to open the mansion front door when the door opens by itself. Jake feels quite afraid; all he wants to do is leave. Joe holds Jake's left hand as they enter the mansion.

After taking their final steps into the mansion, the front door slams closed. Joe and Jake can't see a thing now. Joe knows that someday he is going to need to carry around night vision goggles in case he ever ends up in a dark place with no lights again. Inside, the mansion is slightly dark and full of a bunch of unorganized items.

Haunted Mansion World has been abandoned since 1972, after the person who owned it passed away. Jake doesn't understand why this mansion is still standing; it should have been taken down decades ago.

As they walk through the slightly dark mansion, they hear a weird moaning sound. It sounds like it is getting closer. Joe and Jake are still in the hallway, about to enter the living room. The fire in the fireplace is still smoking hot. Jake goes to sit near the fireplace and take a glance at it.

Joe goes to explore the living room. While Jake is sitting down near the fireplace, something appears behind him. Jake is unaware of it. Joe happens to turn around at the right time, seeing that a mad person with a chain is about to grab Jake. Joe runs to the person to prevent him from attacking Jake, but he is too late. The person with a chain grabs Jake by covering both of his eyes and leaving the living room with him, slamming the living room door. Joe can't get the door open.

Joe repeatedly yells out for Jake, but Jake isn't answering. Joe starts looking around the living room, trying to spot another door, but there isn't another one. Joe starts pulling on the door to get it open. This may take some time.

Inside an unfamiliar room, Jake gets off the floor, wondering where he is. He finds a light switch and flicks it, but no lights come on. This room is slightly dark; it is hard for Jake to figure out which room he is in. He looks out the window and sees that he is still on the first floor of Haunted Mansion World. Jake spots something quite shiny on a cabinet desk. He goes to see what it is, and it happens to be a key. The key is probably to be used somewhere inside the mansion. Jake takes the key, about to put it inside his backpack, when he notices that his backpack is missing.

Jake's missing backpack isn't good; he had all his schoolwork in there. He remembers bringing it inside the mansion, so it is probably still here. The person with a chain who attacked him must have stolen it from him.

Jake still hasn't identified the room he is in, so he doesn't know where he is. There is a door next to a knight statue. Jake opens the door and notices that it leads to the hallway. Jake leaves the unnamed room and goes to look for Joe. He opens another door that leads outside at the back of the mansion. There is a pool, and Jake wants to check it out. When he comes closer, he notices that the pool has no water in it; it is completely empty.

When Jake finishes looking at the empty pool, he turns around and is grabbed by the T-shirt. The person who grabbed him has one eye, a thumb missing on the left hand, and a left foot that is turned backward. Jake starts to understand that this is a ghoul, and he is terrified.

The ghoul throws him into the empty pool. Luckily, the pool isn't that deep, so Jake doesn't suffer any injuries. The ghoul jumps into the empty pool, about to attack Jake. Jake can't stop staring at the foot that's turned backward. He has to give this ghoul a name; he calls it Reverse Foot.

How is Jake going to escape Reverse Foot from inside the empty pool? He starts yelling out for Joe, but he doesn't hear him. Jake realizes that he has to take on Reverse Foot by himself. Jake goes to attack Reverse Foot, but every time he punches and kicks, his fist and his foot go right through the ghoul.

Reverse Foot grabs Jake by the cheeks, pushing him against the wall of the empty pool. Reverse Foot opens his mouth, revealing some sharp fangs. Jake screams out for Joe again, but Joe still can't hear him. He is still trapped in the living room. Reverse Foot is about to sink his teeth into Jake. Jake struggles really hard to escape Reverse Foot. He reaches into his pocket to take out the key he found in the mansion. He tries using the sharp edges to stab Reverse Foot to see if he will let go, but the plan doesn't work.

The unthinkable happens, however. The key starts reflecting the moonlight, and the light from the key starts shining into Reverse Foot's left eye, since the other one is missing. Reverse Foot lets go of Jake and vanishes into thin air. Jake thinks it lucky that he found a key and that there is a full moon tonight, but he still wants to know which room the key opens. He should be able to find out eventually.

Jake jumps out of the empty pool and goes back into the mansion to see if he can find Joe before something else happens to him. Back inside the mansion, he can hear weird music. Jake follows the music, and as it grows louder, he opens a door, revealing to him a golden auditorium. In the center of the auditorium, the strange person with a chain is playing an organ. Jake realizes that the person is a ghoul, probably the same one that kidnapped him.

Jake slowly closes the auditorium door with both eyes wide open. He had not known that a ghoul could produce such good, creepy music. Jake continues looking for Joe, but he can't remember which part of the mansion he was in before they entered the living room. He is going to explore the mansion until he can find the living room and free Joe.

Jake goes through another door, revealing a dining room. Surprisingly, the dining room doesn't look too messed up; it still looks like a new area. There are plastic foods on a very wide dining table, and Jake thinks at first that the food is real. There is a cool antique grandfather clock against the wall in the center of the room. Jake explores the room to see if he can find some delicious food until he remembers that the mansion has been abandoned for decades, meaning that there isn't any real food left.

Jake leaves the dining room, and now he is back in the hallway. This time he can't hear any music playing. This isn't a good feeling for him, and he starts to hear footsteps that sound close by. When Jake reaches a corner of the hallway, he sees the ghoul with a chain approaching him. Jake could have sworn the ghoul was still in the golden auditorium. He quickly looks around the hallway and spots a cabinet desk, which he hides behind so that the ghoul won't spot him.

The ghoul with the chain comes closer to where Jake is hiding. He doesn't notice that Jake is hiding behind the cabinet desk when he passes by it. When the ghoul disappears, Jake comes out of hiding to see where it is going next, but it is tough to see which room it is. Jake wants to know why the ghoul is carrying around a chain in the first place.

Jake can still hear footsteps, and he knows that they're coming from the ghoul. The door that Jake just came through opens, and who is coming into the hallway? Reverse Foot spots Jake from behind and approaches him. Jake is unaware that Reverse Foot is behind him. A floorboard creaks, making Jake turn around. He spots Reverse Foot right behind him. Reverse Foot is about to grab Jake, but Jake manages to dodge him and starts to run away.

Reverse Foot starts to moan and goes after Jake again. Jake has a plan to make sure that Reverse Foot doesn't spot him. He takes off his sneakers and places them near the door that leads into the golden auditorium. Reverse Foot falls for it and goes into the auditorium to find Jake, but he doesn't know that Jake is still in the slightly dark hallway, making sure he enters the auditorium.

Jake turns around, making sure that another ghoul isn't behind him, and he spots another door that leads into the kitchen. He wonders how many rooms there are in the mansion. He has already found quite a lot, and he hasn't even explored the second floor yet. The kitchen on the first floor is a complete mess. Nasty things are on the floor, and dirty dishes are in the sink. The stove looks normal, but the microwave doesn't. Jake opens up the stove and thinks that Joe should take it; he doesn't like the ugly burnt-up stove back at home. Jake calls out for Joe to make sure that he is okay, but Joe still doesn't answer.

Jake looks out the window, checking out the graveyard. It looks a bit spooky, with crows flying around. He hears more footsteps, so he quickly puts his head back inside to check out where the footsteps are coming from. Outside the kitchen, he sees the ghoul with a chain coming. Jake has no idea why, as soon as he goes to that part of the mansion, a ghoul has to be there.

Back in the kitchen, Jake is quickly trying to find a place to hide. He looks at the counter cabinet and wonders if that's a good place to hide. He will give it a shot. He hides inside the cabinet as the ghoul with a chain comes into the kitchen, looking out the same window Jake had been looking out from. Without touching the window, the ghoul closes it all the way.

The ghoul with a chain opens the refrigerator and puts something inside there while Jake peeps through the cabinet door, wondering what it was. The fridge door closes by itself, and the ghoul with a chain leaves the kitchen. Several seconds later, Jake comes out from inside the cabinet, about to open the refrigerator to see what the ghoul put in there.

Jake opens the refrigerator door and notices that the ghoul put a tin can in there. That's it? Jake doesn't find that to be very important. Jake laughs, closes the fridge door, and is about to leave the kitchen. Once Jake takes a step away from the refrigerator, the ghoul with a chain pops out from inside the fridge, grabbing Jake from behind and making him fall to the floor.

Jake thinks this ghoul must be mad for bursting out of the refrigerator like that. The ghoul holds Jake on his back and takes out his chain, about to wrap it around Jake's body from his feet to his shoulders. Jake holds the ghoul by the wrist, trying to prevent him from doing that. Then Jake notices that his hands aren't going through the ghoul, and he knows what to do. He knees the ghoul to the gut, allowing himself to get off the floor.

The ghoul falls to the floor. It is about to pick itself up until Jake runs toward it and spin-kicks its chin. Jake goes to pick up the chain, but it disappears along with the ghoul. Jake finds the ghoul to be a coward, and he still can't believe that he barged so madly out of the refrigerator. He thinks that the tin can might have been a trap. The ghoul probably knew that Jake was in the kitchen, maybe because of Jake's cologne. Because the ghoul barged out of the refrigerator so madly and can play a musical organ, Jake decided to call it Madman Morzician.

On the second floor of Haunted Mansion World, Jake is still calling out for Joe in the hallway. He still cannot remember where in the mansion the living room is located. Jake goes through yet another door, and it leads him into a library. The library features a headless skeleton and a statue of a kid with an evil face wearing a brown cap.

Since Jake can't find anything else inside the library, he goes to the next room, which is the bedroom. There are two bedrooms; Jake doesn't know which one to explore first. He chooses the bedroom closest to the staircase.

There are a bunch of matches and candles, and there is a little, half-broken wooden rocking chair. The chair is still rocking. Jake lifts a dirty white sheet and notices his backpack sitting on the rocking chair. Jake does not dare to think that his backpack was rocking the wooden chair back and forth.

Jake sees a very dusty book on the bed. After Jake blows away the dust, he opens the book and starts to read a few sentences, which keep repeating on every page.

"Once upon a time, there was a mansion called Haunted Mansion World. One day, someone kidnapped a bunch of people and trapped them in there, and they could never escape because they were being held back by ghouls. The ghouls would never let them escape; people would stay there until they died. No one can escape the ghouls. I repeat; no one can escape the ghouls. Ha, ha, ha."

Jake feels that the book he just read is not a real book. It doesn't show the author's name. Jake drops the book on the floor and is about to explore the bedroom. Apparently Jake doesn't know that Joe is standing right behind him. He gets scared and pushes Joe, making him fall to the floor. Jake had no idea that it was him, so he apologizes. At least Joe knows that Jake has the strength to push him to the floor.

All that time, Jake had been trying to find Joe, but he couldn't remember where in the mansion the living room is located because the mansion is big. Joe reminds him that they are near the entrance of the mansion. Joe explains to Jake how he got out. He heard footsteps, thought it was Jake, knocked on the door, and yelled out for him, but then he heard moaning. He saw the doorknob shaking, so he hid, and when the locked door opened, he saw a person with a chain and realized that it was a ghoul. He quickly ran out of the living room and closed the door, leaving the ghoul in there. Joe isn't too sure if the ghoul is still there.

Jake explains to Joe how he escaped the ghouls many times. He did fight them, but mostly he tried to escape from them.

Now that they have reunited, they can continue searching around the mansion for the missing future sighting crystal, which is one of the six Crystals of Power. Inside the bedroom, there is a king-size bed with purple bed sheets and a caramel-colored headboard. There is a window that is closed, but the curtains are slightly blowing. The room is so small that the bed looks like a fire hazard.

Jake goes to sit down on the bed while Joe looks around the bedroom. He is looking at a few pictures in there. One of them is a picture of the mansion itself. The next picture is of a kid with an all-black eyeball and a dark brown cap on his head. It looks like the kid has the same face as the statue Jake saw while he was in the library.

The next picture after the kid is of a dark graveyard with cracked tombstones. It looks like the graveyard outside the mansion. The next picture catches Joe by surprise. It is a picture of the six Crystals of Power that he keeps inside the black and gold jewelry box back at his house. Joe looks at the picture carefully. For some reason, he thinks that the picture was taken in his attic.

Joe turns around and looks at the last picture. This time, the picture is moving. While Joe is looking at the moving picture, a head with a full body that is wearing black and red pajamas is moving backward. Is it coming closer? The person is walking inside a dark forest with a full moon that has clouds passing by it. When the person comes close enough, Joe moves closer to the moving picture to see who that person is.

The person's whole body does a fast 180-degree turn, facing Joe with his head down. Joe moves closer to the moving picture to see if he can spot the person's face. When he is close enough to the picture, the person lifts his head, and Joe jumps back a little. Joe is still looking at the picture when something catches him by surprise. The person in the picture is . . . Joey?

The Joey inside the picture opens his eyes. He has no corneas, irises, or pupils. Both of his eyeballs are all white. The picture of Joey says, "Attack them" in a loud, echoing whisper. A few seconds after the echoing has stopped, two hands come from underneath the bed, grabbing Jake by both of his ankles and making him drop to the floor. The hands pull him under the bed.

Joe grabs both of Jake's hands to pull him back to safety, but it is too hard to pull him back out. Jake is screaming with fear. When he looks back, he notices that it was Reverse Foot that grabbed him. Reverse Foot opens his mouth again, exposing his fangs. Jake starts fighting his way out of there while Joe is still trying to pull him out from underneath the bed. Jake's left sock comes off, and after that Joe manages to overpower Reverse Foot to get Jake from underneath the bed. Jake takes back his socks.

It isn't over yet. Reverse Foot comes through the box spring and the mattress, creating an enormous hole in both of them. He crawls out from the hole and drops to the floor. He slithers back up with his backward foot. Reverse Foot starts to moan and goes after Jake. Joe stands in front of Jake so that Reverse Foot won't hurt him. Unexpectedly, Joe flies against the wall, knocking down the framed picture of the graveyard. No one touched him. Joe looks at Reverse Foot, wondering what just happened. Thunder and lightning begin. There is no light inside the bedroom.

Lightning keeps flashing in the bedroom. Every time that happens, Reverse Foot gets closer to Jake. When the lightning stops, the room is completely dark. They hear a loud breaking noise. Jake lights the bedroom candles, and he notices that Reverse Foot is gone. Joe sees Jake still inside the bedroom. Where did Reverse Foot go? Jake looks at the floor, not remembering such a big hole being there before. That tells him that Reverse Foot fell through the wood floor. Jake starts laughing.

When Joe and Jake are to leave the bedroom, Joe doesn't notice that he has his back to the moving picture, which allows the picture of Joey to grab him and try to drag Joe into the picture. Jake is stunned at what's going on, and he doesn't know what to do. He tries to get Joey off of Joe, but Jake's hands go right through Joey's arm. Jake thinks that Joey must be a ghost.

If Jake can't touch the ghost of Joey, what can he do to get him off of Joe? He starts to think and remembers that he brought along that mega flashlight. He reaches into his backpack to take out the flashlight and flashes it in the ghost of Joey's eyes. The ghost gets off of Joe and disappears from the moving picture.

Joe is lucky that Jake found his backpack in time; otherwise, the ghost of Joey would've taken him.

They leave the bedroom. Jake puts his socks back on and goes downstairs to retrieve his sneakers, which he left near the golden auditorium. Joe wants Jake to meet him on the top floor of Haunted Mansion World. When Jake gets his sneakers back, he quickly runs up to the top floor of the mansion before he ends up getting attacked by those two ghouls again.

On the third and final floor of Haunted Mansion World, there seems to be one last room for them to visit: the attic. When they go up to the attic, they see a chain resting on the wood floor and someone standing near the window.

Chapter 16

Secrets to Behold

The person standing near the attic window looking at the graveyard sees that Joe and Jake have made it through all his wonderful traps. Since he said "his" traps, Joe figures that it was he who caused all the madness in the mansion. He nearly got him and his son hurt.

"Your son?" the mysterious guy says to Joe while looking Jake in the eyes. "Ah, Jake Fallon, you made it, as well."

"How do you know me?" Jake asks. "Wait, everybody knows me. I'm famous—well, I will be someday. But still, how do you know me?"

"Scram told me all about you. Scram, come. You've got a visitor."

Scram enters the attic, looking at Jake. Jake wants to know how Scram figured out his last name. He finds it impossible because nobody has told Scram what his last name is. Joey told him that it was never to be revealed. Scram tells Jake the truth: that he wasn't the one who figured out his last name, that it was his mother. Scram's mom comes out laughing like a crazy hyena.

Jake calls Scram's mom an evil witch for controlling Scram's mind, making him do some dirty work for her. Jake doesn't understand why she would do that. Scram's mom doesn't like the way he is talking to her. One more word of nonsense from him and she will have Jake buried alive in the graveyard.

The mysterious guy has no idea what brought Joe and Jake to the mansion at this time of night. Joe explains that they are in the mansion to answer some questions. Joe asks the mysterious guy who he is, but the mysterious guy isn't going to answer that.

"I understand," Joe says to the mysterious guy, taking out the picture of Haunted Mansion World with a portrait frame. "Do any of you guys mind explaining to me why this portrait frame is featured in this photo of Haunted Mansion World?"

Scram asks, "How did you find that picture? It was in my bedroom stacked with other papers. I bet it was you, Jake."

"Not really! But you did help me and my friends last week. You gave us a lot of information about your dad, where he is, and what you two are up to. Scram, did you really think that the five kids would be your friends? Did you ever notice that we've been asking you tons of tricky questions about you and your dad?"

The mysterious guy knows that Scram's mom should have let Bianca do this. He wants Scram to go straight back to Georgia; he thinks Scram is the worst son in history. Jake gets confused. That mysterious guy is Scram's dad? He knows that this is too good to be true. Something is bothering him. Why does Scram's mom look familiar to him?

Scram's mom admits to Jake that she was the phony security guard at the school. Jake realizes that all this time Scram had his mother inside the school, but he doesn't understand how they were able to communicate through the smartphone.

Scram explains to Jake that his mother was rarely inside the school; she was only there on Monday, Friday, and then Monday on the second week of school. On the first Monday, Scram's mom was in the monitor room, and Scram wasn't allowed to go in there so he decided to call her instead. Something doesn't make sense to Jake; he and the other kids never saw Scram and his mother on Friday. They weren't in school then.

That's what Jake thought, but Scram explains to him that he was in school, along with his mother. They were in the monitor room watching Joey and Jake get attacked by Leonard in the school laboratory. Because they were dealing with the school security cameras, trying not to get Frankie and Baron in trouble, it was safe for Scram and his mom to enter the monitor room while the security cameras weren't recording. Scram already knows what the five kids were up to; that's how he knew the five kids were dealing with the cameras.

"How did you know what my friends and I were up to?" Jake asks Scram.

Scram is thrilled to explain this to Jake. On Thursday, when school was over, before Frankie was speaking to the other four kids in the hallway, Scram told his former partner, Laurence, the other person he was working with, to hide inside a locker next to the five kids in case they were talking about Scram. When Laurence found out from Frankie that they had been spying on Scram all this time, he went off to tell Dennis so that Dennis would tell Scram.

Once Dennis told Scram that he was being stalked by the five kids, he noticed who the five kids were, and Scram figured out what they were up to. He realized that they were trying to find out why he needed to find this Fallon kid and why he needed to find his house.

"By the way," Scram says to Jake, "you guys never knew that I was working with two partners? I heard that you guys were looking for one."

"You are actually a smart goon," Jake replies. "So tell me, how come Dennis turned on Laurence and attacked him in school today if they are working with each other?"

"They *were* working with each other. I found out on Saturday evening from Dennis that after Laurence lost the HC Mind

Chip, Dennis tried to continue working with him, but Laurence refused and Dennis gave up on him. He ended up making fun of him because of the sneakers he was wearing."

Jake wants to know why Scram forced Dennis and Laurence to put the HC Mind Chips inside their ears. This is one of the reasons Scram wasn't in school on Wednesday; he was looking for two kids to help him find this Fallon kid, which is actually both Joey and Jake. Scram chose Dennis and Laurence because they looked like they might get the job done. Scram never knew that they go to Sea Sight Elementary School. There is a little secret Scram wants to hand over to Joe and Jake that he isn't going to regret: the reason Leonard agreed to attack Joey and Jake with a Taser is that he's being controlled by an HC Mind Chip.

"Wow, it is so obvious!" Jake yells. "I can't believe that I never guessed that Leonard had an HC Mind Chip inside his ear. If only I had heard a beeping sound coming out from his ear. Okay, explain this to me. Where did Leonard get a Taser from?"

Scram's mom replies, "From me, at my husband's apartment building! If you would like to know how I met Leonard, Scram introduced him to me since he looked like someone who could get our dirty work done."

Jake bets that Rodney has an HC Mind Chip inside his ear, which is probably why he asked Scram how he was going to find this Fallon kid when Jake was in the school office getting a medical form from the printing machine. Jake is very mad at himself right now.

"Hmm, speaking of machines!" he says. "Hey, woman, I remember what you said in school earlier this morning, since it's still Monday. You said that you had the technology to make the duplication system work. I'm thinking that it was you who created that machine."

Scram's mom asks, "How did you know that I was talking about that?"

"I'm not stupid. You tried to be slick with your words, didn't you? I also figured it out because of the question my friend Baron asked, and also because of this picture of you eating a chicken wing." Jake takes the picture out of his backpack. "The system in the background of this picture has to be the duplication system."

"This boy is so smart," she whispers to Scram. "Yes, I created it, and it was to duplicate a dark pendant made by my husband on Saturday night. Then this foolish system broke down after the duplications because the wires Scram took from the lab back in that filthy old school building had spilt chemical on them. They sparked and blew the whole system up."

"That's what you get," Jake says.

There is something else Scram wants to explain. During gym on Thursday, he happened to leave the locker room where Joey and Matt were. When he reached the gym, he was sitting on the bleachers until he ended up hearing voices on the backup smartphone his mother gave him before school started last Monday. He always keeps his voice recording app active on each smartphone just in case of burglary. The voice recording app is connected to both of his smartphones. This means that he had been listening to Joey and Matt when they were talking about him and his dad, and about the places they go during their free time. They were also talking about the S.S. Security building. He guessed that Jake didn't know that he had two smartphones with him.

He was right; Jake never knew that. As Scram talks about the S.S. Security building, Jake wants to know what they were planning to do in there. Scram and his mom were going there to shut down all the security cameras around southern Florida, but since the plan wasn't necessary, they decided not to go through with it.

Jake knows that every plan doesn't always work, and it was lucky that Scram never fooled any of the five kids. But he was wronged by Scram. On Thursday, Scram asked Frankie during lunch why they were looking for the person he was working with, and of course Frankie gave him a false answer. Frankie didn't say anything about that, but he did because Scram thought that the five kids would get the idea that he already knew what all of them were up to.

Jake gives Scram credit for being the sneakiest person ever. Speaking of being sneaky, he wants to know why Leonard crept into the school laboratory and attacked only him and Joey, but not Baron, when they were in the school lab on Friday.

This is the best question Jake has asked Scram. Leonard only aimed for Joey and Jake, and not Baron, because they want to kidnap everyone in Joey and Jake's family—their cousins, aunts, uncles, nephews, everyone in the family. Scram is surprised and impressed that Jake blocked most of Leonard's attack.

"That's why my dad kept making me do all this physical training when we went to Everyday Gym almost all last week," Jake says to Scram. "Wait a minute, did you just say cousin? Does this mean the third person Leonard was supposed to attack was Frankie?"

"So slow to catch on," Scram says.

"I can't believe that you guys are trying to kidnap all of my family. I actually want to know why. Look what you did—you made Leonard attack Joey and me with a stupid Taser so that he could stun us. And since you said that you and your mother were in the monitor room watching Joey and me getting attacked, I bet that once Joey and I were stunned on the floor, you guys would have come to the lab and kidnapped us. Then you would have brought us to a dangerous place where we could be tortured or, worse, killed by these ghouls."

"How did you figure that out?" Scram asks.

"Ha, because you just told me. Geez, Dad, this boy hardly thinks."

Scram's mom says, "Watch your tongue, you half-wit dunce."

"I wasn't talking to you. You know, I think we should capture you right now because all the things we had to do in school were such a pain. It's your fault, pea brain, and don't call me a half-wit dunce."

Scram's mom says, "That wouldn't have happened if your stupid dad hadn't revealed where you guys go to school. Nothing would have gone on inside that building. Your cousin wouldn't have had that panic attack. Scram told me about that. Your brother wouldn't have ended up in the hospital. Again, Scram told me about that. Also, you guys wouldn't have been attacked by Leonard and had that fire."

"What you don't know is that my 'stupid' dad actually did the right thing. When I found out that Scram was looking for two kids to help him find out where I live, I realized that if they found the house and took one of the six Crystals of Power, whatever those are, and used them, everyone in my house would probably have been kidnapped and taken to this mansion to be tortured by these ghouls until we died."

"I see that you saw the book that I wrote in. That took me a couple days to complete," Scram's mom says.

"Shush, I'm not done talking, and your handwriting is nasty," Jake replies. "If you didn't send your son with a stupid last name to our school, giving my friend a panic attack and making my friend Dakota tell us to find out what Scram was up to, we wouldn't have been here in this mansion right now."

"How smart are you?" she asks.

"Very, but Frankie is still smarter. I just remembered something—none of you guys has answered my dad's first question. What is the point of this portrait frame in this picture of Haunted Mansion World?"

Scram's dad gives Jake a little riddle and explains that the portrait frame is to be hidden in a greenish place in the United Kingdom.

Jake doesn't like riddles, but since Scram's dad mentioned a greenish place, he believes that the portrait is going to be hidden somewhere in a forest of the United Kingdom. Scram's dad can't believe that Jake has figured out what he meant, but he knows that the portrait won't be found that easily because it will be hidden deep in the forest.

Another important question that Jake wants to ask is how Scram found out where he and Joey live. Scram wants Jake to listen to this little story. On Friday, when Joey was going home after being in emotional pain, Scram followed him since Joey already knew what Scram was up to. Once Joey was inside the house, he locked the front door. Scram tried opening all the windows, but they were locked. There was a basement window that he thought might be unlocked, but it wasn't. He kept making noises. Every door and window was locked.

Jake thinks it lucky that he told Joey to make sure all the doors and windows are locked when he's home by himself. Scram thinks it clever, but not clever enough. Joey didn't close and lock the front door when he went out of the house an hour later. As soon as his back was turned, Scram quickly ran inside the house, closed the door, and locked it.

Scram heard Joey trying to open the door and saw him peek through the window, but he didn't see Scram. Scram was glad to be hiding underneath the nice, lush couch in the Fallons' living room. While Joey was sitting at the front door, Scram had enough time to look around the house for the Crystals of Power, but he had no luck.

Moments later, Scram saw a handle on the ceiling in a mini hallway, pulled it down, and noticed an attic. He looked around in there for a while. When he saw a strange-looking case, he opened it and the six Crystals of Power were revealed to him. He made sure to think carefully and pick up the right crystal, and he did. He took the crystal, closed the attic, and ran out the back door since Joey was in the front. He hopped over the fence in the backyard and made his escape.

Saturday morning when Scram woke up, he realized that he'd been sneaking around the house while he was being watched by the front door security camera. He quickly went back to the Fallons' house, noticing that the front door was already open. He sneaked inside and noticed that no one was awake. Inside, near the front door, he looked at the security camera and noticed that a white wire was stapled to the wall. He followed the wire, which led up to the attic; he hadn't noticed it the other day.

When Scram went up to the attic, he found where the wire ended. While he was up there, he found a pair of scissors and cut the wire. To be smart, so nobody would notice, he wrapped it with clear tape so that none of the Fallons would figure out why the camera wasn't working. It was taped very well.

Jake found that amazing. Judging by the story Scram gave him, he bet it was he who moved Joe's ladder, which disappeared when he was on the roof last Saturday.

"Yep, I did that later that afternoon," Scram admits. "Your dad couldn't see me because I was wearing the invisibility Crystal of Power. Don't worry—it's back inside the black and gold jewelry box since it isn't necessary."

"You rock for moving that ladder. It was a funny joke. Where did the ladder go?" Jake asks.

What happened to the ladder is that Scram and his mom took it so that they could sneak into Frankie's house window with dark curtains. They took his parents while they were sleeping in their bedroom. Scram kindly reveals to Jake how he found out where Frankie lives: Rodney told him through the smartphone after he finished beating up Frankie in the bathroom last Wednesday during school. Scram was shocked that Frankie actually revealed where he lived.

Scram and his mom took Frankie's parents because Frankie never gave Scram back the twenty dollars after he gave him Uriah's lunch, which he bet that Frankie gave back to him. Frankie was supposed to give Scram twenty dollars after school ended on Tuesday. He broke his promise.

"Never trust anyone with money," he says to Joe, shaking his head.

Joe replies, "See, Jake, this is why I don't loan your mother my money."

"Let me guess—it's because she never pays you back?"

"Exactly!"

Now that Joe has mentioned Kay-Lo, Jake asks Scram what he did to the attic staircase because his mother has been blabbering about it, and it is annoying him. Why won't it close? Scram explains to him that he loosened two screws in the attic staircase, but they shouldn't worry; he didn't take anything else from the attic besides a Crystal of Power. One thing he remembers is that he was the one who trapped Joey inside the garage and made him think it was Jake. He only wanted to play a little prank on him.

Joe remembers what Scram's mom said about Joey being in the hospital. There are two things he wants to know: how the clown doll that Jake received two weeks ago came to life and where the future sighting crystal is.

Scram's dad explains to Joe and Jake that the clown doll is somewhere in Florida. They will never find it, so he is kind enough to tell them that there is an HC Mind Chip inside the clown doll. That is how it's alive. The HC Mind Chip doesn't just make people heartless; it also brings nonliving things to life. There is no explanation of how the HC Mind Chips were accidently released from the High Production factory since it was a failed experiment.

Scram first noticed the clown doll inside Jake's closet when he was searching for the future sighting Crystal of Power. When Scram returned to the Fallons' house on Saturday morning to deal with the house security camera, he crept inside Joey and Jake's room while they were sleeping, opened up Jake's closet, cut a little hole in the clown doll, and stuffed an HC Mind Chip inside it.

Scram doesn't know how the HC Mind Chip was able to bring something that is made out of cotton to life. He admits that the clown doll's HC Mind Chip was originally for Joe, but plans changed. Scram's dad wanted Scram to put the HC Mind Chip inside the clown doll instead once Scram told him about it. Scram's mom ordered the clown doll to attack Joey late in the morning.

"So you guys *were* looking for my dad," Jake says. "You wanted to find him so that he could be controlled by an HC Mind Chip for unknown reasons. You guys also made Scram look for my brother, Joey, so that he could spit out where he lives, and once he does, Scram will ask him some tricky questions so he will reveal his secret. If Joey revealed his secret which is now known as a pendent, Scram would go to Joey and I house and take it, which of course he did without trying to trick Joey into revealing the secret pendent. Scram, I love how you and your rat face mom manage not to think whether the pendent was in the house or not.

Jake remembers that, before Joey got attacked by the clown doll, he wanted to know what happened to the faulty wiring inside the house. Scram's mom has a reason for all of that, and eventually they are going to find out why the lights were acting up.

Joe thinks that if he finds that clown doll and takes the HC Mind Chip out from inside of it, the clown doll will no longer be alive. It seems like he is definitely correct, but Scram's dad knows that he will never find the clown doll.

The next answer Scram's dad gives out is that he has the future sighting crystal; it is the only Crystal of Power he needs.

"Hold on!" Jake says to Scram's dad. "What is the point of taking the future sighting Crystal of Power? Why only take that crystal but not the others?"

Two very smart questions from Jake. Scram's dad gives Joe one heck of a surprise. Scram's dad holds the number three locket that was attached to the future sighting crystal and opens it, revealing the secret pendent that features a red eye. Joe now understands why the factory worker he spoke to said something about a hidden secret inside one of the crystals that he couldn't talk about. Joe never knew that the future sighting crystal number locket could open. Now he wonders if the other Crystals of Power number lockets can open as well. But something doesn't make sense to Joe: how did the factory worker know that a red-eyed pendant was inside the crystal?

Jake says, "Dad, you owned that crystal necklace for about two decades, and you never knew that the number locket could open? I don't blame you for that. I wasn't expecting it either."

Joe replies, "I never knew that it was a locket, not from the moment I laid my eyes on it. Now the question I would like to ask—what is the purpose of that pendant?"

Scram's dad says, "Come; follow me downstairs."

Downstairs in the bedroom, Scram's dad shows Joe and Jake something interesting. This is the same bedroom where Jake was attacked by Reverse Foot. Scram's dad shows Joe and Jake the moving portrait of Joey. Jake doesn't understand why this portrait is the only one in the bedroom that moves.

If Joe or Jake looked more closely at the bottom of the portrait border, they would notice that a pendant has been placed on it. Does this give Joe and Jake a clue? They guess not. Scram's dad wants Joe and Jake to listen carefully. Scram's mom made this red-eyed pendant, which is now known as the Oremonia pendant. Scram's dad cannot explain how the pendant managed to get inside the future sighting crystal.

"Wait a minute!" Jake says. "If you can't explain how the Oremonia pendant got inside the future sighting crystal, how on earth did you guys know it was in there?"

Scram's mom answers, "Ms. Parkinson! That's all I have to say."

"No! I know Ms. Parkinson. She is a sweet lady who would never harm my family," Joe exclaims.

"I didn't say anything about her being harmful. It's what she said to me once when I visited her."

"What did she say?" Joe asks.

Scram's mom replies, "I don't remember! This is why I always write notes to myself to remember things. Now, let my dear husband explain more about the Oremonia pendant."

Scram's dad has a few more things to say about the purpose of the Oremonia pendant. The main purpose of it is to power up the portrait so that the picture can move. One surprising fact is that there is a huge chance to gain entrance into the portrait. There used to be only one Oremonia pendant, but now there are ten, thanks to the duplication system in the mansion's attic. There are also ten portraits created by Scram's mom, each of which contains one Oremonia pendant. There are two known moving portraits: the one they are standing next to right now, which features Joey in a dark place, and one that is featured in the picture of Haunted Mansion World that is to be sent to the United Kingdom forest.

"Okay, so you explained the purpose of this ridiculous pendant. What is the purpose of these ten portraits?" Joe asks.

Scram's dad says, "The ten portraits release ghouls every five months. It actually should have been every month."

"That explains the two ghouls that attacked me," Jake says. "What's the purpose of these ghouls? How was I able to fight Madman Morzician but not Reverse Foot? Yes, I gave them names."

Scram's mom explains to Jake that Madman Morzician is the most recent ghoul to come out of the portrait, meaning that he hasn't completely developed yet. Reverse Foot came out of the portrait before Madman Morzician did, so he has already developed fully.

Scram's dad will answer Jake's first question later. He will be helpful: the only way for the ghouls to vanish is to destroy the pendant that was placed on the same portrait it was powering up. He doubts this will happen because Joe and Jake don't know where the rest of the moving portraits are. Once the pendant is stored in the portrait frame, it won't come out.

Now that the Oremonia pendant has become a success, he doesn't need the future sighting crystal anymore, so he takes it out of his left pants pocket and throws it. Jake catches it with one hand. Scram's dad knows for sure that nobody will be able to find the portraits, other than the one in the bedroom they are in right now.

"Wait a second," Jake says to Scram's dad. "How do you know all about the Crystals of Power? Who told you about them?"

Scram's dad will hold that question for later. Joe has one last question about the clown doll. He wants to know why it attacked Joey. Scram explains to him that Joey is afraid of clowns. Joey told Scram in school that this was his fear.

Jake looks at the moving portrait of Joey and shakes his head. Jake has no idea what games Scram and his parents are trying to play. He still wants to know why those three boneheads are trying to kidnap his family.

"Why don't you ask your dad's kidnapped parents?" Scram's dad blurts out, and then he covers his mouth.

Joe realizes something. He asks Scram's dad how he knows that his parents were kidnapped. Scram's dad is still covering his mouth; he has said too much. Joe snaps his fingers as he realizes that it was Scram's dad who kidnapped his parents. Scram's dad laughs, denying Joe's theory. He wasn't the one who did the kidnapping.

Joe has had enough fun and games. He is about to attack Scram's dad, but Jake stops him because he doesn't want any violence to happen in the bedroom. After calming Joe down, Jake wants to know more about when Joe and Scram's dad used to work at Empire Hall. He wants to know if they really worked together at Empire Hall in New York.

Scram's dad says, "For one day only. Then he happened to disappear. He started working there on January sixth and then left the next day, on the seventh. I noticed him on the second day because of a voice communication. I got so mad when he didn't come back because I wanted something from him. You already know what that is."

"Now I remember why I left and never came back. Jake was born that day—that's why. My wife wanted to start a new life with both of us on the beautiful southeast coast. My brother didn't want me to go, but since he was my brother, I entrusted Jake to him. I didn't want Joseph to feel lonely. A few weeks later, we moved, and it was already February. Months passed, and we made life even better. Then, some months later, Joey was born."

"Okay, I may be a nine-year-old, but I think you just spit out too much information," Jake says. "Hmm, I find it weird how Joey was born months after me... Dad, are you hiding something?" Then Joe will say, "No!"

Scram's dad really wants this interview and explanation to be over; it is wasting his time, and he needs to get more work done. Since nobody has spoken for five seconds, he is about to leave the bedroom, but Joe isn't letting him go anywhere. He closes the bedroom door. He needs to know where Frankie's parents are, and where José and Joanne Fallon are as well.

Scram's dad says, "First of all, Joe-Loser, your answer lies in a forest in the United Kingdom. And second, if you want to know where this kid's parents are, they are inside this mansion, but you don't know where. I am now officially out of here."

"Hang on a second. You just called me Joe-Loser. Where is your partner, the one I chased down last week?"

"Ah, you must be talking about Raymond."

"Raymond? Who's that?" Jake asks.

Jake hasn't realized that Raymond is actually right behind him. He turns around to look at him. Jake moves back toward Joe so Raymond won't hurt him. Joe notices that Raymond is the same person he chased last week. Now that Joe has figured out who he is, Raymond is going to tell Joe and Jake who his partner is: Scram's mom.

Before Raymond met Scram's mom, he was at a community speech in New York. He saw two people walk up to the podium with two little boys. He knew who the adults, José and Joanne Fallon, were, but he didn't recognize the kids. Raymond was in shock when he saw their faces, because José and Joanne tortured his people when they were in the military.

José and Joanne terrorized Raymond's relatives because they had a bad plot to change the world. The plot was to invade the world with evil robots, but that plot was foiled. Raymond's relative was left to suffer and zapped with multiple Tasers.

Raymond is a criminal who works with people. While he was on a social networking site, he happened to make friends with Scram's mom, a robotic engineer. Scram's mom saw his name and his occupation, so she made every effort to meet him in person. They met in New York a few months later. Scram's mom wanted Raymond to do business with her and get paid lots of money. After planning a few things, Raymond received his biggest assignment yet: to kidnap former soldiers and factory workers José and Joanne Fallon. He decided to let Scram's mom do that.

Scram's mom searched around New York for months trying to find them, and then, in late December, she finally did. That night, José and Joanne were awake in their living room watching television. Scram's mom sneaked inside the house and wrapped tape around their mouths, legs, and wrists. She carried them over to the Finger Lakes National Forest in New York.

Scram's mom and Raymond had a few words with them, and they discussed what they did at the High Production factory. They created a lot of things that weren't released to the public. Then they mentioned something called the six crystals. Scram's mom and Raymond were curious to know more about them.

José and Joanne explained the crystals to them, and this gave Scram's mom and Raymond a smart idea. They thought of all the things they could do once they found those crystals. José and Joanne weren't going anywhere because they knew that something bad was about to happen to them. Joanne wanted to say one last word to her friend. Raymond gave the phone to her, and she called some woman named Ms. Parkinson. After that call, that was pretty much it for them. Raymond told Scram's mom to take them away.

Somewhere in New York, at the next community speech a month after the kidnapping, the two boys came up to do a tribute to their parents. Once they mentioned their last name, Scram's mom and Raymond remembered that they were José and

Joanne's kids. They assumed that the kids had the six Crystals of Power.

The day after the community speech, Scram's mom went to Joe and Joseph's old house, but nobody was there; the house was completely empty. For years, Scram's mom and Raymond looked for the two kids, but they never found them. Eventually they gave up on finding them and the Crystals of Power.

On August 10, 2009, Raymond saw one of the kids, now an adult: Joe Fallon. This was the first time he had seen him in two decades. He recognized some of Joe's facial features; that's how he knew who he was.

Jake says to Raymond, "So it was Scram's mom who kidnapped my dad parents because his parents kidnapped your crazy relatives, because they were trying to make evil robots take over the world. I find that impossible. I think my dad's parents did the right thing taking away your relatives."

Scram's dad surprises Jake with something, supposedly the master plan. They are planning a huge robot invasion since the last plot was foiled. Now that Raymond has told his story, Scram's dad can answer Jake's question from earlier about the ghoul. The purpose of these ghouls is to haunt all the members of the Fallon family, kidnap them, and bring them into this mansion to suffer just as Raymond's relative had suffered.

Jake knows that Scram's dad has another master plan because one of his friends overheard it during a smartphone conversation and told him. Jake doesn't mention Baron's name, to keep him safe. Scram's dad reveals his second master plan: to hide ten portrait frames with finished paintings. Ghouls will rise out of the paintings, thanks to the power of the evil Oremonia pendant. As Scram's dad mentioned before, the ghouls will kidnap all of Joe and Joseph's family, bring them to an unknown place, and haunt them for the rest of their lives.

Jake has one last important question: how will the ghouls be able to kidnap all of Joe and Joseph's relatives if they don't know what they look like? Scram's mom knows the answer to that question and has it written on a memo, but she will not reveal her answer. Jake seriously doesn't like it when people know the answer to something but don't reveal it. He promises that he's going to expose Scram's mom, and he is going to make sure that his question about the ghouls knowing which person to kidnap will be answered.

Scram's dad explains that if anybody unrelated to the Fallon family finds out about these ghouls, that person will be haunted as well. It's best not to tell anyone about them. It has been a pleasure for Scram's dad to see Joe and Jake. Now he wants the ghouls to haunt their souls.

Scram's mom and dad run out of the bedroom so they won't get caught. Scram is about to do the same, but Jake quickly snatches him and points the tweezers at his head. He looks inside Scram's ear and finds out that there was actually an HC Mind Chip inside his left ear. Jake uses the tweezers to take out the mind chip. He looks at it and then gives it to Joe.

Joe tells Jake what he remembers about Ms. Parkinson after the story Raymond just told them. Ms. Parkinson was the one who entrusted the Crystals of Power to Joe and Joseph. While they were living back at her house, she told Joe and Joseph that it was a request from Joanne before she was taken away with José. That is all Joe remembers.

Chapter 17

Freedom

Joe and Jake are still in the bedroom with Scram and Raymond. After taking an HC Mind Chip out of Scram's right ear, Jake wonders if all the mind chips will be found. He wants to be the one to find all the HC Mind Chips, but he knows that isn't going to happen because he can't go on a mission by himself. Still, he is grateful to Laurence for telling him how many mind chips there are.

Jake explains to Joe that Laurence told him and the other four kids that a cyborg went missing from the High Production factory, along with the eleven HC Mind Chips. After the cyborg and all the HC Mind Chips are found, they must be returned to the High Production factory. Laurence also said that all the mind chips are in Florida. There are a total of eleven, and so far three have been found. Who else besides the clown doll holds a mind chip?

"How come you never told Joey and me about this cool crystal necklace?" Jake asks Joe, swinging the future sighting Crystal of Power. It is a long story for Joe to tell. When the time comes, he will explain it to Joey and Jake.

Scram gets up off the wood floor. His head is hurting and he wonders what he has been doing all this time.

"You were being controlled by an HC Mind Chip," Jake tells Scram, helping him up off the floor. "Your mind couldn't escape from this evil device, so it made you act heartless and very smart, I must say. But don't worry, Scram. I know you are a nice kid. The HC Mind Chip destabilized your common sense."

"Enough saying my nickname," Scram says.

Jake freezes for a moment. "Whoa, Scram is your . . . nickname? Then what's your real name?"

"My real name is Gunner, and my last name is Torres. You actually thought my parents had the last name Bumbleberry? While I was being controlled by the HC Mind Chip, I was forced not to mention my real first and last name to anyone."

"Your real name is Gunner? Well, I'm still calling you Scram. I like it."

Joe says, "You hid an HC Mind Chip inside a clown doll. Where is that doll? I would like to find it and get the HC Mind Chip out from inside of it."

Scram doesn't know, but his dad from Georgia may know. He's been there for ages. Scram's not sure if he will know where the clown doll is, though. He apologizes for giving the clown doll the HC Mind Chip; he couldn't control his actions because of the mind chip that was inside of his right ear.

"This is confusing, and it's getting me really annoyed," Jake says to Scram. "If you're saying that your real dad is in Georgia, then who were that man and woman?"

The woman is Scram's real mother, but the man is some mysterious person she met. When Scram met him for the first time, his mom told him to hang around with him for a few days. Scram offered the mysterious guy some water because his voice started acting up, but he didn't want the water. Scram doesn't want to see either of them again because of the way they act. He's going to see if he can move back to Georgia with his real father. He thanks Jake for saving him.

"You're welcome . . . friend." Jake starts to smile. "Wait, one more question. Do you remember this? Why did you bully my friend Dakota's cousin?"

"Oh, you must be talking about Brooks," Scram says. "That's his cousin's name. I know who you're talking about. I used to bully him because one of his friends was an instigator from back in the day."

Brooks's friend instigated him to pick on Scram because his mother kept coming up to the school to make sure that he got pampered so that he would feel more comfortable there. That was before the time she became a berserk human. Scram isn't sure if she was like that before he was born. He doesn't know; he just doesn't want to see his own mother again. He's not quite sure if he still loves her, but when she acts outrageous, that makes Scram lose all respect for her.

"You're ten years old and you still wear Pampers?" Jake asks Scram.

"No, not that kind of pampering. It's different, and I was eight years old at the time."

"A little advice for you—boys don't get pampered. And why do it at school?"

"Can I continue with the story, please?" Scram asks.

After Brooks bullied Scram, he'd pretty much had enough. They ended up fighting after that; one smack in his face and Brooks didn't know where he was, and he looked a bit dazed. The next day, when Brooks came to school, he looked at Scram with nervous eyes and walked away. Scram decided that if Brooks wasn't going to pick on him again, this was his chance to get his revenge.

It was a bad move on Scram's part, and he regrets it a lot. A week later, Scram got tired of being a bully and left Brooks alone because he knew that bullying is the worst thing to do, but Brooks was still afraid of Scram. Also, when Scram was being controlled by the HC Mind Chip, he saw Brooks panicking and didn't care. Scram actually knew what was happening.

Scram finds the HC Mind Chip to be very disturbing. He knows that he's not the type of person to give someone a nervous breakdown and act heartless. He loves people very much, including kids. He really doesn't like evil people. He is very sorry that Dakota's cousin panicked. If Jake sees him, Scram wants him to give Brooks his apologies. Scram hopes to see Joe and Jake sometime in the future.

Jake is so shocked that he has nothing to say since he found out Scram's real name. Gunner "Scram" Torres leaves the bedroom. Jake is still going to call him Scram; he thinks that the name suits him well.

Raymond is about to sneak away with Scram, but Joe pulls him back. It is time to deal with him now. Raymond sees a chain on the wood floor and wants to use it to destroy Joe. Raymond is going to make sure that Joe doesn't hurt him. Jake, on the other hand, wants that to happen to teach him a lesson: that it is awful to kidnap kids and adults.

"Jake, get out of the bedroom and go find Frankie's parents in the basement. Be brave—you have a lot of bravery, and I believe in you," Joe says.

"Oh, man! I wanted to see you knock out that jerk. Oh well." Jake gives the future sighting crystal to Joe. "If I get attacked by Madman Morzician or Reverse Foot and don't survive, I will haunt you at night. Hope to see you in front of the mansion, Joe-Loser." He exits the bedroom.

Joe and Raymond are staring one another down to see which one of them will get the chain first. Raymond does a sneak attack on Joe and he retrieves the chain. Joe and Raymond start fighting in the bedroom. After one kick to the stomach, Raymond drops the chain. The chain ends up falling through a hole in the wood floor.

Raymond gets up quickly and runs out of the bedroom. He might want to find that chain. Joe notices something inside Raymond's pocket. He wants to see what it is, so he starts chasing after him for the second time this month.

Raymond is running as fast as he can so that Joe won't catch him. The mansion is still slightly dark with no lights on, making it hard for Joe to see Raymond. On the second floor, Madman Morzician breaks through the wall, creating a big hole in it. The ghoul catches Joe by surprise and holds him against the wall, making him drop his future sighting crystal.

Madman Morzician has one hand on Joe's shoulders, chaining him to the wall, and now Joe won't be able to escape the mansion. His hands are free, but it his wrist is chained to the wall. Madman Morzician disappeared, leaving Joe chained against the wall. Joe was trying to break free.

While Joe is trying to break free, he hears footsteps coming from the side of the hallway. While looking around, he noticed that it was Reverse Foot. Reverse Foot saw Joe chained against the wall and went right near him. He was staring at Joe eyes even though Reverse Foot only had one eye. Joe looked down to look away from Reverse Foot face and saw the future sighting Crystal of Power on the floor right next his legs.

When Joe's eyes were down, he also saw that Reverse Foot only had four fingers on the left hand; he is missing a thumb. Joe just found out that Reverse Foot is a ghoul, but already Jake knew.

Reverse Foot didn't waste any time, he opened his mouth exposing his fangs about to bite Joe. Joe came up with a plan. He told Reverse Foot to look, "There's another human."

Reverse Foot fell for it, which allowed Joe to quickly take off the chain from his wrist and pick up the future sighting Crystal of Power.

After that, Joe starts to run away, only to get caught by Reverse Foot again. Reverse Foot grabs Joe again and is about to attack him, but something happens. Reverse Foot looks up, feeling as if someone has just thrown something at him. He turns around and sees Jake.

It looks like Jake has thrown some rubble at Reverse Foot. Reverse Foot runs fast at Jake, grabbing him by the cheeks and squeezing them. He has him against the wall. He opens his mouth, about to try and bite Jake again since his last attack was unsuccessful.

Joe lifts up his head after falling on the wood floor. He is going to make sure that the ghoul doesn't hurt Jake. He runs toward him, takes out Jake's mega flashlight, and shines the light at Reverse Foot's one eye. Reverse Foot lets go of Jake and scurries away from them. Jake falls on the wood floor, trying to calm down, and then he gets back up in peace.

"You're lucky that I didn't leave the mansion with Frankie's parents," Jake says to Joe. "They were tied up against each other on two chairs and covered with white sheets in the cellar. They've already left the mansion. You're also lucky that I found you, or else you would have been bitten by Reverse Foot, turning you into a ghoul. It would be so cool if that actually happened. Do you believe in ghouls now?"

"Yes, I do!" he says to Jake.

"Good! Thank you for saving my life. Now can we please go? This mansion is too wicked."

Joe and Jake leave the gloomy mansion. When they are outside, it is clear to Jake that Scram's dad isn't Scram's real dad. Scram's real dad lives in Georgia. Since Scram's fake dad's name has never been mentioned, Jake might as well give him one. He calls him Pablo.

"I'm giving him a name because we can't call him Scram's dad anymore, and if we end up bumping into him in the future, we won't know who he is. That's why I named him Pablo."

"Good thought," Joe says. "It is good to keep track of people's names. C'mon, we've got to go find him."

"Oh great, more things to do? Look, Dad, he already escaped and I just want to go home. I had a really fun night with you, but it's almost midnight and my perfume hour has already passed."

"It's curfew!"

Jake sighs. "See? This is why I should be sleeping. Now my brain is all messed up."

Jake has mentioned that Pablo has already escaped, and there is no chance of finding him. Joe's new mission is to search for José and Joanne, who are trapped in a forest in the United Kingdom. Joe cannot go alone; he will have to bring Joseph with him to explore the forest and see if they can find their parents. Which part of the forest are they in, and how long will it take to find them? Joe still believes that José and Joanne cannot be dead.

Chapter 18

True Story

Haunted Mansion World is no place for Jake. He is so glad that he has survived the ghouls' attacks. Outside the mansion, Joe and Jake made their way through the closed graveyard. Near the gates Joe needs to use the bathroom desperately after drinking a whole cup of coffee. Once Joe and Jake pass by the closed graveyard near the gates, Joe needs to use the bathroom. He would've gone into the mansion, but he doesn't trust the toilet water and doesn't want to have to solve a mystery about a haunted toilet. There is a restaurant that's close to Haunted Mansion World, so Joe decides to use the bathroom there.

Inside the restaurant, Jake is sitting with his left elbow on the counter and his hand on the side of his face, watching the chefs cook some food. He starts to think about the ghouls. He knows for a fact that the ghouls will be roaming around the streets or will be inside someone's house at night since they can't come out when there's light, unless they are in a dark place when it's light outside.

It feels stuffy inside the restaurant due to the high temperature and the steam coming from the chefs' food. Jake starts to make his way out of the restaurant to get some fresh air until Joe comes out of the bathroom.

A male restaurant employee says to Jake, "Hey, you; don't walk out that door. Aren't you a bit too young to be in this restaurant and roaming the streets by yourself in the middle of the night?"

"Didn't you just see me come in with someone, you broke buffoon who works with a silly fast food hat on his head?" Jake asks.

"That wasn't very mature of you."

"What would you expect from a nine-year-old? Right now I have two requests for you—take off that nerdy hat and turn off that record player. Who still uses a record player in the twenty-first century?"

The employee says, "Kid, you have no idea how many people still use them."

Jake replies, "Back in New York, my uncle had some awesome classic tunes. 'Tiptoe Through the Tulips' was the best, and it rocked this world. I couldn't even tell if it was a man or a woman singing."

"Back then music was totally bogus, dude."

Jake starts to shake his head, not even caring what the employee is saying anymore. As soon as he looks out the window, he notices someone walking past the restaurant. Jake catches a glimpse of the face, and it is Raymond. He is holding something in his hands. Jake gets up and leaves the restaurant.

"Hey!" he yells, making Raymond turn around and notice that Jake is following him.

Raymond started to run away, and Jake starts chasing him down the street. Later on, inside the restaurant, while Jake is chasing Raymond, Joe comes out of the bathroom wondering where Jake is. He asks the employee if he has seen a kid with long, blond hair. The employee tells Joe where he went. Joe exits the restaurant, making the employee think that night shifts are so weird.

Joe goes in the same direction Jake went, looking for him. A few blocks down, Raymond captures Jake. He calls Jake a little twerp, pokes him in the eye, pushes him on the ground, and runs away. Jake gets back up and continues chasing after him. Joe is still wondering where Jake has gone until he notices that he is across the street, chasing Raymond.

Joe runs across the street, not noticing that the stoplight is green, and a big, black, out-of-control, truck unexpectedly moves toward him, about to crash near him. Joe looks petrified and can't move. The truck starts crushing some cars. Then it falls and crashes right near Joe, and a few tires come off. But where is Joe? Suddenly he is nowhere to be seen.

When the dust starts to clear up a little, Joe is lying down on the sidewalk. He is so lucky; he can't believe he is still alive after that. He looks at the truck driver's seat and notices that the driver is still alive. People try to get him out before something happens to the box truck.

Joe wants to help the truck driver, but he has to make sure that Jake is all right. Joe runs away from the box truck and searches for Jake again. Jake is still chasing after Raymond, and it looks like he hasn't stopped running. His training has paid off big time, even though it was just for a week. He had already been training before he moved to Florida. Jake continues chasing after Raymond until they reach Village Park. It looks like Jake has finally caught him.

Raymond wants the twerp off of him, but Jake isn't going to let him go until he suffers. He holds Raymond down on the ground by both of his shoulders until someone appears behind him. Jake turns around and noticed a guy. He doesn't know him, but the guy is Lance Perkins.

Jake is distracted by Lance, and Raymond pushes him off of him. Raymond gets up to run away, but Lance happens to catch him and makes him lie on the ground on his stomach.

Joe finally finds Jake. Jake is so glad that Joe made it. He shows him who he caught all by himself. Joe doesn't believe him because he sees Lance holding down Raymond. Lance wants Joe to believe the kid; it was actually Jake who caught Raymond.

"Wow, Jake," Joe says in shock. "How long did you chase after Raymond before you caught him?"

"For about four minutes. Thanks for the training."

"You proved it to me, Jake. You proved to me that you are a tough kid. That's all I wanted from you."

Jake says, "I don't consider myself weak anymore after fighting with Leonard, the two ghouls from Haunted Mansion World, and now Raymond. I didn't think all this training was going to pay off, but like they always say, you must believe in yourself. It's that simple! If people criticize you about your dreams, don't listen to them because you have something worth living for. Don't let them discourage you."

"True," Joe says. "Do me favor, though. I don't want you using your toughness against people who are way bigger than you."

Jake respects Joe's words. Jake looks at Raymond and sees that he is still holding something in his hands. He snatches it away from Raymond, and Jake discovers that it's an Oremonia pendant. He thinks that Raymond was on his way to put it in a portrait so that the portrait would move and release evil ghouls. Jake wants to see if it is really possible to access the portrait— or was Pablo just making that up? Jake has found one, meaning that there are nine more to find. Joe takes the pendant to keep it safe until he gets home, where he will inspect it before destroying it.

Raymond is going to court. Lance handcuffs him. Lance is a detective in Florida, so he is licensed to use the handcuffs. Sid is still in eastern Florida with his wife for their anniversary. Once the vacation is over, Sid will go back on duty and work with Lance once again. For now, Lance has Joe and Jake's back.

"It's lucky you were here at the park," Jake says to Lance, patting him on the left shoulder.

"Like I told your dad a few days ago, I usually come here at midnight while I am on duty," Lance replies.

"You shouldn't stay here at midnight. You might get attacked by two ghouls. If you see a person with a chain, that's a ghoul right there. Reverse Foot is also a ghoul, and so far he's the scariest one I have witnessed."

"You watch too many horror movies," Lance says. "Now excuse me, guys. I have to bring this person to court. See you both in the future."

"Wait, before you leave," Jake calls after him. "Because you're a detective, you should be able to answer this. How come all the police officers are on strike?"

"I can't say much, but I can tell you that the police are on strike because of the force's low funding."

"I never knew that could happen!" Jake exclaims. He thinks that the police will be back very soon. Jake still has no idea why Lance wants to see a ghoul. He thinks that Lance is a creep. Jake has had enough excitement for one night; he can't wait to tell the other four boys what has taken place tonight. Jake is also glad that he caught a kidnapping criminal. He thinks that he deserves to get paid lots of money.

"You know, Dad, if both Joey and I were kidnappers, I would try to figure out why we were like that. That mansion is not the right place for kidnapped people. Luckily, we didn't get kidnapped. Mr. H. would be all over us if we missed that in-class essay tomorrow. Luckily, Joey and I finished reading *The Mysteries of Captain Broach* before Joey got attacked. Attacked by a clown doll—that's stupid."

"So you would find it stupid if you got attacked by a robot?" Joe asks.

"Ah, be quiet, Joe-Loser. Now you see how it feels when you call me Little Moth, right? Joe-Loser will be a good nickname for me to use on you. Revenge is mine!"

On the way home, Jake reaches inside his backpack to look at a few things. He takes out Scram's drawing of the ghouls he wished were real. Jake immediately figures out that those were the ghouls he saw in the mansion, but there were only two. There are three on the paper. Jake wonders where the other one is.

They make it back home a minute before midnight. Jake starts to get ready for bed. He is glad that he doesn't have any injuries after the things he went through tonight. He will probably dream about it. Frankie comes out of the bedroom with his parents, thanking Jake for saving them. Frankie says he made a bad wish when he wished that his parents would leave the house and never come back. He needs his parents more than ever, even though they make a mess of the house all the time.

Frankie didn't mean to tell Rodney where he lived after he got beaten up in the school bathroom last Wednesday. He meant to give Rodney a false answer, but the truth slipped out because he was very nervous. At least everything went okay. Frankie thanks his cousin Jake and says he will see him in the morning for school.

Joe enters the house and sees Joseph sitting on the living room couch next to Sasha. Sasha was at the party for Joseph and Jake last week; she is Joey and Jake's cousin. Joe wants to know why Sasha is in the house past midnight. Sasha is there waiting to go to some club with her girlfriends and her sister, Trish.

After Sasha has left, Joe explains to Joseph everything that happened while he was out with Jake. At half past midnight, Joe notices something. He asks where Kay-Lo has gone and when she left.

"She went to get Joey from the hospital," Joseph answers. "He was free to go, so she left here about an hour ago, while you and Jake were out. She forgot that we have the car back, so she went out to take the bus. She's been gone for quite a while."

Joe remembers that it's dark outside, and he hopes that his vision hasn't come true. He knew he should've left the car outside. He leaves the house in a rush and takes off in the car, about to try and find the bus.

Kay-Lo is sitting next to Joey on the local bus, reading a book called *Mechanization Annihilation*, which she's been reading this week during her break from the hotel where she works. The book is about robot development and what kind of destruction robots can do.

While Kay-Lo is reading the book, she asks Joey a couple of questions about the hospital and what they did to him. Joey doesn't answer any of her questions; he isn't saying anything, nor is he happy to see her again. He just sits there with his sunglasses on and minds his own business.

Kay-Lo notices that Joey's hair is straight; he must have gotten tired of the spikes. She liked it when Joey had spiky hair. She also sees that he is wearing a cool pair of sunglasses. The nurse must have given them to him as a gift. It's dark outside, so there is no need for Joey to be wearing them. Kay-Lo takes them off for him. Then Joey randomly starts screaming inside the bus, covering his eyes. He quickly takes the sunglasses away from Kay-Lo, puts them back on, and becomes calm again. Kay-Lo doesn't understand what that was all about. She apologizes to Joey.

Kay-Lo asks Joey the same question about the hospital. Joey has yet to answer her. Kay-Lo doesn't mind. She understands that it is after midnight and that Joey is very tired and doesn't feel like talking. Once the sun rises and he wakes up in the morning, he should feel better than ever. Still, she wants to know why Joey had such a bad reaction when she took off his sunglasses.

While Kay-Lo and Joey are on the local bus, Joe is driving through the streets in his car to see if he can find the bus. Back on the bus, nothing seems to be going on. They're stuck in traffic. Kay-Lo can't believe it. Later, while they are stuck in traffic, they hear a creaking noise. Kay-Lo is reading her book when she hears it.

The creaking noise stops for a few seconds; then it happens again. It is even louder than the last time. People on the bus start to hear it and look around the bus. Some of them are sitting down and some are standing up. The only person who isn't looking around, and who is ignoring the sounds, is Joey. He just sits there next to Kay-Lo, not worried about what's happening.

Joe is still roaming around the streets trying to find the bus. Meanwhile, the bus driver starts to whistle, making music while looking at the traffic. When he looks in his rearview mirror, he notices that Joey is staring at him. *Freakish kid*, the driver says to himself.

What the bus driver doesn't know is that Joey actually heard him from the back of the bus. He is still staring at the bus driver. A few seconds later, the lights on the bus start flickering on and off. They flicker for a few seconds. Then they shut off, making the inside of the bus dark. Kay-Lo and the rest of the passengers can't see a thing other than the outside.

The bus starts to shake as if there was someone outside shaking it. It shakes so hard that a few people fall to the floor. When the shaking stops a few seconds later, the bus lights come back on and people get back up from the floor.

One woman gets back up with her wig covering the left side of her face. Once the woman has fixed her wig, she looks around and notices that the bus driver is gone. He couldn't have escaped through the window because it isn't broken. The woman screams, "Where is the bus driver?" Other people start to scream, and Kay-Lo holds Joey to protect him. Joey pushes Kay-Lo off of him. She can't believe what he just did.

People start punching and throwing things at the windows, but they aren't breaking. They can't escape the bus. A few seconds later, the lights go out again, and the bus starts to shake even more. Joe has now found the bus; it looks like it's out of control. He wonders if Kay-Lo and Joey are on this bus. He quickly gets out of the car and watches the bus shake. Other people get out of their vehicles as well. Joe waits to see what will happen.

On the bus, there is a lot of fear. Kay-Lo has no idea what is happening. People on the bus are paranoid. The only person who isn't afraid is Joey. It's almost as if he doesn't know what's going on. What did the nurse and her assistant do to him while he was in the hospital? It must've been the medication the nurse gave him.

The bus stops shaking yet again, but all the lights are still off. About ten seconds later, the lights come back on, and there is a creature standing in the center of the bus. Everyone but Joey is screaming. The creature has black and silver hair down to the floor of the bus with a nice curl at the end. The whole body is covered in hair, including the face.

The people on the bus are staring at the creature, whose hair starts flying in the air, revealing its face. It's a gray and black female creature with huge pores on its entire body, not just the face. The pores start making a lot of movements, and then a burst of gray fog flies out of the pores and covers part of the bus. People on the bus start losing consciousness. Then they all get knocked out by the fog. Strangely, Joey is the only one who is fine.

The creature covers her whole body with her hair again. Now she seems to be looking at Kay-Lo's sleeping body. The creature starts to glide very slowly toward Kay-Lo. Joey looks at the creature and starts to smile. When Joey looks back at Kay-Lo, the creature grabs her with her claws.

The creature moves her hair to the side and shows her face to Kay-Lo once again. It is possible that this creature is a ghoul. She is about to attack Kay-Lo's sleeping body, but, lucky for her, people spring into action to get on the bus. Joe quickly goes to the door, but it won't open.

A local citizen who is helping Joe open the bus door picks up a huge rock and breaks the door's window, releasing some of the fog. The fog makes contact with the people, causing them to drop to the ground. Joe quickly moves away from it; he knows what the fog is: sleeping gas. Kay-Lo and Joey are in trouble. If Joe wants to rescue them, he must enter the fog. He gets on the local bus and sees a lot of sleeping bodies on the floor. He finds Kay-Lo and Joey and quickly pulls them off the bus.

Once they are back outside, Joe starts to feel very woozy from the sleeping gas. He kneels on the ground and looks at Joey, and then he gets knocked out by the sleeping gas. Sometime later, inside the Fallons' house, Joe wakes up on the living room couch. Joey and Kay-Lo are okay. Kay-Lo explains that Joseph came to get them when he was watching the news on CC7.

Kay-Lo is still terrified of the event that happened two hours ago. Joe gets off the couch, and Kay-Lo gives him a big hug, telling him that there was this wicked thing inside the bus that caused innocent people to get knocked out by sleeping gas.

"Was it you who saved Joey and me from the bus?" Kay-Lo asks Joe nervously.

"Yes, it was me," he answers.

"Did you see that horrible thing inside of there?"

"No, but I did see it in my second vision, which I thought was the first. It probably disappeared when it saw me coming.

That thing is a ghoul. It must be the one who flipped over the bus in my vision. Kay-Lo, I believe that ghoul's purpose was to kidnap you and Joey."

"But why Joey and me? How did it know who to kidnap?"

Joe says, "It couldn't have been Pablo, Scram's mom, or Raymond because they don't know what you guys look like. I don't know how the ghoul knew who to kidnap. Joey, how come you were the only one who was still awake on that bus?"

"Joey isn't talking. I don't think he knew what was going on inside the bus. Maybe he was holding his breath and that's why he didn't pass out. I think this has something do with the medication the nurse gave him."

Joe notices the sunglasses on Joey's face. He realizes that it was Joey who gave the report about the bus flipping over in his vision. Joe can't believe it.

Joe explains to Kay-Lo everything that occurred while he was out with Jake. Later, inside the house, Joe destroyed one of the Oremonia pendants that Raymond had earlier. When he destroyed it, purple smoke came out of it and he could hear an eerie sound.

The questions that Joe must answer while he's in the forest are how the Oremonia pendant got inside the future sighting Crystal of Power and how Scram's mom and dad knew that it was in there. One of the questions has something to do with Ms. Parkinson. Joe hopes to get some information from her.

They need to find and destroy nine more pendants before more evil ghouls arise from moving portraits. Joe also needs to find the HC Mind Chip that's in the clown doll; Jake has no clue where it is. He wants to take revenge on the clown doll for attacking his brother, Joey.

Jake wonders if Joe is really going to the United Kingdom to find out where his parents are. Joe is serious about it; Joseph is going with him too. They have a long journey ahead. This is just the beginning. Since Joe is leaving, he is going to quit his job at the day care. He loves little kids a lot, but he doesn't think the job suits him. He's trying to become a mechanical worker. Tomorrow, he will head down to the day care and thank them for the time he spent in there.

Kay-Lo really doesn't want Joe and Joseph to go, but for the sake of their family she prays for both of them. Joe doesn't know when they're coming back to Florida, but he hopes that it will be soon. Jake thinks that Joe is the best father he's ever had. He wants him to come back safe, to take photos during his travels, and to continue writing his blog when he has time. Joe will do so.

Jake remembers something. He reaches inside his backpack and takes out the funny picture of Scram's mom eating a chicken wing and shows it to Joe, Joseph, and Kay-Lo. Joseph looks at the photo and recognizes the person. That's Ophelia, the woman Joseph told Joe about during the reunion party. Joseph now sees how that woman knows him and Joe. Raymond told her about him and Joe during or after the community speech. Raymond took a photo of him and Joe to show Scram's mom what they looked like.

Joe is surprised that his features haven't changed that much. He thanks Jake for the photo. Someday he will bring Jake to the United Kingdom with him. For now, he wants him to do well in school and try to remember what happened at his old school that caused him to have so much fear.

It is lucky that Joe brought along Jake to Haunted Mansion World after they left Star-Bright coffeehouse. That reminds Kay-Lo of something. She smacks Joe across the face and tells him never to bring Jake on a dangerous mission again. Jake is way too young to be doing these kinds of things. Joe sees her point.

Later, outside the house, Joe and Joseph are ready to go. This is a sad moment for Jake; he had a lot of fun with Joe during their father-and-son time. Joe promises him and Joey that he will buy them a cool racetrack when he returns. Jake wants him to enjoy his vacation. He will try to have a normal day at school.

They all hug. It seems like Joey doesn't want to get hugged; he moves away. Joe and Joseph will see their family in the near future. They both leave the house and head to Orlando Sanford International Airport to book a ticket for tomorrow's flight. They will have to stay at a hotel for now.

Kay-Lo has tears coming out of her eyes. She is nervous about what will happen to them. She is afraid of something extremely bad happening to her family. To keep up to date, she will call often to make sure everything is okay. Also, she is going to make sure the house is secure while they are away so that no one sneaks in there again.

Jake is going to miss Joe; he hopes they will do detective work together again someday. Kay-Lo and Jake both go back inside the house. Joey is still standing outside in front of the house, still wearing the sunglasses. He watched Joe and Joseph leave for the airport, but he hasn't moved yet to go back inside the house. What is going on in Joey's mind? What kind of hospital medication did the nurse give him? Why did he have such a bad reaction when Kay-Lo took off his sunglasses on the bus? There is something strange about Joey.

Review Requested:

If you loved this book, would you please provide
a review at Amazon.com?

CPSIA information can be obtained at www.ICGtesting.com
Printed in the USA
BVOW04s0504301115

428782BV00002B/117/P